GRAVEYARD SHORE

Tom Edge #1

Glenn Eric

Beachfront Entertainment

GRAVEYARD SHORE

1

"We got another dead body, Chief!"

I looked up from my desk, which wasn't far enough or private enough from the desks of my team. Not that I have anything against them, but a man's got to have a little personal space. "I keep telling you, Frenchie, I'm not a chief, I'm a Sheriff."

And some days, some times, like this one, I wished I wasn't even Sheriff. It was time for the annual budget review and I was hip deep in paperwork.

Actually, as Jenkins over at the Currituck County Finance Department liked to remind me, it was past time for the annual budget review. If I didn't get the paperwork turned in soon, he threatened to slash our budget to nothing.

Wasn't there some kind of law against threatening a public official? A sheriff, no less?

"Right, sorry, Chief. Uh, Sheriff." Frenchie, not his real name, poked his head in my door.

I don't actually have a door. I do have a small office. I had a door but some clown high on PCP managed to break free of the two deputies who'd brought him in late one Saturday night. He'd ripped the door off its hinges and busted it into itsy bitsy bits. Gave one of my deputies a concussion that he still hasn't recovered from completely when he cracked said door over said deputy's skull.

I'd come a little unhinged myself when I found out about the fracas and ensuing damages the next morning.

That was weeks, no, make that months, ago. Time flies around here. Mostly in the wrong direction. And budgets being what they were, no new door was in sight. No old door either, of course.

"Where is this body?" I asked.

"Out by the harsis."

"Houses?" Sometimes I got the feeling the only thing thicker than Frenchie's accent was his skull.

Frenchie, born Pierre Depardieu in the Loire Valley of France, knighted Sergeant of the Currituck County Sheriff's Office, further obfuscated. "Not the howsis, Chief, the harsis."

"Harsis?" Where Sergeant Depardieu had learned to speak English was anybody's guess. I was guessing it was not the Berlitz Method.

"With the four legs, Chief." Sgt. Depardieu raised his arms and cocked his elbows, bobbed up and down. He opened his mouth wide, let the word fall out in slow motion. "Haarrr-sis."

Was he imitating a bunny rabbit?

"I'm not the Chief, I'm the—" I let my boots slide off my desk where I'd been giving them a rest. "Oh, you mean horses."

"Right, Chief. Harsis."

"So we got a drowning?" Horses run wild up in the Currituck National Wildlife Refuge. So do the drunken tourists in the summertime flocking to the beach to gawk at those horses and horse around a little themselves in and around the Atlantic Ocean.

This being the fall season, the tourists, like the migratory birds, had mostly fled—the birds south, the tourists to the four points.

"Did you call Lizzie?" Elisabeth Gutierrez—née Bergqvist—was in charge of Beach Patrol.

"Cap'n Lizzie is already on the scene, Chief."

"Fine, Frenchie. You let me know if you need anything else. I have a budget to work on."

"You not interested?" Frenchie looked confused, maybe a little saddened.

"No. Can't you see I'm drowning in paperwork? The captain can handle one little drowning."

Truth is, we get a few of those each year. Lousy swimmers, hungry sharks, nasty undertows, and those folks too drunk and/or too stoned who temporarily, and fatally, forget how to swim.

Now, if we got a victim who ticked all those boxes, I'd drop everything and go take a look. Until then... paperwork.

Frenchie scratched his nose. And with a nose like that, there was plenty of acreage to scratch at. His shiny hair was as black and curly as any carpeting a Portuguese Water Dog.

"Could be he drowned," allowed Frenchie. "But how d'you suppose he got that knife in his back?"

2

Frenchie's bombshell would have had my feet hitting the floor but since I'd done that earlier, I skipped that part and scrambled past him. "Address?"

Frenchie scurried behind, turning a stickie note this way and that as he tried to read his own scribble. "South of the Carova bitch, Chief. That sound right?"

"South Carova *Beach*, got it." That was out in my part of the Banks. I snatched the keys to the 4x4 from the case by the door and headed out.

The Refuge lies out above Corolla on the far tip of the Outer Banks. It, like our jurisdiction, ends at the Virginia border. As Sheriff of Currituck County, I hold the somewhat dubious honor of policing an area of approximately 540 square miles with just about half of that area being water.

A lot of that water stood between me and my destination. The Sheriff's Office is located on the Inner Banks. Maple, North Carolina, to be precise, pretty much due west of the Refuge.

Since Gutierrez had the patrol boat, I had to take the long way, south down the 158, Wright Memorial Bridge—named after a pair of amateur inventor brothers who thought they could fly—across Currituck Sound, then up north Highway 12.

A chopper would have been convenient. But no

point requisitioning a helicopter when the county won't even give me a new door for my office.

A light cold misty rain came and went. My windshield wipers went click click click. It wasn't the best day for the beach, so there was little traffic and I made good time.

With the tires heated up after the long drive, I was taking no chances. I stopped at the Corolla Village Road public access facility to let some air out of the things.

The public facility sits at the edge of North Beach Access Road, which actually is just that, the beach, as in sand and lots of it—and the only road into the Currituck Banks.

I climbed out of the Bronco, grabbed the tire pressure gauge I keep in the glovebox, and danced around the truck, fiddling with the valve stems, getting the pressure in each tire down to the 20-psi range.

Not only was the low pressure necessary for driving along the soft, sandy beach, it was the law. Still, we got our share of morons who insisted on hitting the beach with hard tires, and sometimes two-wheel drive. Both of which is stupid. And pricey. Because you'll pay through the nose for a tow.

And you will need a tow.

With the tire pressure adjusted and my radio in the Bronco squawking "Tom! Tom! Tom!" and "Where the hell are you, Edge?" I hopped in and flew up the beach. The speed limit is 35 mph, 15 if within 300 feet of pedestrians, horses, turtles or anything else you might squish, dent or cause the untimely demise thereof.

Being Sheriff, I have some leeway.

I took that leeway up to 50 mph.

Being careful of the wild horses, of course, but at the moment there were only three in sight and these were nibbling sea oats growing atop the dune up ahead on my left.

The Banker horses, magnificent Spanish-blooded beasts, a remnant of the presence of the Conquistadores who'd once plied these lands and shores, leaving behind their horses and their smallpox, exist in a controlled population of approximately sixty.

Sadly, we lose a few each year due to car-horse collisions, random disease or knuckle-headed tourists who decide to feed the horses something that doesn't agree with them.

We have laws against two out of three of those things too.

To maintain the herd size, new horses are judiciously brought in. There's been an ongoing tug-of-war between groups including Fish and Game on one side who think the horses are a detriment to other hunting and fishing resources, and proponents of increasing the herd size to a number they consider something more genetically suitable to the herd's long-term viability.

No end of that war was in sight.

With the drizzle gone, I could see my chief deputy and three wild horses crowded around a body being licked by the incoming surf.

"It's about time you got here." Chief Deputy Nathan Midgett held his arms across his chest, a favorite pose of his, at least when eying me. "Shoo!" He waved his arms. I assumed he was talking to the horses, not me. The wild horses must've assumed this too because they trotted off.

"Stopped for a parade," I quipped. "You know I love a good float." I stepped around my second-in-command to inspect the corpse. "What have we got?"

Our unmanned patrol boat bobbed at anchor a hundred yards off shore. A small dinghy, proudly bearing the seal of our office, sat like a beached whale a dozen yards south of us.

We'd had a beached baby whale about a mile south of here my first year on the job. All the king's horses and all the king's men, plus the combined forces of the volunteer fire department, Sheriff's office and every Good Samaritan within spitting distance, hadn't been able to push her/him out to sea again.

Not that I'd thought there was any real chance of saving the stranded beast. The VW Beetle-sized humpback looked pretty much gone from this world when it had been discovered washed up in the surf that sunrise.

"One John Doe," Nat said, voice monotone and serious as the bubonic plague. "Rolled up on shore. That family over there spotted him."

Nat pointed. My eyes followed. A shellshocked family of four huddled on a striped beach blanket beside a late-model blue Toyota 4Runner. Snorkels, kid-sized body boards, one adult-sized surfboard, a bean bag toss set, a couple of kites, and other beach supplies filled the rear of the truck and spilled over the open tailgate.

"I'm gonna want to talk to them."

"Sure." Nat's Ray-Bans blocked the light and my reading of his mood. He's six-two and wiry, spending an hour or more in the gym each day.

Nat's by the book and by the clock. He maintains

a strict number 2 haircut, keeping his reddish-brown hair to a quarter of an inch all around. If it grows more than an eighth over, he makes an appointment with his barber.

When I'd teased him one time about the Sheriff's office moving to require a number 3 haircut, he'd practically peed himself. And soiling his uniform would have broken yet another of his many self-imposed rules.

I bent down for a closer look, letting the cold saltwater splash at my protesting knees. Our victim, a white male, appeared about forty years old, dressed in Wrangler jeans and a black parka over a green plaid shirt. Bare feet. "Strange way to dress for a swim. At least he had the sense to take off his shoes first."

Nat sniffed. Not liking my humor. I could tell. Sometimes a sniff is worth a thousand words. Especially when Nat is the one doing the sniffing.

Nothing unusual about the corpse, markings or otherwise, that I could see—barring the knife sticking out between his shoulder blades. As for his face, that was half-buried in wet sand so I couldn't say anything yet about that.

I stood and wiped my hands on my pants. "Lizzie was first on the scene?" Tire tracks ran up and down the beach. Footprints dotted the shore, some human, some dog, some horse, some bird, and some I didn't recognize. It was going to be hell making anything of it all.

"Yes, sir. I arrived about ten minutes after her. She already had the area staked."

Foot-tall wooden stakes jutted up in an approximately twelve-foot by sixteen-foot rectangle. Crime scene tape, wrapped neatly around the stakes, fluttered in the ocean breeze. Gutierrez liked things neat.

"Where is she now?"

Nat pointed once again. One of his favorite moves. I looked again. This time, towards the dunes as Lizzie came down in a controlled slide, managing to stay on two feet.

"Tom." She pulled off her sunglasses and wiped a hand through the sweat accumulating on her brow. Replacing the sunglasses on her button nose, she said, "What do you think?"

I shrugged. "You see anything up top?"

"Nada."

"Either of you talk to our witnesses yet?"

"Only to take their names." Nat patted the notepad in his shirt pocket.

"I had a quick word with them, Tom," Lizzie said. "They weren't much use. Mom and Dad were munching on ham sandwiches and red potato salad while the kids played in the surf. One minute our victim wasn't there, the next minute he rolls up on the beach. Screams followed."

"He was still alive?"

"Nah. The kids." She glanced at the corpse, her boot nudging his calf. He did not appear to mind. "This one looks like he's been swimming a while."

"Yeah." The victim's skin was white and puckered rather like he'd fallen asleep in his bathtub.

Curious sand crabs—tiny egg-shaped critters half the size of a finger joint with light gray-pink shells and pairs of antennae the better to see you with—hovered nearby, incredulous at the windfall Neptune had gifted them, and hungry to let the feast begin.

3

I cast my eyes up and down the beach. The sky was dirty gray streaked with blue, the seas relatively calm. Not the best day to work on your skin cancer or ride your long board. "Any other witnesses?"

"I haven't seen anybody, Sheriff," replied Nat. "You, Captain?"

She shook her head, hopped two steps toward shore to escape a breaking wave. I wasn't so lucky.

"Damn." I flapped my wet trouser cuffs.

"You'll have to go up and down the beach, ask everybody you see." I gazed up at the dunes. "Better check the houses too." An uneven string of houses, most of them beach rentals, rested uneasily on the ever-shifting sand.

More homes sat between the dunes and the Sound. A large number of those were seasonal rentals too. Misfits and outcasts occupied a smaller number year-round.

I should know. I was one of them.

"All of 'em?"

"Somebody might have seen something. Only way to know is to knock on doors."

"All right." Lizzie didn't look happy about it. She was happier knocking on heads than doors. "Mind if I call in Flo and Eddie?"

"I'd mind if you didn't." Deputies Florence Pinder and Edward Wu were fine officers and had nearly twenty years of on-the-job experience between them. "But don't wait on them. Could be somebody up there saw something or someone. They might be checking out and heading home. Then we're screwed."

"Speak for yourself," Lizzie replied. She turned aside to call the deputies.

"Recognize the make of knife?" Nat tested me.

"Benchmade Griptilian," I replied. "I've seen plenty of them. They're not uncommon." A popular folding knife over eight inches long with a blade nearly three-and-a-half inches sharp. Lightweight and, in this case, probably lethal. This one was gray handled. I'd once carried a black one in the USCG. "There's a bit of fiber on the lanyard hole. Let's make sure we don't lose it."

"Yes, sir." Nat replied.

"Where's Tracy?"

"Got held up. Doctor's appointment. Be here in five."

"The baby?" I asked. Tracy Zefferelli, our pathologist, is working on child number four when she isn't working for us.

"Yeah. If it doesn't pop out soon, Tracy says her gyno is going to force the little bugger to come out and greet the world. Such as it is." Lizzie stiffened and pushed past me. "What are you looking at? Show some respect!"

A young couple standing several yards from us, snapping pics with their smartphones, was her target.

"You want pictures? Shoot the damn horses!" Lizzie flapped her arms. "Go on, git!"

The captain can be imposing even when not flapping her muscled arms at passers-by. She's physically fit with short blonde hair, blue eyes that can smile at you all beguiling one minute and have you trembling in fear the next.

She looked all woman but underneath I was pretty sure she'd been put together with titanium bones linked to advanced high-tech polymer muscles.

The couple beat a retreat.

Lizzie has a way with folks.

"Morbid," Lizzie exclaimed. "Leave 'em be and the next thing you know they'll be snapping selfies and posting them on who-gives-a-fuck-a-gram."

"While you're controlling the mob, I'll go talk to —" I turned to Nat. He's one of those guys who have all the answers. Right or wrong.

"The Leftkowitzes, Sheriff. Up from Tulls Bay for the day."

"Those are the folks who called it in," added Lizzie.

Located a good sixty miles away and fed by the Northwest River originating in Virginia, Tulls Bay sits over on the northwestern shore of the Currituck Sound.

I ignored my waterlogged boots and highly water-absorbent socks, so much for waterproof leather, and started up the beach.

"Hey," shouted Nat. "What do you want me to do?"

Like a gnat buzzing my eyes when I'm trying to read in bed with my book light, this homonymic Nat had a way of getting on my nerves—justifiably or not. "You search his pockets yet?" I called back.

"No."

"Have fun." The look I received from my Chief Deputy told me the idea of poking around in a dead man's pockets was not his idea of a good time.

Mine either, to tell the truth. That's why I was talking to the living.

4

Approaching the witnesses, I winked to the two children kneeling in the sand. They appeared to be sculpting a replica of the dead man in sand, three-quarter scale.

A picnic spread was laid out on an empty standup paddleboard bag near the sandman or should I say sandcorpse.

"Mr. and Mrs. Leftkowitz?" I decided on a friendly yet not happy face as being most appropriate to the occasion.

"Yes." The mister of the pair stepped forward. "I'm Jeff. That's Jinny in the cab. I'm the one who called."

The missus sat behind the wheel of the Toyota 4Runner. The door hung open. A local Montessori school sticker, featuring a gray dolphin reading a book, sat in the right corner of the back window.

The scent of sunblock rode on the air. The day being what it was, it seemed like a waste of sunblock to me.

"I'm Sheriff Edge. I'd like it if you'd tell me what you saw."

"Nothing much really," said Jeff Leftkowitz, a slender red-haired fellow several inches shorter than me, in tan cargo shorts and a loose-hanging white shirt over a white T-shirt.

"Nothing at all," Jinny Leftkowitz chimed in, peering at me through a pair of wide-rimmed glasses. "We were picnicking. Then the kids started yelling."

"Screaming bloody murder," Jeff Leftkowitz said.

"Can't say as I blame them," I replied, if not for the dead body at their feet, then for braving swimsuits on a less than perfect day at the beach. I often admired kids their resilience. Something I didn't think we so-called grownups often gave them enough credit for. "My Chief Deputy tells me you're visiting from Tulls Bay?"

"That's right. Thought we'd come to the beach for the day," Jeff Leftkowitz explained. "Now I wish we'd stayed home. Like I wanted to," he said, turning to his wife. "I mean, between the weather and now this."

I ignored the all-too-familiar husband-and-wife dynamic. "Yes, sir. What time did you and your family arrive?"

"Early. About ten?" He turned again to his wife. "Would you say?"

"Something like that. Maybe a little earlier." Jinny Leftkowitz slid out of the cab. A loose pair of knee-length denim shorts rode low on her hips. An unbuttoned blue shirt over a modest bikini top kept her decent. Short brown hair poked around the edges of a red Carolina Hurricanes-branded cap.

The girl started bawling. "Bobby threw sand in my eyes!" Her fists smashed against her eyes.

"Did not! It was the wind, Mommy!"

"Did so! It was you!"

"Quiet. Mommy and Daddy are busy," ordered their father.

Jinny took the girl's hands from her face. "Let Mommy see." She wiped sand from her daughter's face.

"The kids are getting restless."

"Probably traumatized for life," put in Jinny Leftkowitz. "Here." She rummaged inside an insulated cooler and pulled out a package wrapped in crinkled aluminum foil. "Who wants brownies?"

"I do!" the kids shouted in unison, tears and dead bodies forgotten, at least for the moment.

My stomach growled. I wanted a brownie too but I kept my mouth shut, at least in that department. "Did either of you happen to see anybody else on the beach this morning?"

"Not me," said Jeff Leftkowitz. "You, dear?"

"Sorry, no. I mean, a few people walked by earlier but nothing special. Here." She handed each child a big, thick brownie chock full of walnuts. No need for plates. They gobbled down their treasures hungrily and quickly, licking their fingers afterwards. The pair were as efficient as the sand crabs.

"Right." This conversation was getting me nowhere.

"How much longer you going to need us, Sheriff?" asked Jeff Leftkowitz. "Your man Midgett has our contact info and we told that lady all we know. Again, not much. We'd like to go home."

"Amen to that," said Jinny, linking her arm with her husband's. "This isn't exactly the outing I was hoping for."

"I don't think it was exactly a day at the beach for our victim, either," I quipped.

"Any idea who he is?" Jeff Leftkowitz peered over my shoulder at the body in the surf.

"Not a clue. But we'll get there," I promised.

"Good," replied Jinny Leftkowitz. "All this crime

and murder. It's getting so you can't even take your family to the beach for a nice time."

"Yes, ma'am. Believe me, things like this don't happen every day."

"I should hope not."

"So are we free to go?" Jeff Leftkowitz asked. "I took a day off work for this. May as well try to enjoy the rest of it at home."

I grinned. "What do you do for a living?"

"I'm a broker. If you're ever in the market—"

Seeing the hungry salesman look begin to glow in his eyes rather like the beginnings of the Big Bang, I cut him off quickly. "And you, Mrs. Leftkowitz?"

Jinny Leftkowitz pointed to the children, now adding a skull and crossbones to the head of their sand sculpture. "What? Isn't this enough?" She clapped her hands. "Stop that, you two!"

Yeah, that was more than enough.

5

I tromped down to the crime scene, passing Lizzie on her way up the dunes behind the wheel of my Bronco.

I waved at her to stop and she did—within inches of my toes. "Where are you going with Bronc?"

"Gotta take your truck, Tom. You want me to start knocking on doors until Flo and Edie show up? I can't do it on foot. That would take me ages. And in case you haven't noticed, the patrol boat doesn't tread sand so good."

"Yeah, but my truck—"

"You giving me permission to ride one of these horses cluttering up the beach?"

"That's illegal and you know it."

"Yeah, yeah. What's the big deal with the horses, anyway? A horse is a horse."

"Of course, of course," I quipped. "But these horses can trace their lineage back to the time of the first Spanish expeditions to the New World."

"Yeah, yeah. And I could trace my fingers with a crayon when I was three years old. Big deal."

"It is a big deal."

Lizzie shrugged. "You're the history buff. Me, I'd rather run around in the buff or eat at a good, cheap buffet." She gunned the motor twice. "So, am I taking your truck?"

"You already did." I wanted to protest the theft but she had me and I knew it. Nobody drives my truck but me. Except for now. "Swing by and pick me up when you're finished."

"Yes, sir." She touched her index finger to her eyebrow, brought her hand down and transformed it into a gun in one smooth move. "Pow. Later."

"Wait. What about our patrol boat?" The thirty-footer bounced atop the water some distance away. We couldn't afford to lose it.

The county wouldn't even let me replace my damn door. There was no way they'd sign off on a new patrol boat. And I didn't even want to think about the amount of paperwork involved in reporting the loss of our boat. Those folks at county counted every paperclip.

The public humiliation, that I could imagine.

"It ain't goin' nowhere." Lizzie revved the engine, slid the Bronco into gear.

I stepped aside as she roared past.

"Find anything?" I asked Nat Midgett.

"Nothing. His pockets were empty."

"Huh. Ever seen him before?" The ocean had sculpted a space around the victim's face, revealing more details, a slight moustache, long chin and thin pale lips. Nicotine-stained teeth.

"Not that I can place."

"Here's Tracy."

We stepped aside as the pathologist came rolling up the beach in a black Range Rover. She scooted to a stop in the hole in the space-time continuum where my Bronco used to be and jumped down, lifting her gray skirt.

"Hi, Tracy. Thanks for stopping by." I gave her Range Rover a meaningful look. "Should you be driving in your condition?"

"Should you be hounding a pregnant woman who's out here at the end of nowhere to do a job that you asked her to do?" The frizzy brown hair surrounding Tracy Zefferelli's cherubic face bounced in the ocean breeze.

I raised my hands and took a step back. Nat took two steps. The coward.

Tracy kicked off her sandals and approached the victim. "What new manner of hell have you for me today?"

"No ID. No witnesses," clipped Nat.

"No breathing," I added. A little gallows humor. Neither seemed to appreciate the effort.

"So," Tracy dropped to her knees over the body, "just another day at the beach."

"First impressions?" I made the mistake of asking.

"My first impression is that I've been about eight and a half months pregnant for what feels like the past fifteen months. And I've about had enough. My second impression," she said sharply, "is the one I do of Amy Schumer giving birth naked on the beach with Don Q and his sidekick, Sancho Stick-In-The-Mud, tilting uselessly at windmills—or in this case, should I say lighthouses?"

The pathologist paused briefly for a much-needed breath of air. "Instead of making themselves useful." Her eyes flitted to me and Nat. "Trust me. You do not want to see it."

Nat and I shared a rare comradely look. A look

that said *Let's get the hell out of here.*

"Sorry. Guess I'm a little cranky," allowed the pathologist with the beginnings of a smile. "One kid on the way and three more that won't be out of the house and out of my hair for who knows how many more years."

Nat reread his notes, not daring to make further eye contact. One day any of us could end up under her scalpel, dead or alive.

"I understand," I replied. "Take your time. The ambulance is on its way and will be ready to go when you are. Tide's coming in."

"Thanks for the beach report, Tom. I've only lived here all my life."

"Right." I blushed, a very undignified thing for a man in my position as Sheriff to do. Everybody in the whole damn county seemed to know I was an incomer and loved to rub my nose in that little fact as if it were a blemish on my very manhood.

"Now, you two want to stop breathing down my neck and let me do my job?"

Okay, it had been a short truce.

"Call me later," I said/asked/begged.

"Don't I always?"

I bent my neck and looked at the gray sky. Not a good day for the beach at all.

"I'm out of here." I started walking uphill, wind whistling through my ribs, wishing I had my jacket but my jacket was in my truck and Lizzie had my truck.

"Where are you going, Sheriff?" Nat hollered.

"Home."

"It's barely midday."

I turned. "If that's an invitation to lunch, thanks,

but I'm not hungry."

"What about this?" The Chief Deputy waved his hands at the staked scene and the slightly agitated pathologist as she examined the corpse.

Nat Midgett was not one to give up easily. Or gracefully but that's another matter. Some people resented me being Sheriff of Currituck County. Some hated me for it. Nat sat firmly in the latter category. Either way, it went with the job.

Of course, a few people maybe sort of liked me being Sheriff. That was the category I fell into.

"I've got a monster headache," I said. That wasn't a lie. "Getting an aspirin."

"But—"

"You've got this. If you come up with anything, bag it, tag it or bury it. Call me with your report."

I resumed my death march.

I did have a headache and it was a doozy. I don't mind a bar fight. I mean who doesn't love a good drunken brawl?

I don't mind so much the errant teenybopper who's hooked up with a local Outer Banks boy and the parents are teary-eyed and threatening to sue the county.

And I enjoy stopping drunk drivers and speeders.

But murder? That's not my thing. I mean, as Sheriff it was my thing, but that didn't mean I had to like it. I'd seen more than my unfair share of unpleasantness during my nineteen years in the US Coast Guard, the bulk of those years in the USCG Intelligence Service.

In the Coast Guard, the job is to save people.

After retiring, I'd sort of stumbled into being

Sheriff and often regretted the fall.

I spotted my Bronco a couple hundred yards away, parked in front of an eight-bed, nine-bath vacation house sitting high on a dune overlooking North Carolina's little old slice of the Atlantic Ocean, and boasting a bird's eye view of our crime scene. Captain Elisabeth Gutierrez was on the job.

And driving my truck while I was stuck plodding through the soul-sucking sand that we call roads out here.

I don't live high on a dune. Too pricey. I live in the wooded flats, closer to the Currituck Sound side to the west. Closer to the mosquitoes too. And I could mention the greenhead horseflies with their bulging green Martian eyes and insatiable appetites for human blood. If you're going to have horses, you're going to have flies.

It seems to be one of those immutable laws of nature.

Like my toast always landing jelly side down when I accidently drop it on the kitchen floor.

6

"Hi-ya, Boy." This being the middle of my so-called normal working day, my dog was surprised and happy to see me. But then, he was a dog, what choice did he have?

I gave him a few minutes of my trademark brand of affection, topped off his water bowl, and threw him a dog biscuit. Not that he needed anything, simply to show him I cared.

With the black and white dog following along, I went to the bedroom and changed out of my wet clothes and into a clean, dry uniform—gray-blue shirt and charcoal slacks. I swallowed a couple of aspirin from the plastic bottle in the kitchen cupboard just so nobody could accuse me of being a liar.

I brewed a cup of strong coffee and carried it out to the deck above the carport. There wasn't much sun but the coffee kept my hands warm, and the dog settled over my feet kept my toes toasty. It was a start.

The next thing I knew somebody was banging on the door. I looked around, bleary-eyed and feeling more tired now than I had before I'd fallen asleep. I hated that. And it happened a lot. Goes with getting older, I suppose. My empty coffee mug sat on the deck collecting ants. The dog was gone.

Bang. Boom. Bang. Rattle.

I yawned and checked my watch. "Shit." Two o'clock. "All right, all right!" I leaned over the railing but couldn't see the front door from where I stood so I decided I'd better go and stand at the front door.

To the sound of incessant knuckle banging and toe kicking, I threw the door open before the Big Bad Wolf managed to blow it down.

"Yeah?"

On the weathered front deck, a five-eight woman looking very fit, and looking back at me with very impatient hard blue eyes huffed. "It's about time."

"Oh, it's you," I said. "Here I thought I was being raided." I stepped aside. "Come on in, Lizzie."

"Nat told me you were here. I was beginning to wonder. You sleeping or—hey, you got a dog!" Cracking the first grin I'd seen on her all day, she bent to pet him.

"No, don't! Please!" I frantically waved my hands but it was too late.

Bladder Boy was peeing all over the rug in the entry meant to catch dirt, not pee. This wasn't the first time.

"Oops." Lizzie chuckled. "Clean up on aisle one!"

"Very funny."

"He always react like that or are you not letting this poor little guy out enough times a day?" She reached down and scratched Bladder Boy behind the neck. "Oops." Bladder Boy obediently peed some more.

"I don't know where he gets it all. I'll get some paper towels."

"Roger that."

"And please stop petting Bladder Boy!" I called from the narrow galley kitchen.

"No worries. He's fled to the great outdoors."

Lizzie followed me to the kitchen and started exploring the interior of my cabinets. "That really his name?"

"Yep."

"What kind of dog is he and what kind of name is Bladder Boy?"

"Bladder Boy is a Springer Spaniel. I picked him up at a shelter down in Kill Devil Hills. Turns out he pees when he's shown affection."

"Takes after you, does he?"

"Again, very funny. I was going to call him something manly, like Spartacus," I said, unrolling a mile of paper towels, wrapping them in my fist, "but the name's got to suit the animal. So Bladder Boy it is." I returned to the scene of the crime and tossed the wad of towels atop the spillage. "Watch where you step."

"You just gonna leave it there?" Lizzie stepped across.

"For now." I'd pick up the soggy mess and dispose of it later.

I popped out on the front deck, put my fingers to my lips and whistled. Bladder Boy came racing up the rickety stairs and bounding through the open door, which I quickly shut to keep out the horses and the skeeters, some of the latter of which were nearly as large as the horses.

Most homes here in the far northern banks, those that wanted to hold up for more than a season anyway, were built above ground level, which was pretty much on par with or below sea level. Homeowners reserved ground zero for storing cars, boats and any crap that they didn't care about getting ruined or swept away when the next round of floods hit or the next hurricane blows through the area. Flooding and power outages are but two of the inconveniences that come with living in this inconvenient land.

Lizzie threw herself down on the thirty-year-old brown leather sofa with a million-dollar view of the smoke-scarred stacked stone fireplace.

It, like most of the furniture, had come with the house, wrinkles, stains, cracks and tears included.

"Smells in here." Lizzie waved a hand in front of her nose.

Smells included too. Although, to be honest, some of those smells might have originated with me.

I leaned back in an antique rocking chair that made me feel like I was about a hundred years old every time I sat in it.

"Come up with anything?"

"Some shack," Lizzie picked at a loose thread protruding from a pale blue pillow on the corner of the sofa. "For a shack. So this is where the great man lives."

"Been in the family for years. Home sweet tomb."

"Yeah." Lizzie nodded. "It does sort of have that graveyard vibe going for it, doesn't it?"

I let the comment go. My grandfather had passed away in this house. Lizzie Gutierrez didn't know that. I wasn't sure if it would have made a difference as far as her comment went but it made a difference in my response to it. "Let's try this again." I rubbed my knees. "Did you come up with anything?"

Lizzie cocked her arm over the side of the sofa. Bladder Boy leapt out of nowhere and laid down beside her, settling his head in her lap.

Lizzie'd been warned. Any new puddles, I was going to make her clean them up.

"What's with all the dusty old books filled with

dusty old history?" Her eyes scanned the oak bookcases lining each side of the fireplace and the longest wall.

I followed her gaze. "Dad and Granddad built those units." I rubbed my knees some more. I was doing that a lot these days. "Many moons ago. Most of the books belonged to them. I dragged a few here. Some are still in boxes."

My ex had gotten most of my books and all of our history in the divorce. Or so it seemed sometimes.

"That's quite a collection."

"Granddad was a history buff. My father taught high school history thirty years. My mom's father, Grandpa Bill was a professor of North American history at Cornell."

"So you're the black sheep." Lizzie smiled at me.

I wouldn't have taken offense even if she hadn't softened the blow with a smile. I sort of was the black sheep.

"So," I said, once again trying to steer Lizzie back to the business at hand. "Let's talk contemporary history."

"Right. I hit about half a dozen of the nearest vacation rentals," Lizzie explained. "Flo and Eddie have taken over, thank god. Half of the homes I tried, nobody answered the door."

"We'll have to check with the rental agencies to see if the current occupants are off playing tourist for the day or if those properties are unoccupied at the moment."

"Right. I made a note of the firms' names."

Most of the rentals have signs displaying the name and contact info of the company managing the property screwed to the front of the house and another on the beachside. It always pays to advertise.

Except in the case of murder.

"Good." I sighed. "But no luck then?"

"If you mean finding witnesses, no. I did get an invitation to dinner though."

"Think your husband will mind?"

"Separated, remember?"

"Does that make a difference?" In my experience, men and women didn't view the concept of a separation in quite the same way.

"Who knows? Oh, I did get one thing."

"Do tell."

"Back at the first property, a young white female by the name of Kelly Bates claims to have seen two fishing boats out early."

"How early?"

"At least since a few minutes before sunrise."

"Let me guess, Ms. Bates was up to watch the sun come up."

Lizzie nodded. "She and about seven others are staying at the house. They're on a retreat."

"What sort of retreat?"

I pictured flowing orange chiffon robes, soft chanting and yoga poses on tatami mats laid out on the beachside deck whilst these retreaters twisted their bodies and brains into all sorts of unnatural positions, all while seeking the rising sun's blessing.

What can I say? We all have our prejudices.

"They're a bunch of grad students."

"Grad students?" I hadn't seen that coming.

"Studying astrophysics."

That put a whole new spin on things. Edgar Rice Burroughs novels of Mars, Vincent Van Gogh, and Don

McLean's poignant Vincent (Starry, Starry Night) song spun into my head.

We all have our influences too.

"Anyway," Bladder Boy gave her a lost puppy look and she scratched his side, "Bates was the only person awake. The boats were present when she stepped out on the deck."

"Were they together?"

"The boats? No. She says the boats, both motorboats, were about a hundred yards apart. Of course, she said she couldn't be sure because it's hard to judge distances on the water."

I nodded. "Yet she could see they were fishing?"

"She says she could."

"Could they have dropped something in the water?"

"Like a guy with a knife in his back? Not that she noticed." Lizzie pulled a pack of spearmint gum from her slacks, unwrapped a foiled stick and popped it in her mouth after biting it in half. "Want one?"

"Nope. Did any of the others see it?"

"I spoke with everyone staying at the house. Three males, four females. They all say exactly what Bates told me. Everybody else claims they were tucked in bed at the time she spotted the boats. They were all out on the deck later when the body washed up and the kids started screaming. That's it."

"How long are these students going to be on this retreat?"

"Till the end of the week."

"Friday?"

"Saturday." I nodded some more to indicate I was thinking but the truth was I was stumped.

How did Mr. Nameless get here?

Why dump him here?

Why now?

Lizzie scrubbed her face. "So, any idea how we're gonna find this snuffer of human life?"

"Sure." I rocked back in my chair. "I'm going to use my finely-honed skills of abduction, deduction, and seduction."

Lizzie snorted.

"Thanks for your vote of confidence," I replied. "Let's go see what Nat and Tracy have come up with and whether they share your rather unkind view of my skills."

7

Nat sat behind the wheel of his county-issue Jeep Grand Cherokee 4x4, one bony elbow sticking out the open window, radio receiver pressed to his lips.

I pulled up beside him in the Bronco—in far worse condition but bought and paid for without benefit of taxpayer dollars—facing in the opposite direction, and cranked down my window.

"Where is everybody?" I asked Nat once he'd ended the call.

The incoming tide had erased our crime scene, wiping all traces of the murder out to sea. A good or bad thing depending on your POV—cop or killer.

"Officers Pinder and Wu are knocking on doors, as per your order." Nat Midgett did not deign to be as informal as the rest of us in the Currituck County Sheriff's Office. "Dr. Zefferelli's gone back to her office. She said she'll call you later. EMT hauled the body off to the morgue." He turned his attention to Lizzie. "You come up with any leads, Captain?"

"Not a thing, Chief Deputy, sir." Lizzie saluted in a way that let you know she didn't mean it. She turned to me. "What do you want me to do, Tom?"

I stared at the near-flat steel gray sea a moment. Three dolphins pushed through the surface then submerged quickly, as if reconnoitering. During WWII,

Nazi U-boats regularly plied these waters attacking merchant ships, as did marauding pirates hundreds of years before them. "Check out the marinas on your way back in."

"All two of them?" Lizzie quipped. "You're thinking about those two boats Kelly Bates saw?"

Currituck County's home to two small commercial marinas, both on the mainland side. The pair are located along a straight and narrow stretch of the Intracoastal Waterway connecting Coinjock Bay and the North River.

"What boats?" Nat needed to know.

Lizzie explained about their only lead.

Nat sniffed. Unimpressed. "You know how many people fish around here? You know how many people own fishing boats? Those boats could be privately owned and docked behind their owners' houses. You going to check every house on the Banks next?"

"Got any better ideas?" I asked him, my left arm dangling out the window. A little further and I could reach out and wrap my fingers around his scrawny neck. Not that I'd do it, of course.

Nat kept his mouth shut but his expression said it all.

"Off you go, then," I said to Lizzie.

She wasted no time throwing open the passenger-side door and leaping to the ground. "Don't just stand there, Twinkle Toes," she ordered Nat as she pulled the anchor from the sand and set it down gently in the raft. "Give me a push off." She jumped in and shoved against the sand with an aluminum oar.

Nat scrambled to the raft and struggled to push her out to sea, not easy when the object you're pushing on has sides the consistency of a marshmallow and you're up to your ankles in wet sand.

I left the two of them to their games and headed north, towards Carova Beach.

Carova, one of Currituck's many unincorporated communities, is the last chance for civilization at this extreme north end of Carolina where it butts up to the Virginia border. With less than a thousand homes and maybe fifty or so permanent residents, myself included, it's not what you might call bustling. No roads, no restaurants, no shops.

From what I'd heard, Carova sprang up like a tenacious weed in the 1960s and refused to die.

Being an eight-mile or so slog up the beach, this is 4x4 land. Despite the beach being the only access, hungry developers have been trying to sell lots and build more homes up here for years.

Most locals rooted for them to fail.

The locals tolerated me because I'd inherited my granddad's house, not because I was county sheriff.

We've got a volunteer fire and rescue station out here. But that wasn't where I was headed.

I was headed to Milepost 21 and the Carova Beach Park public boat ramp. The ramp only provided access to Currituck Sound but if a person, such as a knife-stabbing-drop-him-in-the-ocean killer, had a mind to, and the time and proper vessel to, that person could have entered the ocean from the ramp.

Unlikely as it was, I wanted to check it out. Even though I held out little hope, the drive and the mental exercise gave me time to think.

That was usually worth something.

Even more unlikely was that our corpse had

washed up from someplace further north or south but I'd have Nat check with whatever authority could tell us about which way a body might and might not be pushed up and/or down the Carolina coast.

I pulled into the quiet unpaved parking area and killed the motor. Two pickup trucks sat deserted, empty boat trailers hitched to their bumpers.

A sixtyish angler in a red plaid shirt, baggy blue overalls, and hip waders turned to look at me. Seeing I wasn't a fish and therefore not worth his time, he returned his attention to the brackish water and his dangling line. His graying hair was just long enough to flap around his protruding ears in the stiff breeze.

I climbed out and approached him. "Catch anything?" Asking an angler about his fishing, I'd learned, was a surefire way to get on his good side.

"One whole sea mullet," he replied without turning around. "You can check the bucket." He gestured towards a blue pail a couple feet to his right. Inside, a foot-long silver-gray fish, with dark bars marking its sides, swam in small circles.

"I plan to let him go when I pack up. I only keep him around for company. If you came to fish, you should try someplace else."

"Why do you stay?"

This time he did turn around. Thin with sharp, dark eyes. "Because I'm already here." He scraped a heel across the dirt.

That made sense.

"You see anything odd today?"

"Such as?" His fingers toyed with his line.

"Suspicious activity."

"You got my attention." The angler planted his

pole in a rod holder spiked into the ground. "What's up, Sheriff?"

"You know who I am?"

"No, but I can read a badge. What are you looking for?"

"An unidentified male was found dead on the beach late this morning."

"You do say? First I'm hearing of it."

"You're not local, are you, Mister—?" With so few locals about, I knew a lot of the faces.

"No need for formalities, Sheriff. Call me Larry. And to answer your question, nope, not local. Down from Virginia for a couple of weeks. I didn't know we were going to have to worry about dead men floating up on the beach. Only seashells and the occasional whale carcass. My wife's not going to like this."

"Tell her not to worry," I said. "It doesn't happen every day." Visitors are required to get a temporary fishing license. I didn't bother asking Larry to see his license because that wasn't my job. Such things were the North Carolina Wildlife Resources Commission's bailiwick.

I turned my eyes on the two pickups, one silver, one white. "Either of these trucks yours?"

"Nope. I came on foot."

"Know anything about them?"

"The trucks? Nope. They were parked there when I got here."

"What time might that be?"

"Tenish."

"You know the fish bite better early."

"Yeah." The angler spat into the water. "But you see, I don't care for mornings."

"I haven't cared too much for this particular morning myself." I said goodbye, walked over to the trucks and made a note of the two NC license plates so we could run them.

Another slim to nothing lead, but that was all I had to work with so far.

8

It was day two of our murder investigation and day fourteen or fifteen of my budget report blues. Either one of these things would normally put me in a foul mood—the two of them together was sheer hell.

I wasn't exactly feeling on top of the world when I stepped into the Sheriff's Office and the first thing I heard was my title being mangled. Yet again.

"We got a name, Chief," Frenchie proudly announced.

"Great." I wasn't in a stable enough frame of mind to correct him. "Here, I've got your coffee."

I handed the sergeant a twelve-ounce paper cup filled with espresso bean coffee, too much milk and too little sugar—exactly the way he likes it.

Before coming to the office, I'd made a pit stop at Salt of the Earth, a local diner next to the Old Courthouse up in the unincorporated community of Currituck. I'd dropped some paperwork off at the new courthouse regarding Captain Jefferson's temporary leave of absence.

Being the county seat, Currituck's where most of the county services reside. The politicians and civil servants decided to keep the Sheriff's Office at arm's length down in Maple. Smart.

I liked things better that way myself.

"Thanks, Chief." Frenchie took his coffee, lifted the chocolate brown lid up under his nose and inhaled deeply. "Parfait."

I knew he didn't mean ice cream.

Sgt. Depardieu liked to give things a good sniff before eating or drinking them. He claimed not only could he tell if any potential solids or liquids he contemplated absorbing were spoiled or not but that this action increased the flavor and consequent savoring of those solids and liquids. For all I knew, it possibly prevented intestinal gases too.

I just assumed this extravagant sniffing was a French thing because I'd never seen anyone else around these parts or any other parts I'd lived in doing anything quite like it.

Not that I was judging but it got to be embarrassing when you ate in a restaurant with him and he stuck his nose in his salad bowl, took a big whiff and came up with an oily lettuce leaf dangling from his chin.

Frenchie popped the lid on his cup and flipped it in the trash can. "And Monsieur Jenkins from Finance called again to remind you about those budget projections."

"Jenkins wants projections? I'll give him projections and then some."

"You want me to tell him that?"

"Yes. No." That might be pushing things too far. "If he calls again, tell him I'm working on it."

"Oui." Frenchie unwrapped a fresh, buttery croissant he'd brought from home—his wife's a baker —and proceeded to spill buttery crumbs all over his desktop.

"What's this name you got?" I leaned over the pony wall separating Frenchie from the masses, resting my own coffee cup on the ledge to give my fingers a break from the heat.

Our office wasn't big or plush but it served its purpose. A few desks and some filing cabinets nobody used any longer what with all the computers and high-tech gadgetry the county had gifted us.

A coffee pot, microwave oven and minifridge served as de facto command and gossip central.

Besides being a handy place to set your coffee down, the pony wall kept the civilians at bay. Two stiff-backed chairs near the door gave them someplace to sit.

"Ryan Deering. Thirty-nine years old last month."

"And I forgot to get him anything for his birthday."

Frenchie looked up from his computer screen. "You knew him, Chief?"

"No." I gave it a minute to let that fact sink in. Enjoyed my coffee. "And I still don't. Who is he?"

"The body on the bitch, Chief."

I focused on my coffee, took a drink, let it hit my empty stomach, roil around some. I'd fed Bladder Boy this morning but skipped breakfast myself. It felt like one of those jelly side down days and I wasn't taking any chances.

The gears in my head turned a couple of times and all became clear. "The murder victim?"

"Yes. Ryan Deering. Age thirty-nine—"

I held up a hand to stop him. "No need to repeat yourself. What else have you got on him?"

The sergeant pulled a sheet of paper off his printer and handed it to me. I read while he quoted.

"Two misdemeanors for possessing and operating video poker gaming machines."

"Old," I said, noting the dates in both instances were more than a decade ago. "Clean since then."

"It would seem so."

"You call this wife of his yet? Ariadne Deering?"

"No, Chief. I felt you'd want to handle it yourself."

"Right. Merci beaucoup," I said. "I hate handling this shit. Nobody ever likes hearing that a loved one is dead."

"Hey, I'm only a sergeant. You're the chief."

"I'm the Sheriff, Frenchie. The Sheriff." I threw open the front door. Cold hard rain hit me in the face. One more obstacle I didn't need. I turned, grabbed a rain jacket from the hook on the wall and wrestled with it until it surrendered. I settled it over my shoulders.

"Where you off to, Tom?" Capt. Lizzie Gutierrez came running from her squad car to the door, wet but wearing a smile.

Was it wrong of me to hate her for it?

"To pay my condolences to the widow."

"Widow?" She stomped her feet on the rubber mat outside then pushed past me.

"Let Frenchie explain it to you." Served her right if he did.

9

Ryan Deering's new widow—whether she knew it yet or not—resided down in Grandy, a community on the west side of the Sound. This meant driving fifteen miles south through the heart of the thundershower.

I didn't know which I was hungrier for, clues or sustenance, but I opted for breakfast, if only to put off having to tell a woman that her husband was dead.

I hit the drive-thru at Duckees and ordered a breakfast burrito and another coffee to replace the one I'd forgotten back at HQ.

I ate in the parking lot, with a splendid view of the passing vehicles, what few there were in the heavy rain, and ignored the speeders because I didn't want to get wet or my food to get cold.

I tossed my trash behind the seat then drove to the address provided. The Deerings lived in a small white cottage with a gabled roof sitting on a flat lot backing up to a narrow canal a couple blocks from the Sound.

A Harley-Davidson motorcycle hid from the rain under a cluttered carport. A rusting beige Camry sedan blanketed in wet pine needles and with a dent the size of a small deer in the left rear quarter panel stood in the driveway. A black 4x4 pickup parked on the weedy lawn.

Two overflowing trash cans in the carport told

me that either nobody here cared much about the weekly garbage collection schedule or that they created a hell of a lot of trash on a weekly basis.

I pulled in behind the Camry, took the kind of breath I always needed before informing a relative of bad news, then scrambled from my truck to the front porch.

I shook the rain off my uniform as best I could, wiped my face dry and pressed the bell.

A barking German shepherd stuck its forepaws on the window ledge and mashed its wet black nose to a pane of glass nobody had cleaned since man first walked on the moon.

A big man in a weathered black leather jacket, soiled jeans and black motorcycle boots, opened the door and greeted me.

"Who the hell are you?" he asked through the stormdoor. The German shepherd squeezed between his knees and growled at me.

The big man growled at the dog. The dog retreated a couple of steps.

"Sheriff Edge." I unzipped my coat and revealed my badge. "I'm looking for Ariadne Deering. Is she here?"

"What do you want with her?" The man rested his arm against the doorjamb. He had a wide face, dark bloodshot eyes and several days stubble.

"That's between me and her."

He looked for a minute like he was going to dispute the matter then apparently thought better of it. Maybe it was my magnetic personality. Maybe it was my uniform. Maybe it was the Glock 22 hanging on my belt.

"Hey, babe!" The dog barked at me some more and

the man wrapped his fingers around its leather collar. "Come here you."

He dragged the dog to a door at the back of the narrow house. It was all I could do to keep from wringing the asshole's neck.

"Go!" He pointed. The German shepherd hesitated and I couldn't blame him. It was raining cats and dogs out there and he was the dog. But out he went and the man slammed the door on him.

"What?" screamed an impatient woman's voice from a room to my left.

"Some cop here to see you."

"A cop?"

An attractive brunette, if a few pounds overweight, with a tan that only comes from days in the sun or hours in a tanning booth, stepped into the room, carrying the smell of cigarettes with her.

She twisted up her lip. "What do you want? Neighbors complaining again?"

"I gotta go," said the big man. "You got this, babe?"

"Yeah, yeah. Go to work. And don't forget, Shelly's giving me a ride so that means you've got to pick me up at five." I recognized the uniform, distinctive light gray button-down shirt and charcoal trousers, as standard issue for one of the local supermarkets.

"I won't forget." He planted a rough kiss on her cheek.

"You always forget."

With a grunt, he threw open the stormdoor and ran across the front yard, making a beeline to the truck. Looking back at me in the house, he cranked the engine, spun the tires, creating huge muddy divots, and sped off.

"My car won't start," explained Ariadne Deering, although I hadn't asked. "This is what I've got to put up with."

"Right."

"So what do you want, Mr. Policeman?"

"You are Ariadne Deering?"

"You came all this way to ask me that?" She pulled an open pack of Marlboros from a side pocket of her slacks and lit up with the cheap plastic Bic lighter she lifted from the pocket on the opposite side. "Yeah, that's me."

"I'm Sheriff Thomas Edge," I said evenly, trying desperately to work up some compassion for the woman, remembering her husband had met a violent end. "I wanted to talk to you about your husband, Ryan."

The worry lines on her face eased up a bit. "Is that what this is about?" She puffed, blew smoke at the ceiling. "He ain't here. Try the Slowater."

"The Slowater?"

"The Slowater Motel in Corolla. That's where he works." She laid a hand on the front door. "Look, I've got to get ready for work and—"

"Mrs. Deering," I began, "I really need to have a word with you."

She frowned, cigarette dangling from her mouth. "Why? What's he done? No, no. Whatever he's done, I don't wanna know." She mashed the cigarette in an ashtray that should have been emptied weeks' ago, spilling ash over the sides and onto the table. "His problem, not mine."

"Mrs. Deering," I said more forcefully, "your husband's problem is that he's dead." That wasn't exactly the way I'd meant to break the news to her but that was the way it had come out so there was nothing I could do now but to go on.

"Dead?" Her green eyes took on a new and interesting look. I couldn't quite get a read on what they were saying but it was well worth noting.

"Yes, dead. I'm afraid his body was found washed up on the beach in Carova and—"

"Washed up?" Tears formed along the edges of Mrs. Deering's eyes. A reaction to the cigarette smoke or the news? "Drowned?"

I sighed. "I'm afraid it's not that simple."

"I need a drink." She scooted to the kitchen and I followed behind.

She grabbed a bottle of scotch off a glass and brass cart and poured some into one of two coffee mugs resting on placemats atop a cheap wooden kitchen table with a hundred-dollar view of a brown canal. Two pale blue melamine plates, scarred with toast crumbs, catsup stains and smeared egg yolk, set the scene of breakfast past. A small fishing boat bobbed at the dock in the backyard. "You want one?"

"No, thanks."

Ariadne Deering turned her back to me while she lifted the cup to her lips and sipped. "What do you mean 'not that simple'?"

"It means somebody stuck a knife in his back."

Ariadne Deering turned and faced me, her eyes narrowed, her expression unreadable.

"That your boat out there?"

Her brow went up. "Belongs to Donny."

"That the charm school graduate who let me in?"

She smiled. "Yeah, that's him. Why you asking?

You think one of us did it?" She wasn't giving me time to answer. "Because if you are, I was at work all day yesterday. So was Donny. You're gonna have to find somebody else to pin Ryan's murder on. Shouldn't be too hard."

What was it that I'd said to the sergeant earlier about nobody liking to hear that a loved one was dead?

There really was an exception to every rule and Mrs. Ariadne Deering was the exception to this one. Probably plenty of others too that we hadn't reached yet.

The house was cold and I was soaked. Not a good combo. I zipped up my jacket. "When was the last time you saw your husband? I mean, he is still your husband, or are you divorced?"

"In the process," Ariadne Deering frowned, refilled her glass with an inch of scotch, adding a splash of water from the tap and drank. "That's lawyer talk for let's drag it out until we suck your bank account dry."

"I see. How long have you been separated?"

Ariadne Deering performed some mental calculations. "Eight, nine months."

"So the last time you saw him?"

She appeared annoyed that I was still asking questions. "I don't know," she sighed. "Maybe a week ago."

"Where was this?"

"At work." She pulled a face. "He showed up when I was working my shift. I'm a cashier."

"What did he want?"

"Same thing he always wants. Me." She shook her head to let me know that was a bad thing. "I've got to deal with people. I can't have him coming in and harassing me when I'm on the clock. I've got customers, I've got a manager. You should do something about that. Harassment."

"Ryan won't be harassing you anymore, Mrs. Deering."

"Oh, yeah." She looked like she wanted to smile but was holding back on account of me. "I don't suppose he left me anything? Like money?" Greed did a little two-step across her eyes.

"I'm afraid I wouldn't know, Mrs. Deering."

Through the glass, I saw the German shepherd looking like the posterchild—or dog—for the term *hangdog*. I felt bad for him.

"About your husband. Records show this as Ryan's address."

"Well, it's not. Like I said, he's been working at the Slowater. Owner gives him a room there."

I was going to want to check that room out. "Do you and Ryan have any children?"

That earned me a snort. "No, thank god."

I agreed but knew better than to say so. "How long had the two of you been married?"

"Ten years, give or take." She carefully lit another Marlboro with a trembling hand.

"Do you have any personal effects here that belonged to your husband, Mrs. Deering? If so, I'd like to take a look at them."

"What for?" She blew a spout of smoke over her left shoulder.

"It might give me some leads on identifying his killer."

"Then I guess you're out of luck. When I threw him out, I gave him a choice. Take it with him or I'd toss it."

"How long have you known Donny?"

"A couple of years."

"Does he live here?"

"You the Sheriff or the morals police?"

I waited her out, folding my arms across my chest. Mostly to keep warm but she didn't know that.

"Yeah." Her lips tightened around the Marlboro, lines radiated out from her lips in all directions. It wasn't a pretty sight. "He lives here."

"What's Donny's last name?"

"Shit, what do you need that for?"

"I'm afraid I have to talk to everyone."

"He's not going to want to talk to you."

"You let me worry about that."

"I know you're a cop but worry about it you should."

"The last name?"

"Fine. Clark but don't say I didn't warn you."

"Where might I find him?"

"You might find him here. You might find him at some bar."

"And right now? He said he was going to work. Where is that?" This woman was trying my patience. Had she tried Ryan Deering's patience too? Maybe they had tried each the other's patience and there could only be one winner in that battle of wills and egos.

Maybe she'd gotten tired of the divorce dragging on, as she put it, and grown equally tired of her lawyer sucking her bank account dry. By the look of things, it wouldn't take much of a money vacuum to clean her out.

Courts move slowly. Knives, on the other hand,

can move quite quickly.

"Clark's Body and Paint, a couple of miles south of here on the Caratoke." Ariadne frowned. "The man can fix a fender and paint a whole damn car in a day when he wants to. But can he get my car started when he's had the whole weekend to do it? No."

A car honked several times in quick succession.

"That's Shelly. I gotta go." She let the German shepherd inside. He shook himself, sending water all over us, the walls, the windows and the outdated yellow kitchen appliances.

The dog shot me a warning look but was too miserable to make trouble for me. He curled himself into a brown dog bed in the corner and closed one eye.

Ariadne Deering marched into the front room, snatched a coat and a purse from a tiny front closet and waved me out the door.

The rain was easing up.

"Thank you for your time. I'll let you know if we learn anything new."

"You do that."

10

I wasn't halfway on my way to interview Donny Clark when my radio squawked. I hit the receiver and slowed, falling further behind the semi I'd been using as a rain shield. "What is it, Frenchie?"

"Chief? Zefferelli wants you."

"Yeah, well tell her I want her too. Just don't tell her husband about us, okay?"

"Okay."

We played the game of silence for a few seconds as another tenth of a mile rolled by on my side. "Anything else?"

"She says the body won't be available much longer because they have to sheep it."

"Roger that." I knew we weren't talking about Little Bo Peep and Company.

"You don't want to see it before they sheep it?" Frenchie asked me.

We don't have much by way of forensic facilities here in the county. Ryan Deering would get shipped to the big boys for a proper autopsy. Tracy only handles the prelim.

"Only if there's a reason to."

"Dr. Zefferelli, she says is very strange."

That got my attention. "Strange how?"

"Strange that a man drowns with a knife in his

back."

My foot hit the brake pedal and I skidded onto the apron of the road. Cars honked their displeasure. I wasn't feeling too pleased myself.

"Did you say drown?"

"Ms. Zefferelli says drowned. I'm telling you what she said, Chief."

I threw the Bronco in neutral. "How long have I got?"

"For what?" Frenchie wanted to know.

"To see the body before it catches a ride to ECU or wherever the hell it's going." The Eastern Carolina University Brody School of Medicine handled most of our business.

"About an hour. Depending on traffic and whether the driver stops for a bite."

"Call Tracy and tell her I'll be there in twenty. That it?"

"Switch called for you, Chief."

My stomach dropped six inches. Switch was the not-so-flattering nickname that my team had branded Sonia Ranganathan with. Sonia has been my on again/off again girlfriend for the past eighteen months or so. Hence the nickname, unflattering as it was. Right now, things were rather off again. "Did she say what she wanted?"

"She wanted to talk to you. She said you should call her but, if you don't, she'd try again later."

"Great." Of course, she hadn't dialed my mobile. Most likely because she expected I wouldn't answer. And I wouldn't have.

I hated that she knew me so well. Probably because of her training. She was a professional psychologist with an office in Manteo.

Mom should have warned me never to date a psychologist.

"Chief?"

"Yeah?"

"What should I tell her if she calls again?"

"Tell her I'm the Sheriff."

"I don't get it. Switch knows you're Sheriff, Chief."

"At least somebody does, Frenchie. And Frenchie?"

"Yes, Chief?"

"Don't ever let her hear you call her Switch."

"Roger Rabbit that, Chief."

I cut the connection with my sergeant before my migraine killed me, swung the Bronco around, setting my sights for the second time that day on the community of Currituck, specifically, the Currituck Community Clinic, Tracy Zefferelli's workplace and the nearest thing to a hospital we've got.

Currituck's got more animal hospitals than it does medical facilities for humans. Shows where our priorities lie, I guess. Not that I was judging one way or the other.

By the time I reached the clinic, the rain had stopped but the gray sky seemed to keep going forever. A jumble of cars filled the slots, patients and staff. Ryan Deering had caught a lift, probably in the very same EMT response vehicle parked toward the side doors.

I came to a stop in front of the main entrance right under the big sign with the boldface red letters that said it was illegal to park in this spot and violators would be subject to a $250 fine, and hurried inside.

A boy nursing his left arm, with a woman who

I assumed to be his mother, huddled in a couple of scalloped plastic chairs near the sixty-five-gallon aquarium swimming with brightly-colored tropical fish, and one lone brown seahorse. A plastic diver hovered over an open treasure chest, bubbles burbling from his miniature scuba tank.

I gave the child a smile and crossed to the reception window, unzipping my jacket as I went. "Tracy available?"

"Hi, Sheriff," greeted the receptionist. "You here about the—" She urged me forward with a bent finger. "Deceased?"

"Since I'm six months early for my yearly physical, that would be a yes. He hasn't checked out yet, has he?"

"Nope. Go on back. Tracy's with a patient. I'll tell her you're here. I'm sure it won't be long."

I swung through the door leading to the medical examination rooms and offices and took the hall to the far right corner of the single-story building. An unmarked door indicated the end of the road, in more ways than one.

I entered a small anteroom with a computer-equipped desk and a couple of chairs. A locked windowless steel-clad door led to a special room reserved for the likes of Ryan Deering.

I'd been inside only a few times since taking over as Sheriff a little more than two years ago. It felt longer. Then again, that was fourteen Bladder Boy years.

I sat at the desk and was about to boot up the computer and play a hand of virtual solitaire when the door to the anteroom shot open and Tracy came plowing in, being led by her very extended belly.

"Hey, Tom. I don't have a lot of time. Let's do this."
She rolled me and the chair I rode on out of her path,
yanked open a desk drawer and extracted the keys to the
kingdom or, in this case, the keys to the inner sanctum.
The place where bodies went to be ogled, prodded and
marveled at before being sent along to their final resting
places or the ECU lab down in Greenville.

With more than a little reluctance, I followed her
into the windowless room. Cold, sterile and disturbing.
A room like this makes a man think. At least, it made
this man think.

Life was too damn fragile. For all of us.

Three built-in drawers clad with stainless steel
doors and long handles, stacked one atop the other,
occupied a section of the wall to the left. Tracy picked
door number two in the middle and rolled it open.
"Voilà."

I found myself not breathing.

"Note the contusion on the right side of the
skull."

"I noticed that at the scene. Didn't know what to
make of it." I still didn't. "My first assumption was that
he struck something in the water."

"Or something struck him."

"That's a thought."

I studied Ryan Deering's pasty corpse for longer
than I cared. "What are those marks?" She knew what I
meant. The legs, a few inches above the ankles, bore red
rings. So did the chest.

"You tell me. Look like abrasions."

"Abrasions?"

"Go all around the body. My guess is he was
bound."

"Bound." I scratched the top of my head. "And, did I hear right, are you figuring he drowned and then he was stabbed?"

"Definitely."

"I'll be damned. Frenchie got it right."

"How's that?"

"Doesn't matter." I eyed the puckered gash in our victim's chest. "And the stab wound?"

"Occurred some hours after death."

"Time of death?"

Tracy shrugged. "I'd guess two or three days."

"Care to guess again?"

"What can I say? You done?" I nodded and she rolled the body out of sight. "He's been submerged for some time. Things don't develop the same in water as they do on land."

"If he'd been floating around in the Atlantic all that time, pardon my saying because I'm just a cop and no expert like you, but wouldn't the fish have been making a feast of him? I mean, he looks in reasonably good shape. For a dead man."

"He is. I can give you a couple of reasons for that."

"Please do." I was at a loss for answers but could think of a million questions.

"Firstly, he didn't drown in the ocean."

"Come on, Tracy, I saw Deering. He was lying on the friggin' beach—"

"And he had a knife wound that you thought was the cause of death," she interrupted.

"Yeah, well. Not exactly. It was only a theory. And a damn good one considering." I massaged the back of my neck, which had sprung a knot the size of a softball.

"No trace of salts, no—"

"Spare me the details. He did drown?"

"There's no doubt in my mind."

"So he drowned in what?"

"Freshwater."

"Fresh?" I gave the idea some thought. "Like his bathtub?"

"I don't think so."

"So then what?"

"There are any number of bodies of freshwater around here. Take your pick."

"Gee, thanks." But it still didn't explain how the victim was relatively in one piece, his flesh generally undamaged by sharks or other seafaring scavengers.

"You're welcome. Need anything else?"

"When's the baby due?"

"Same time she was the last time you asked me."

My cheeks heated up. "Sorry. I'm not good with dates."

"So I've heard from every girl you ever went out with."

11

Nat Midgett threw himself down onto a thick oak chair across from my desk. The cumbersome chairs had come from the Old Courthouse up in Currituck. Before that, who knew? Maybe the chairs had come across the ocean from England in the bowels of some leaky tub with the Lost Colonists or Sir Walter Raleigh himself.

We had a good dozen of the clunky chairs sprinkled throughout the office. They were quite comfortable—so long as you remained standing.

Keeping a couple of those chairs in my office tended to keep visiting hours on the short side. Just the way I liked it.

I glanced up from my computer, which at the moment was antagonizing me with Excel tables a thousand cells long and a million rows wide, all related to official vehicle usage and maintenance costs.

Eyes glazing over, I was beginning to think it might not be a bad idea to dump the motorized vehicles and start riding the wild horses of Currituck. How much of a spreadsheet could maintaining those critters require? One column for oats and a second column for horse manure disposal?

"Hell," I found myself saying aloud, "we could probably sell the horse shit for fertilizer." I flicked off the monitor. "Break even that way."

"What on earth are you talking about, Sheriff?"

"Huh? I almost forgot you were here." Wishful thinking, I guess. "What's on your mind, Nat?"

"Sergeant Depardieu tells me that Dr. Zefferelli believes our victim was drowned and then stabbed. That true?"

"Yep. Believe it or not."

"There have been Deerings living on the Banks a long time."

"As long as you?" Everybody familiar with the Outer Banks knew that the Midgetts' family tree went way back in these parts. They were some of the first settlers here in Carolina. To be a Midgett was to be somebody.

Midgett blood ran particularly thick in the Banks, especially on Hatteras Island. There was also a long history of Midgetts serving in the Coast Guard and its predecessor, the US Lifesaving Service, as well risking their lives assisting at the many coastal life-saving stations.

It was no surprise to me, or anybody else for that matter, that Nat resented me being Sheriff. It was something he felt he deserved, not me.

Then again, it had always been his choice not to run, preferring the security of a steady job.

"Hardly. Two or three generations is my guess."

"An incomer like me." I grinned. "Did you know Ryan Deering?"

"No, sir. I believe the Deerings are mostly down in Dare County. Of course, I have no idea if he's actually related to any of them. I did a little checking. None of those Deerings have been in any trouble with the law. I mean, a traffic ticket or two. Commercial crabbing without a license. That's it." Nat squirmed. My chair had worked its magic.

"Maybe somebody in his family got tired of him showing up for the holidays."

"Maybe."

"Call 'em up. Interview them. Maybe they can shed some light on his recent activities. Maybe one or two of them might even know who'd have wanted to see him dead."

"Yes, sir."

"Besides his wife, that is."

"You spoke with her? I haven't seen your report."

"That's because I haven't had the chance to type one up yet. It'll get done. In time. Just know that she's not shedding any tears for Ryan. She's shacked up with a man named Donny Clark. She and Ryan are, were, separated and in the process of getting a divorce."

"And now she doesn't have to bother." Nat nodded. "Gives her motive."

"The boyfriend too. See? Sometimes we do think alike."

I could see by the sour look on my chief deputy's face that he didn't very much like that idea.

Since he made no sign of leaving, I had to ask, "Was there something else, Nat?"

"The sergeant told me that Dr. Zefferelli also said there were some anomalies regarding the body."

"A contusion on the right side of the head. Above the ear." I indicated the position using my own thick skull as a demonstrator model.

"A blow to the head." Nat nodded.

"But it didn't kill him. Must've hurt like hell though."

"And then he drowned." Nat narrowed his eyes, bit his lower lip. I could see he was thinking hard. If smoke started coming out his ears next, I'd really be impressed.

"Plus, our boy had been bound."

"Bound?"

"Tied up. Lacerations from rope or something above his ankles and around his torso."

Nat pressed his knuckles into his aching spine. "What do you think, Sheriff?"

"I think somebody really didn't like Ryan Deering." I stood. "All we have to do now is figure out who that somebody is."

12

What with all the interruptions, I never had interviewed Donny Clark one-on-one yet but I figured that could wait. If I knew his type, and I was sure I did, he wasn't going anywhere.

What I really wanted next was a look at the room at the Slowater Motel that Ryan Deering was supposedly living in at the time of his murder. Assuming Ariadne Deering was correct. Assuming she wasn't lying.

I also wanted to talk to some of the other employees of the motel and the manager. Somebody there might know something, seeing how the man lived and worked there day in and day out.

The Slowater Motel was on Highway 12 up in Corolla. Easy enough to stop on my way home and still get to my house before the tide made it hard to get in.

Sometimes, when the storms were brewing just right—driving the churning waves up tight against the dunes—I parked my truck at the end of the pavement and slept inside the cab, waiting for things to settle down.

The sun was beginning to think about sinking now, not that a person could tell since the sky never had been any color but gray all day.

Two flags fluttered one above the other atop a shiny aluminum flagpole planted in a small patch of lawn outside the two-story Slowater Motel, the US flag and the NC state flag.

I slotted Bronc next to the office, saluted the flags, and made my way inside. A wave of dry heat blasted me head-on. I took a moment to savor the feeling of warmth rolling over my flesh.

The Slowater was one of the first of the new motels built in the northern Banks. It's been around since the early nineties, when tourism really started to rear its many-dollared head around these parts, after the roads got paved and infrastructure started springing up almost as if by magic or some unwritten law of nature.

An unbroken line of pavement hadn't stretched this far until 1984. That was when the state decided to connect Corolla up with the rest of the known world and extended Highway 12.

Now it looked like the road had been here forever. Nature fought daily to make it and all it had wrought disappear into the briny deep.

It was anybody's guess who was winning, Mother Nature or Mother Development. My money was ultimately on Mother Nature. Like Vegas casinos, nature would always come out the big winner in the end.

"Can I help you, Sheriff?" A woman clad in a blue sweater over a white blouse and blue slacks greeted me, her eyes welcoming. Her hair was dark and straight, accentuating her long face. "If you're looking for a room for the night, I'm afraid we're all booked up."

"Congratulations," I said. "I wouldn't have figured you'd be full this time of year." Summertime, the population here swells from a very manageable few hundred to an unmanageable pain in the ass fifty thousand or so.

"We're having a good year."

Thick braided rugs sat atop deep orange-red wide plank pine floors. More rugs hung from the walls on black iron rods. These rugs featured a number of North Carolina's most well-known and most-visited lighthouses, like the Currituck Beach Lighthouse right up the road here in Corolla, and the Cape Hatteras Light Station less than one hundred miles south.

All very homey. Cozy. Painted duck decoys occupied floating shelves on either side of the fireplace. Decoy carving and duck hunting used to be all the rage around these parts.

I laid my hands on the counter. "Would you be the manager?"

The middle-aged woman stuck out a hand. "Caroline Frazier. I'm one of them. We," she hesitated, her eyes flickered, "recently lost our night manager."

"Tom Edge. So you heard about Ryan Deering's death?"

"Yes." She nodded. "It's all everyone is talking about."

"Did you know him well?"

"Not really. Excuse me."

I stepped aside while she dealt with an arriving couple. After getting them settled and giving them their room keys, she gave me back her attention. "About Ryan Deering."

Caroline Frazier stepped from behind the waist-high counter and came to a stop beside the freestanding gas fireplace with glass doors and a black powder-coated chimney. She turned her palms to the heat. "Ryan and I didn't have a lot of contact, working different shifts as we did. But he did his job."

"Do you remember when you last saw him?"

Caroline Frazier lost no time replying. "Late Friday afternoon. We were busy. I was here until six."

"Mr. Deering never caused any trouble?"

"Ryan? No. None that I ever heard of. I mean, guests complain about no hot water or the power going out or occasionally other guests, but I never heard anything negative about Ryan personally. Not from the guests or the staff."

"Any of those staff around now?"

"One or two housekeepers and Joe, from maintenance."

"I'd like a word with each of them. Are there any employees in particular that Mr. Deering might have confided in, been closer to?"

She gave my question some thought. "I'm sorry. Nobody comes to mind."

"Who owns the Slowater? Are they around?"

"Sorry, no. The owners are two dentists. They reside in Danbury. Connecticut. They only come down once or twice a year."

"Either of them here now? Or been here lately?"

She gave her head a little shake. "No, not for several months. I don't expect either of them again until January. I telephoned Paul soon after I heard about Ryan's death. I'm supposed to find his replacement." She pushed her hands through her hair. "As if I don't have enough to do now with Ryan gone."

"Working a double shift?"

"Yes, but I have a friend. She works part-time as a desk clerk for a B&B in Southern Shores. She's agreed to help out until we can find Ryan's replacement."

"I'd like to see his room. I assume it hasn't been touched."

"No, Sheriff. I don't believe housekeeping has even been in since…"

"Good. How about his car? Is it here? I didn't see it out front." According to DMV's records, Deering owned a 2005 Pontiac Grand Am.

"Now that you mention it, the car's been gone several days."

"Just like him?"

Caroline Frazier nodded. "Just like him. His parking space is next to mine, around back, near the dumpster. That's where all the employees park."

"Thanks, I'll take a look anyway."

She returned to the counter and plucked a keycard from a drawer. "This will get you into his room. Room 204. Right above us." Her eyes moved to the ceiling.

"Thanks. Do you live on the premises also?"

"Are you kidding? In one of these tiny rooms? No, I live in Duck. I've got a husband and three kids. We barely fit into our house."

The Slowater Motel was shaped like the letter L. Offices and facilities occupied the smaller section nearest the highway. Guest rooms spread out the longer wing.

I climbed the concrete steps. Room 204 stood at the top of the stairs. I saw a laundry to the right, plus an alcove with an ice machine and two vending machines —one for junk snacks and one for soda. Pick your poison.

I slid the keycard across the lock and went inside. The draperies were pulled tight. I fumbled for a light switch, found it and flicked it, to reveal pink walls, flat sand-colored carpet and a full-size bed with a plush white comforter.

A room AC unit clung to the outside wall, not making a peep. A 32-inch flatscreen faced the bed and requisite night tables. The alarm clock was off by approximately five minutes.

I took my time searching the small room top to bottom and snapped a number of photos with my smartphone. Maybe it would see something I was missing. Because so far what I was missing was any clues to Ryan Deering's murder.

Inexpensive clothing filled the narrow closet. Bottles, pastes and lotions—all cheap generic supermarket brand stuff—cluttered the bathroom counter. All of it had come from Old Union, the same regional chain of grocery stores his widow was employed with. A lonely pack of condoms sat on the shelf under the sink, its plastic wrap unbroken.

I pulled back the white plastic curtain on the fiberglass tub/shower combo. A half-filled shampoo bottle, a razor and a sliver of soap.

I yanked open the night table drawers and dug around. Lots of junk, socks, underwear and a pair of flip-flops in the first one. Things went downhill from there. Until I got to the top drawer on the far side. Among the dollar store treasures, I uncovered a box of .22 long shells. No gun.

What was he planning on doing? Tossing the bullets by hand?

In the bottom drawer on the far side of the bed, I found a few old magazines curling around the edges and a copy of Think and Grow Rich written by Napoleon

Hill.

I flipped through the pages. The book had once been the property of the Currituck County Public Library system. Somebody had stamped 'discarded' on the title page.

Now, somebody had discarded Ryan Deering too. Had he been thinking about growing rich?

If so, the book had failed to work its magic for him.

I straightened, rubbed my back. I'd spent over an hour in the room and come up empty-handed. If a room said something about a person, then there was nothing much special to be said about our victim.

Except that he was a victim—of murder. That made him someone special in my eyes. That made him someone special in the eyes of our killer too. Special enough for our killer to have wanted him dead.

I'd had enough of the tiny room.

I took the book with me on my way out, thinking it couldn't hurt.

I ran into a housekeeper rolling a cart up the second-floor walkway. All she did was cry and say what a wonderful man Ryan Deering had been.

Joe from maintenance turned out to be Joelene Hislop and she was working on the heater outback. While she twisted a wrench, she explained that Ryan Deering pretty much kept himself to himself.

"He was a decent manager, considering he had no experience when he started."

"When was that?"

Joe sniffled, wiped the crescent wrench under her nose. In a lavender and black plaid shirt, heavy dungarees and soiled work boots, she was suitably-dressed for the cold and wind accosting us like a mugger behind the motel. A fawn brown OBX ball cap featuring the silhouette of a prancing horse kept the brown hair from her brown eyes as she worked. "Less than a year ago, I'd guess."

"If he had no motel experience, how did he get the job?" I made a mental note to learn what previous jobs Ryan Deering had worked at.

"Like most of us, I guess. He was willing to work cheap."

"Did he have any friends that you know of?"

"Nope."

"How about enemies?"

"Like Ariadne and Donny?"

"You know about them?"

"Sure. Hard not to. He pined for that woman. Why, I'll never know. As for Donny, he came by a few times."

"What for?"

"To warn Ryan to keep the hell away from Ariadne."

"Has a temper, does he?"

"Only when he's mad." She tossed the wrench into her metal toolbox and pulled out a screwdriver. "And he was born mad. Hand me the tape, would you?" She worked at a rusty screw sticking out of the side of the heater.

"This?" I bent my knees to reach into the toolbox for the black electrical tape on a tray inside.

"Yep." She held out her free hand palm up. I dropped the roll in her hand. She twisted a pair of wires together, yanked a couple inches of tape from the roll, bit it off with her teeth and wound it quickly around the wires. "That ought to hold."

I stood, anxious to be on my way before Joe turned me into her unpaid apprentice. "Thanks."

"No problem. Oh, Sheriff."

"Yeah?"

"You might as well know. Donny used to be my old man."

"Small world."

"Too small," Joe amended. She picked up her toolbox and marched off.

Returning to the lobby, I found Ms. Frazier seated at the desk tucked into the corner to the right of the counter, reading blue columns of data on a computer screen.

I settled my elbows on the counter. "Seems I'm not the only one who's cursed with looking at numbers."

Caroline Frazier swiveled round in her chair and smiled. "Going over the week's upcoming check-ins. I don't mind." Her hand settled around a mug that she brought slowly to her lips. "Did you find anything interesting in Ryan's room?"

I held up the book. "Some late night reading."

Ms. Frazier squinted. "Think and Grow Rich? Maybe I should take it home and have my husband give it a read. Mind if I borrow it?"

"Sorry, evidence."

"Of course."

I fumbled in my pocket for the keycard and set it atop the counter. "Here you go."

"I'm sorry you couldn't find anything to help you with your investigation. Ryan was okay. I hate to see whoever did this to him walk free."

"It's my job to see they don't."

"How's his wife taking it?"

"Better than you might expect."

She leaned against the counter across from me. I could smell the minty sweetness of her hot tea. "Poor Ryan. He really wanted her back."

"He talked about her? Ariadne?"

"Is that her name? I don't remember. Yes, he spoke of her. Not often, but every once in a while, he mentioned he hoped they'd get back together. Work things out."

"I guess it just wasn't in the cards." I thought about Caroline Frazier's picture of Ryan Deering. This was not quite the same as the picture Joe painted for me but there was nothing surprising about that. Two people, two perspectives.

"Again, I'm sorry you couldn't find any clues."

"Sometimes it isn't about what you find. It's what you don't find."

"That's rather cryptic."

"I don't mean to be." I pressed my arm tighter against me to keep Think and Get Rich safely tucked into my armpit. "I did not find a phone or a PC, or any kind of electronic device at all in Ryan Deering's room. Not even an electric toothbrush."

"That's funny." Caroline Frazier slipped a lock of escaping hair behind her left ear. "I'm sure he had both. I mean, who doesn't have a cellphone? And I know he had a laptop. Motel issue." Her face showed concern. "You say it's missing?"

"Seems to be." I glanced behind the counter. "You sure it's not here someplace? Could he have left it in the office? Under the counter?"

"I haven't seen it." The manager turned, planted her hands on her hips. "I suppose it could be here." Turning to face me, she said, "If I find it, shall I give you a call?"

"Please do." I gave her my card and headed for the door.

"Sheriff?"

"Yes?"

"I don't know if it means anything but there was a gentleman in here a couple of days ago looking for Ryan Saturday."

"Did he give his name?"

"No, I don't think so. He looked familiar though." Caroline Frazier gave a description that matched thirty percent of the tourists, older male, balding, on the short side and armed with a tan.

"Do me a favor, if you see him again, try to get his name and number, and add him to the list of reasons to give me a call."

13

Nights are for me, unless there is some pressing need for a sheriff. Tonight there wasn't. Truth be told, Chief Deputy Nat Midgett rarely found a pressing need for my presence. To put an even finer point on the truth, he very much preferred my absence.

Nights were for Bladder Boy too, of course, but that should go without saying. The spaniel spent most of his evenings snoozing, legs twitching as he chased after one-eyed wild cats and squirrels too busy chasing the acorns of their own dreams to see him coming. That gave me a lot of time for myself.

Myself and my thoughts.

Probably not the best combination. In fact, a toxic and dangerous one, according to my ex-wife, but such is life.

I gazed at the stars. All two of them visible through the clouded-over night sky. Actually, I was pretty sure one of those dim lights was Venus, so one star and one steamy planet—possibly crawling with Venusians or microbes depending on your beliefs and the science of the day.

Cold wind swept across from Russia and made the three empty chairs on my deck dance and rock. My weight on the fourth kept it from joining in.

I pictured a ghost in every chair smirking at me,

goading me to find, if not the meaning of life, then at the very least the reason behind Ryan Deering's death. So far, I was coming up empty. I snugged the collar of my parka up under my neck and tried my best to ignore the ghosts.

But for the ghosts, I faced the night alone. Bladder Boy lay asleep in front of the fireplace in the sitting room. The dog was no fool.

Most days, my dinner came in a box and drinks in a bottle. Tonight, I selected a bottle of red from a local vineyard for company—drink local, that's my motto—although that company was dwindling rapidly.

My eyelids fluttered as sleep strained to push them down. I knew better than to fall asleep and inadvertently spend the night out on the deck. I'd been there, done that, one time too many.

I'd frozen solid in the winter and gotten eaten alive by mosquitoes in the summer. Either way, the story always ended the same, always left me with stiff joints and an even stiffer neck.

The front door rattled and Bladder Boy barked. I figured it had to be a neighbor. The nearest of which was a couple hundred yards away. One came knocking on occasion, invited or not.

I rose, made some groaning noises to go with the noises my knees were making, then stepped inside. Bladder Boy licked my hand. "What's up, boy? Looks like we got some late-night company." Probably some neighbor with a problem. Nobody came by at this hour to chew the fat.

I threw my parka over the nearest chair and went to the door.

No one waiting for me on the front deck.

Either my visitor had given up or it was the ghosts playing tricks. I closed the door quickly only to have Bladder Boy bounce his nose off it, signaling that he wanted outdoors.

"Fine. Don't take too long." I let Bladder Boy out the door and listened to his nails clatter down the wooden steps. Not that I needed to tell him to be quick. It was cold and dark out there. If Bladder Boy could talk, he'd ask for indoor plumbing built to doggy specs.

I shut the front door once more, not so much to keep him out until he'd done his business but to keep in what little heat the house held. With no central heating or air in the house, I rely on nature to be kind to me.

I'd been meaning to add a woodstove to my bedroom but in a world of to-dos, that was exceedingly low on the list.

I brushed my teeth in the bathroom and washed the day off my battered face. I smiled at the man in the mirror to remind myself that I could and should smile once in a while.

Bladder Boy scraped at the front door. No need to add installation of a doggy door to my future to-do list, eventually his scraping would get us one for free.

"I'm coming." I yanked the cold door handle. Bladder Boy shot between my legs. I stared at my late-night visitor.

Not a ghost.

"What are you doing here?"

14

"You didn't call me back." She ran a slender hand through a cascade of long black hair. A white scarf curled around her neck like a pet albino boa constrictor. She dressed in black jeans, black boots and a black coat but she was one of the good guys. Girls. Women. "So here I am."

"Here you are." I was good at repeating the obvious.

"Why didn't you call me?" Green eyes pinned me under the microscope.

"I've been busy." I wrapped my fingers around the thickness of the door, felt the solidity of the weathered oak against my fingertips. Held on.

All the sleep and bone tiredness whooshed out of me. Disappearing out into the night. I felt tense as a wire pulled to the breaking point between the bridge and the tuning peg on an electric guitar. This reminded me of the long-neglected Rickenbacker 360 twelve-string electric behind my boot collection in the closet. I'd been inspired to purchase it after falling in love with George Harrison's Hard Day's Night solo.

I'd become uninspired when I'd attempted to learn to barre chord the twelve-string using my index finger. You might as well have asked me to barre with my chin, I was equally as ineffective.

Bladder Boy padded up and rubbed against her leg. I expected the worst but she refrained, wagged her finger. "I already gave you some love outside. How about you, Tom? Need some love?"

Sonia Anand Ranganathan. The name was a mouthful. The woman herself was a handful. And then some.

My heart played the part of a bass drum. A Ludwig. And Ringo was stomping on the pedal. Boom boom boom. I couldn't remember which of us had broken it off last, me or her. It didn't matter really.

"Come on in. I'll relight the fire." I didn't care if that sounded Freudian. It was cold and cold called for fire, psychoanalysis be damned. And knowing Sonia, there would be some psychoanalysis going on in that pretty little head of hers.

The chorus to The Doors' Light My Fire started circling inside my brain like one of those everything-old-is-new-again thirty-three and a third rpm vinyl records.

"Thanks." Sonia's parents came to the United States from Mumbai. She and her siblings were born and raised here in the good old US of A. Raleigh, North Carolina to put a pin in the exact location on the map. Like her siblings, she was a Duke University graduate. Her English, and maybe everything about her, was better than mine.

I took her coat and scarf and draped each over Granddad's handmade black iron hooks nailed to the wall next to the door. I recognized the fuzzy gray angora sweater I'd given her for her birthday.

I followed Sonia and Bladder Boy to the sitting room. She settled on the sofa. The dog took one look at his cold bed, compared that to my on-again/off-again girlfriend's warm lap, and chose option number two.

I tossed a couple of logs on the dying fire, blew on it some to kick it into gear. I extended my arms and warmed my hands for a minute, watching the flames lick the firebox to see if it was up to snuff, then fell into Granddad's rocking chair.

I decided to go first. "Was there something special you wanted to talk about?" Although I couldn't remember who had broken it off last or the reason why, I was sure that we had agreed we'd break off all contact with each other.

Of course, we'd said that a time or three too. Just because I was Sheriff didn't mean I didn't have some human qualities.

"I heard about the murder. I thought you might want to talk." She ran a gentle finger along Bladder Boy's right ear. I held my breath but he was either acting on his best behavior or he was all out of juice—so to speak.

"Well, I don't." I clasped my knees. Rocked faster.

Sonia smiled a gentle, knowing smile. Ten years my junior and often acted like she was my mother.

"It's so strange," I said. "I mean, I've seen murder before. But this one doesn't make sense." I leaned back, stared at the crackling fire.

"Come on, Tom, what's going on? What's so strange about this murder? I heard the victim was a motel manager? Ryan Deering?"

I didn't ask her where she'd heard all this because it was probably from Nat—she'd known him longer than she'd known me. Hearing that would only annoy me. That she and Nat were friends really annoyed me. That it annoyed me annoyed me all the more.

"That's right. Nothing special about the man at all that I can find so far."

"There's something special about all of us. You have to find out what was special about Ryan Deering." That was the psychotherapist in her talking.

I redirected my eyes to her. "Why dump him on the beach? I mean, if you're going to kill somebody, there are a thousand places to dump a body in these parts and it'll never be found. He was found on the beach, drowned but not in the ocean, with a knife in his back that somebody stuck there after he was dead."

Sonia gasped. "Seriously?"

"Yep."

"That's horrible." She shuddered. Proving that just because she was a psychologist didn't mean she didn't have some human qualities too.

"That's the going theory du jour. Have you got a better one?"

"No, I'm afraid not. Look," Sonia rose, crossed the gap between us and stood beside my chair. She laid a hand on the seatback, stopping my rocking. "Don't let it get to you. Don't let it eat you up."

"It's not," I lied through gritted teeth. I pressed my feet into the floor but the chair chose her over me and refused to rock.

"You'll solve it or you won't."

"I will."

"Perhaps you should take a break, go away for a few days."

"Yeah," I sniffed. "Nat would love that. When I come back, I'll probably be working for him."

Sonia knelt beside me, took my hands in hers. "Don't push me away."

"I didn't ask you to come."

"You didn't have to. I came because you needed me."

"We broke up, remember? What is that? Four times now?"

"Seven. But who's counting?" Sonia smiled and kissed my cheek. Bladder Boy lifted his head, looking like he wanted in on the action.

"You can't keep your past bottled up forever, Tom."

"It's my past, I can do whatever the hell I want with it." If my past was something I could shove into a bottle, stuff a cork in and toss in the middle of the ocean for some poor sap to find drifted up on a beach fifty years from now, I'd do it. That was how much, or how little, the past meant to me.

"You're being difficult." Sonia rose and ran her fingers through my hair, her fingernails massaging my scalp. A current of pleasure skittered across my skull.

"I am not being difficult," I argued. My head wanted to go one way, my body another.

"Think about it. You move from Cape Disappointment—"

"I liked the name." It sounded romantic, in a suicidal sort of way.

Her voice overrode mine. "To the Outer Banks."

"So? My grandfather left me a house."

"You moved from the Graveyard of the Pacific to the Graveyard of the Atlantic, Tom. What does that say about you?"

I cracked a grin. "That I'm cheap. I'll go anywhere so long as it's free and located near a graveyard?"

"And are you free, Tom?"

I shook my head. "Let's not get too deep. I can't handle it right now."

"Are you afraid to talk about yourself?"

"I'm not one of your patients, Sonia."

"Don't be afraid to open up."

"It's late. You need to go." I stood. Being a foot shorter than me, she had no choice other than to look up.

Sonia swung her watch around, looked at it and then at me, defiant and smirking. "It is late. Eleven forty-five. Pitch black on the beach. And the tide is in. It looks like I'm going to have to spend the night." Her fingers walked up my inner arm. "Unless you want me to risk driving out?"

I rubbed the sides of my face to give my hands something to do other than wrap themselves around her and pull her closer, which was what they were contemplating doing. "Looks like you are."

15

I watched Sonia's British racing green Land Rover fade in the distance as she turned off for Manteo and I went on to the office. We made plans to meet up at her place later.

I guess we were on again.

But this wasn't the time to be thinking about me and Switch.

Retrace the victim's life and last days. That was the way to find a killer.

I had to focus on that. I had to stay focused. Put my relationship with Sonia on the backburner, a backburner keeping a stack of pecan-buttermilk pancakes warm.

The police radio under the dash squawked to get my attention. "Accident, Chief."

"Let's hear it, Frenchie."

"Jacques knifed off Shawboro."

"Jacques knifed who? And how was that an accident?" I pictured another grueling day. At least the night had been memorable. I'd gotten a home-cooked hot breakfast out of the deal too. Who knew I had the makings of pecan-buttermilk pancakes in the house? Not me.

"Not who, Chief. It is an accident, vraiment. Jacques knifed truck. Lumber everywhere."

I pulled over to the side of the road to pick at the puzzle Frenchie presented me. I held the receiver in my hand, brought it to my lips. "Okay. Let me see if I understand. We've got this Jacques and he's knifed somebody in a dispute over some lumber?"

I'd heard worse. When I'd first served in the Coast Guard, we had a guy gut his best friend over a walleye each claimed to have plucked from the Columbia River.

"Huh? No, Chief," countered Frenchie. "This trucker—"

"For chrissakes, Sergeant," Chief Deputy Nat Midgett's voice cut between us. "It's a damn lumber hauler, *Sheriff*. Jack-knifed. *Jack-knifed*, Frenchie, get it? It's blocking the intersection of Shawboro Road and the Caratoke."

"Injuries?"

"None reported, Chief," said Frenchie, unfazed by Nat's outburst.

"Got it. Send a couple of units, Frenchie."

"Done, Chief. Flo and Eddie are responding."

"I'm on the 158 heading north. I'll be there in twenty, if the mess isn't cleared by then. If it is, let me know and I'll cut over to the office." So much for my plan to focus on the Ryan Deering case.

"Rojay," said Frenchie.

"Are you heading that way, Nat?" I asked.

"I've got court in an hour, Sheriff, remember?"

"Roger, that." Some people didn't take getting tickets all that well and chose to fight them. A pile of tickets and a passel of unhappy defendants stood on the docket for today.

"Sheriff, we've got another situation you might want to handle instead of the road accident."

"What's that, Nat?" A choice of troubles. My lucky day.

I shut my eyes briefly as I fought my way into the stream of traffic heading north. Some days I felt like a salmon on a spawning run, waiting to get its head bashed in by a primitive fisherman wielding a club or a hungry grizzly bear with razor-sharp claws and an empty belly.

Mornings like this made Cape Desolation sound like Eden.

"I just heard from Captain Gutierrez. She received a report about a car and I sent her to follow up the lead. If the caller got the plate correct, it's Ryan Deering's vehicle."

Now here was some good news. Finally. I nudged the gas pedal and powered up the light bar bolted to the roof.

"Location?"

"The Bells Island Life Campground. Think you can find it?"

"Tell me the damn address. I'll find it." Nat took great pleasure in rubbing my nose in the fact that he knew Currituck County better than I did. Like he believed he knew Sonia better than I did.

"Take the Caratoke up to Bells Island Road. That's right before you come to the Feed and Farm. Turn right and follow until you can't go any further. That's pretty much it, Sheriff." Nat sounded a bit tetchy.

Feed & Farm did business out of a big old red barn repurposed as a feed, seed and supply store. I'd driven past it a hundred times. "See? Was that so hard? Tell Lizzie I'm on my way."

Not only was Jacques and his lumber in good

hands vis-à-vis the Sheriff's Office, the Crawford Township Fire Station stood within spitting distance of the blocked intersection. Those boys got bored playing checkers all day. They'd be on the scene, itching to help out.

With one crisis handled and one persnickety chief deputy tied up in court for the rest of the day, I was free to go car hunting.

16

It seemed to me the brochure and mapmakers had lied. Unless Merriam-Webster had recently revised their dictionary on the sly, Bells Island appeared to me to fit the definition of a peninsula, not an island.

Then again, a good strong high tide or a decent storm surge would sever the slender connections I passed over. The next time the oceans rose a foot or two, my point would be rendered moot.

Homes had some room to breathe here. Many of them sitting along straight canals leading to Coinjock Bay, giving boaters quick and easy access to the watery half of our county.

A quiet road and pleasant drive, if not for current circumstances.

And I'd now reached the end of that road.

I found Lizzie Gutierrez before I found Ryan Deering's car. She waved to me, not that I could have missed her. Her unit stood guarding the entrance to the campground like one of those famous library lions, if that lion was wearing a crown of flashing holiday lights.

I rolled up beside her and rolled down a window. "Merry Christmas."

Lizzie planted her hands on her well-armed hips. "You trying to be funny?" Sweat rolled down her forehead. She'd undone the top two buttons of her long-sleeve uniform shirt and rolled the sleeves up to her elbows, showing off her well-toned forearms. A white T-shirt poked through, keeping her modest.

A clear breach of rules, but I didn't dare say anything.

"Apparently not." The weather girl's stated goal for the day was eighty degrees. Although it was only ten in the morning, it already felt like ninety-five and the sun hung over Lizzie like a brutal spotlight. "You check the vehicle yet?"

"Only to run the tag. It's Ryan Deering's, all right. I haven't searched the vehicle. Nat ordered me to wait for you."

"Hop in."

Lizzie climbed in on the passenger side and we rattled and rolled over the rutted tracks, following her directions. The expansive campground held an assortment of mobile homes, campers and a few pitched tents. Barbecue grills were as common as trees.

A row of boats, some sitting on trailers, others sprawled on the grass, if you could call those weeds grass, created an interesting maritime themed art installation, albeit a primitive one, along the far edge of the campground.

"That's it, there." Lizzie pointed.

I parked the Bronco and eyed the car and the man leaning against its front fender. His belly, and it was a big one, leaned our way. "Friend of yours?"

Lizzie chuckled. "That's Mitch."

"Campground manager?"

"Campground hanger-on and mooch is my guess." Lizzie threw open her door with more strength than necessary. The Bronco groaned as the door reached the limit of its limited range of motion. Thankfully, the hinges held.

We walked over to Ryan Deering's car and Lizzie made the introductions. "This is Mitch Green, Sheriff. Mitch, this is Sheriff Edge."

"Pleased." Mitch came towards me with hand extended and mouth agape. I smelled beer and weeks without bathing.

"Mr. Green." I shook the offered hand. "I take it you reported the vehicle?"

Mitch burped. He wasn't a small man, having a good six inches and hundred pounds on me. His black hair was thinning on top and his black beard sprang from his face like it carried a static electric charge. Baggy blue overalls hung off his rounded shoulders, ending in rolled up pant legs and bare feet.

Mitch had made the unfortunate fashion choice this morning of going shirtless. Being the Sheriff, I felt obliged to maintain eye contact as he spoke. "That's right, Sheriff. This Pontiac's been sitting here forever."

"Forever?" If that was the case, I wasn't sure what help finding it would be. The old heap did have a look of abandonment about it. The kind of look Bladder Boy likes to give me when I leave for work each morning.

"Well, maybe not forever." Mitch dragged his bare toes across the ground. "But days." He banged a fist against the hood. The freshly-minted dent he created wasn't a large one and Mr. Deering wasn't going to complain, considering the state he was in, but I felt it my duty to say something.

"I'm going to have to ask you not to touch the vehicle, Mr. Green. This car is evidence." Evidence of bad taste, for sure. Other than that, it was too early to say.

Hopefully, Ryan Deering's car would give us some leads in his murder.

"Huh?" Mitch seemed nonplussed. "Oh, right. This is the car that belonged to the dead guy?"

"No comment," I answered.

"What happens to it now? I mean, if nobody claims it? Finders keepers?"

"Sorry. I expect it will go to his wife."

Mitch frowned. "Married, huh?"

"I'm afraid so."

I turned and studied the vehicle a moment then did a three-sixty around it. The license plate matched, all right. The DMV had gotten it right. Deering drove a 2005 Pontiac Grand Am, white over dark taupe interior with cloth seats.

Lizzie cupped her hands over her forehead and peered through the driver's side window. "Jeez. I've puked prettier colors."

The captain liked her cars red and their interiors so black she could fry her ass on the driver's seat in the summertime. Her words, not mine.

"Is it locked?" I asked the captain.

"No," Mitch was first to reply.

We shot him a jointly-held dirty look.

"Mitch, have you been inside?" Lizzie got all up in Mitch's face.

"Huh? No, sir. Ma'am!" He took a step back. He should have made it two. "I only tried the handle."

Lizzie grabbed the dangling strap of his overalls and held on. "Which one?"

"Umm, driver's side. Front." Mitch pointed.

Lizzie frowned and released him.

"Think, Mitch. Exactly when did you first notice

the Grand Am?" I asked.

Minutes seemed to tick by as Mitch forced his brain into action. He shook his head. "I dunno. Saturday morning, I guess." He brightened. "Yeah, that's it. I got up Saturday morning and there it was. I didn't think anything of it at the time."

"Right." I looked closer at the tires. The earth showed signs of settling and the grass had grown, barely but perceptibly, where the rubber meets the earth. The timing was right.

"Does the campground have an onsite manager?"

"Yeah." Mitch scratched his belly. "That'd be Isaac."

"What's his last name?" Lizzie demanded.

Mitch shrugged and extended his arms, palms out. "Coors, maybe?"

"Like the beer?" Lizzie asked dubiously.

"Something like that. That's his trailer over there, closest to the boats."

"Has he said anything about the car? Did he maybe speak with its owner? Give him permission to park it here?"

"You'd have to ask him, Sheriff. Isaac keeps himself to himself. I don't see him much unless it's time to collect the rent."

"You didn't ask him about this car before calling us?"

"I knocked on his door. He didn't answer. That's his pickup but that don't mean anything."

Mitch indicated a red Chevy quarter-ton nestled against the side of the mobile home like it was holding up the wall. "Sometimes Isaac's gone for days with his buddies, fishing and drinking. He never invites me, though."

"Okay. I'll have a word with him when we're done here. Let's get to it," I told the captain.

Lizzie slipped on a pair of gloves and pulled the driver's side door open. "Geezus. It stinks in here!" She waved her hand in front of her nose.

"What did you expect? It's been sitting locked up outdoors for the past several days," I replied. "Things ripen."

"Peaches ripen," Lizzie snapped. "This shitty car stinks. Smells like it and everything in it is decomposing."

"Is the key in it?"

Lizzie leaned over and checked. "Nope. Not in the ignition, at least."

"Check the glovebox."

"For what? Ripening body parts?" Lizzie cursed me some more as she fumbled with the glovebox. "A bunch of expired registration papers, old receipts, coupons. An air freshener thingie that you hang on the rearview mirror to keep the fucking smell out which you can see this imbecile never bothered to use."

Lizzie waved a sexy hula dancer on a string at me and Mitch. "See? Coconut scented. The damn thing's still in its plastic wrapper."

"Pop the trunk for me."

She did and I took a look. A flat spare tire, a gray blanket, a red-handled screwdriver with matching red rust creeping up its sides, two soiled Slowater Motel branded bath towels and a length of blue nylon cord. One end had been cut, its tip frayed.

"Did Ryan Deering own a boat?"

Lizzie stuck her head out the door. "I don't think

so. Why?"

I squatted to the height of the rear bumper. "Looks like a new trailer hitch back here." No rust or oxidation and only a couple of scratch marks."

Lizzie shrugged and resumed her search of the sweltering interior.

"Did you see a boat trailer on this car at any point, Mr. Green?"

"No, I can't say I did. Not in all the time I saw it." Mitch coughed up another burp. I suspected his beer level was getting dangerously low and this was his body's way of reminding him it was time for a six-pack. "Maybe he had some other kind of trailer, like for hauling junk or something?"

"Could be." I moved upwind of the Grand Am and the camper. "All those boats belong to folks staying here?"

"Nah. Some do. Other locals pay a few bucks a month to keep 'em here, close to the dock. That's mine over there. That little fishing boat. Third from the right."

Mitch pointed to a twenty-one-foot flat-bottomed boat painted a dull army green. Fishing poles hung fore and aft.

"And this is your camper here?" I shook my chin at a nearby dusty black Chevy pickup hosting a camper shell. The Jack Russell terrier, taking advantage of the irregular triangle of shade thrown by the truck, gave me a quick glance then lapped up some water from a steel hubcap serving as his water bowl.

"Yes, Sheriff."

"What's the dog's name?"

"That's Mutton."

"Interesting name."

"Interesting dog. I found him right here. At the campground. Nobody claimed him. Then he claimed me. Eventually. I had to put food out and get out of his way until he could trust me enough to come eat. The little bugger. Sheepish is what he was, but I couldn't call him Sheep, could I?"

Mitch clapped his hands in time with an accompanying sharp whistle. Mutton ran up and danced on two legs under his fingers as he wriggled them like engorged red worms.

I rubbed the dog's belly. "Hey, boy."

"He's okay now but you should've seen him then. Nothing but skin and bones. You got a dog?"

"Springer Spaniel. Bladder Boy."

Mitch's forehead curled upward. "Hear that, Mutton? Your name's not so bad after all, is it?" He scooped the dog up in his arms. Mutton rewarded him with a lick on the lips.

I figured this was a good time to get the subject back to crime solving before Mitch Green reported me to the ASPCA, Name Enforcement Division, for cruelty to animals. "Is there anything else? Anything suspicious or unusual that comes to mind these past few days, Mr. Green?"

"I've been staying here all summer, Sheriff. It's quiet most times. That's the way I like it."

"I know the feeling. I'd like you to give your contact information to the captain, Mr. Green. And if you can think of anything else, please give us a call."

"Yes, sir, Sheriff. Pleasure."

Since we'd started our conversation on that note, I thought it a good place to end it.

I walked up to the mobile home, a singlewide balanced on cinderblocks. Tall weeds sprouted under and all around. Isaac wasn't much of a gardener.

I climbed the steps and rapped on the door.

The mobile home shook but I heard no ensuing footsteps. "Isaac? This is Sheriff Edge. I'd like to talk to you about a vehicle on your property."

I pressed my ear to the door. "Isaac?" I banged a final time but Isaac wasn't answering. A faded plastic sign screwed into the door indicated this was the manager's office—Isaac Miller, not Coors, but I gave Mitch credit for being in the ballpark—and listed a number to call for assistance. The number was local. I dialed it only to get a voicemail box. And got no assistance.

"Isaac, this is Sheriff Edge, please call the Currituck County Sheriff's Office when you get this message. We'd like to ask you a few questions concerning a car found on the property."

Hopefully, Isaac would call me back sooner rather than later. If he knew something, I wanted to know it too.

I stuck one of my business cards in the crack between the door and the jamb then moved over for a closer look at the row of boats and paced between them. I had no idea what I was looking for. Pacing gave my arms and legs something to do while my brain was busy thinking.

I walked to the end of the wooden pier and back for no particular reason too. So it was no wonder the walk did me no particular good.

I returned to Lizzie standing with her arms crossed and looking pretty cross herself, leaning against the side of the Grand Am. She smelled almost as bad as Mitch—maybe worse—and her uniform floated blotches of perspiration.

"Find anything?"

"A reason to look for a new job," Lizzie replied, running her hands down her blouse.

"Have the Grand Am towed to the impound yard and check it thoroughly."

"What are we looking for exactly?"

"I have no idea. Could be Deering's killer drove the vehicle and left his or her prints on the steering wheel."

"Why would they do that?" Lizzie asked, her usual skeptical self.

"To give us a sporting chance?"

"What do you want to bet they didn't? Lunch for a week?" She extended her right hand, waiting for me to take the five fingers of bait.

"No bet. When it comes to betting, I always lose."

17

"What's happening with Jacques and his lumber?" I teased Frenchie, tossing my coat up on the peg at the entrance to the Sheriff's Office.

"Jacques, Chief?" The sergeant looked at me from his seat behind his desk.

I could see I'd befuddled him. Served him right. What comes around really does go around.

"Never mind." I walked past him to my office. I threw myself into my chair and booted up my PC. I skimmed through the overnight reports. Nothing interesting. I opened the budget file and moved some numbers around.

Call me paranoid but the Sheriff's Office was on the same computer network as the folks over at County. And knowing how devious those kind can be, I had a hunch that Jenkins in Finance had talked one of their IT specialists into gimmicking some spyware on my computer that would let Jenkins know if I was working on those priceless budget projections for him.

Satisfied that I had successfully altered the file enough to look like I'd actually done something—I added a few zeros here and removed a few zeros there to balance things out—I sat back and closed my eyes.

Ryan Deering, night manager at the Slowater Motel. Drowned in freshwater. Knife in the back. Why?

Didn't the killer know he was already dead? Complete autopsy results remained pending and would be for some time. Car abandoned at a campground miles from home. I had a hunch we weren't going to find any traces of violence in the Grand Am either. Not unless Lizzie started slashing the seats and busting out all the windows to let some fresh air inside.

Caroline Frazier, day manager at the Slowater, had seen Deering Friday evening. Had anyone else seen him since then? Besides his killer?

Mitch Green claimed he first spotted Deering's car at the campground Saturday morning. Given Mitch's unreliability and foggy state of mind, that didn't mean it wasn't there Friday night. We'd have to do some more checking on that detail.

I'd need to check with Caroline Frazier again too. See if any of the guests remember seeing or speaking with Ryan Deering later Friday night or early Saturday morning.

I also had to verify Ariadne Deering's alibi. Was she really working all last weekend? That should be easy enough to check out.

That led my thoughts to Donny Clark, Ariadne's live-in boyfriend.

It was time for a friendly visit with my favorite body-and-paint man.

"If anything important comes up, you know how to reach me, Frenchie. I'm heading down to Grandy to interview a possible suspect."

"Sure, Chief." Using his index finger, he held his place in an inch-thick stack of papers he was working on, while he focused on me. "What shall I tell the Commissioner?"

"Commissioner?" My hand automatically reached for my coat as it always did this time of year but, being unseasonably warm, I let it hang.

"Commissioner Jewell."

"Jerry? What does she want?"

"Didn't you read zee email I forwarded you?"

"No, it must've slipped through the cracks."

The sergeant scolded me with his eyes. "There are no cracks in the Internet."

"No? Must be in my spam folder then." I leaned my elbows on the pony wall and my chin on my fists. "What exactly does Jerry want?"

Geraldine "Jerry" Jewell served as Vice Chairman of the Board of Commissioners. Currituck carries a seven-member board, one for each of five proscribed districts and two at-large members.

"She wants to be certain that you are available for zee planning party she is hosting."

I groaned. "Tell her I've got enough work of my own."

"She claims you already told her you'd be there, Chief."

I went back in time. Crap. I had. "That was months ago."

Frenchie brought two fingers to his lips and smacked them. "Poof! Now the time has come, Chief. She says eez important."

"Jerry thinks everything she does is important." Jerry chaired the Tourism Advisory Board. As Sheriff, I felt it my duty to advise her every chance I got that Currituck County already had too many tourists as things stood. "What is it this time?"

"Creaky Carolina is coming up. She's counting on

our support."

"Got it." *Creepy* Carolina was the County's annual Halloween spooktacular. I saw no point correcting Frenchie. If he wanted to think the event was creaky, who was I to burst his bubble?

To celebrate Creepy Carolina, our office handed out treats, gave safety talks and dressed in silly costumes, all in the name of entertaining the kiddies.

"Can't you tell her Carolina's already got enough creeps?"

Frenchie waited me out. The man can really stare.

I exhaled. "Fine. When and where?"

"Check your email." Frenchie's hand went to the ringing phone. "Sheriff's Office."

Sure, that he gets right. Every time.

I scooted out the door.

18

From the chatter on the radio, I knew the accident on the Caratoke was in cleanup stage. I decided to swing by before paying a visit on Donny Clark. Not so much to lend a hand as to talk to Eddie Wu and Florence Pinder about a whole other matter.

A matter of murder.

The pair had gone door-to-door up in Carova looking, not for treats, but for witnesses to the murder of Ryan Deering.

I wanted to talk to them personally.

Like I expected, the fire department was out in force. Half a dozen firefighters fought traffic rather than flames.

The lumber truck had been moved to the side of Shawboro Road. Clearing all that spilled lumber out of the way of traffic, however, was a work-in-progress.

That progress was being furthered along by a pair of bulldozers operated by two local farmers, and two forklifts belonging to the county. If this were a game, judging by the number of logs lying on each side of the highway, I'd have to say the dozers were ahead of the forklifters by four points.

Eddie directed traffic. Flo, to my surprise, ran one of the forklifts. The other driver wore a Currituck County Transportation Department uniform.

I waited for a gap in the slow-moving snarl of traffic and darted to the middle of the intersection. "How's it going, Eddie?"

"Great, Sheriff."

"So, no injuries. That's good."

"Not a one. A woman's car got its nose clipped by a runaway log during the initial event but the driver was unharmed. A tow truck hauled the vehicle off a while ago. I expect the driver and trucking company responsible will be hearing from her insurance company."

"No doubt." I joined Eddie in waving for the southbound traffic to get moving. "Look a little less, drive a little more!" Nobody could hear me so I wasn't in danger of losing any future votes.

"About yesterday afternoon's house-to-house, did you and Flo come up with any leads, Eddie?"

"No, sorry, Sheriff. It's all in our report." Eddie was born in Hong Kong but his English was excellent. Frenchie should take lessons from this guy. He'd worked a few years with the NC State Highway Patrol before deciding to go local.

"I've had a lot of paperwork. Haven't gotten to it yet. Give me the highlights."

Eddie spun and stuck up his hand to stop the southbounders. Planting his left foot in front of him like he was wielding an epée, he whistled for the northbounders to move. Only a couple of logs left blocking the northbound lane and traffic could get back to its normal state of mayhem.

Eddie's a slight fellow, shy of six foot with short black hair and brown eyes. When he wants to, he makes up for his lack of size with an overabundance of gestures. "Flo and I ran into a young couple, a Peter and Chloe Goslin, on their way back to their rental. They've got a cottage a couple rows back from the dunes. They were walking on the beach that morning."

"Did they see anything unusual?"

Eddie shook his head. "No. They were walking up the beach toward the border. They were a hundred yards or more north of the Leftkowitzes when the kids started pointing and hollering at something in the water."

"They didn't go back to look?"

"No, sir. They stopped for a minute but then continued on their walk, figuring it was probably a log or a dead shark or something."

It was something all right. But I couldn't blame them. Our shoreline gets more than its share of debris. Everything from storm uprooted trees and dead sharks to unexploded WWII ordnance.

"They said something else too."

"What's that?"

"That when they turned around and were coming down the beach toward the crime scene, one of our officers started yelling at them."

I chuckled. "I remember. We had a couple taking selfies. A young blond kid and a redhead?"

"That's them."

"Anything else I should know about?"

"The folks we talked to at one house, they reported seeing strange lights."

"Strange lights?"

"Yes, like UFOs, you know?"

I knew. "What time was this?"

"Late Friday night."

"So, before Ryan Deering was found on the beach." Many hours before.

"What sort of witnesses are we talking about?"

"They're having a big family reunion. Came in from all around the country. Canada, too. Vancouver, I think. Staying for the week."

"A big family reunion. I'm guessing a lot of partying. Drinking."

"Let's put it this way, Sheriff, if a couple of those gentlemen I interviewed the other day had been behind the wheel of a moving vehicle, they'd be sitting in lockup now."

"Gotcha. Unless one of those aliens shows up and confesses to murder, let's forget about following up on the UFOs."

We watched as Flo, at the controls of her forklift, scooped up a twenty-five-foot pine at its midsection, lifted it, then spun the forklift a neat ninety degrees. The forklift rumbled to the side of the road. She lowered the pine and watched it roll into the ditch.

"I think our team is catching up," I said.

19

I couldn't put off the inevitable, no matter how distasteful. Time to talk to Donny Clark.

Clark's Body & Paint occupied a large gray Quonset hut set back about fifty yards from the Caratoke Highway. I estimated the corrugated galvanized steel relic to be a hundred feet long and forty wide.

Somebody, my guess was Donny himself, had painted the Clark's Body & Paint name along the top. Wonder of wonders, he'd even managed to spell his own name right. His teachers would be so proud. I knew I was.

Quonset huts have been around since 1941 when the George Fuller Construction Company manufactured the first ones at the request of the US Navy. I'd seen plenty of them.

This one definitely had that WWII vibe. With no structural systems like support beams and walls necessary, these huts are as quick to assemble as they are to disassemble. Relatively easy to transport too.

If memory served, the name Quonset came from the Davisville Naval Construction Battalion Center at Quonset Point, Rhode Island where they had been originally built.

As far as I know, huts like these are still being

manufactured today and can be found all over the world. In my years with the Coast Guard, I'd spent a few days and nights in some myself.

Judging by its aged appearance, the one Donny's body and paint shop occupied was likely military surplus that some enterprising soul had bought, dismantled, and hauled here for some post-war business venture of their own.

Fine orange rust and gray-white bird droppings painted the steel shed's sloped sides. Like a Deep South version of an old-time Currier and Ives scene. The looming oak and maple trees bordering it on three sides would keep the temperature down in the interior during the summertime.

I drove onto the gravel lot, joining a herd that included a Yamaha motorcycle, a muddy ATV, a motor boat sitting on a trailer and covered in a gray tarp, and four cars in various states of disrepair.

A blue-and-gold liveried pickup truck belonging to Axle Auto Parts, a regional auto parts supply chain with stores throughout the county, rolled out as I rolled in. I nodded to the delivery driver.

I recognized the black 4x4 truck nearest the door and window to the right as the same vehicle I'd seen the other day parked on the grass in front of Ariadne Deering's house up the road.

A tall overhead garage door cut a mouth into the middle of the structure. The steel door hung open. The sounds of banging echoed outward.

Reading the sign beside the door, I noticed that the body and paint shop held eight to five business hours Monday through Friday but was closed on weekends except for Saturday mornings.

The sounds of banging and swearing inside muffled the crunching of my boots over gravel as I stepped off the parking lot and onto a pitted and scuffed poured-concrete floor stained with decades worth of oil, paint, and transmission fluid.

A heady smell of perspiration, lacquer and dog piss hit my nose like the flames of a blowtorch being fired up my nostrils.

A two-post hydraulic lift balanced a black, chop-top 1940s era hotrod with fat tires twelve feet off the ground in the center of the vaulted Quonset hut. I identified a paint booth tucked into the far corner next to an overhead garage door in the rear matching the one I'd come through.

Donny's shop was the definition of a hodgepodge. Cars, car parts, and car carcasses, with some motorcycle bits and pieces thrown in for variety overwhelmed my eyes. I'd seen better organized junkyards. A wooden stairs led to an exposed second level of mayhem, including several body shells, two of which were totally rusted out, the other mottled with bondo and primer—a work in progress. Like Donny Clark himself.

Somebody had carved out a small office in the front corner with a door leading through. To the side of the office, a pile of dirty shop rags surrounded a red two-gallon gasoline can holding open the door to a filthy, closet-sized bathroom that I wouldn't use if my life, and my bladder, depended on it.

Donny's back was to me. Busy hammering out a rumpled fender using a loud pneumatic dent hammer, he hadn't noticed me come in. I decided to make my presence known.

I walked over to the portable air compressor

resting on a rolling workbench and cut off the power.

"What the—" Donny turned to look at the glitching compressor and saw me instead with my hand on the switch. "You."

Thick fingers reflexively squeezed the pneumatic hammer.

"Hello, Mr. Clark." I rubbed my palms together. "We haven't been formally introduced. I'm Sheriff Edge. If you don't mind, I'd like to have a word with you about Ryan Deering."

Donny glared at me. "I wouldn't mind if you fuckin' left." He wore an old pair of blue jeans, a black T-shirt bearing the name of his shop, and a black skull-and-crossbones doo-rag wrapped around his sweaty forehead.

"I'll take that for an okay," I said with a grin.

"Ariadne tell you where to find me?" Donny narrowed a pair of dark brown hate-filled eyes at me. "You've got no right coming to my place of business and causing me trouble."

"Who's causing you trouble? Not me. In fact, I'm here to see you don't get in any trouble."

"How's that?" Donny snarled.

"You tell me where you were all weekend, account for your whereabouts, as we say, and I won't have to arrest you on suspicion of murder."

"Murder!" Donny's face darkened. He took a step towards me and I was pretty sure murder was what was on his mind.

He managed to stop himself, lowering the arm that held the heavy pneumatic hammer and tossing it on the workbench rather than at my face. The attached cord caught his boot. He cursed and tore himself free.

Donny marched to the entrance and yanked on a heavy chain dangling next to the door. He pulled hard and the overhead garage door rumbled down and slammed shut. "People see a cop here, it looks bad for business."

Donny snapped a heavy Yale lock through the clasp.

"You telling me all your customers have a problem with the law?"

"Uniforms make people nervous, even if they've got nothing to hide."

"Am I making you nervous, Mr. Clark?" I took a good look at the knife clipped to his belt. "Nice knife you're carrying."

Donny patted the knife snugged against his hip. "It's useful."

"I'll bet it is. Benchmade Griptilian. One of the best. Not cheap."

"I got a good deal on it."

"Oh? Where was this? I might be in the market myself."

"Sorry, can't help you. I picked it up at a garage sale somewhere."

"You remember the house?"

"Not exactly. Me and the old lady—"

"You ever call her that to her face?"

"What?"

"Never mind." Let him find out for himself. "You were saying?"

"Yeah. Me and Ariadne went driving around. Stopped at a few yard sales. I was lucky to find it. Misplaced the old one and picked this one up on the cheap. You know how it is."

"Any idea where the old knife might be?"

Donny shrugged. "I'm sure it's around the shop someplace. I'm always putting it down and forgetting it."

"I'll bet." I took in the crammed and cluttered surroundings. "A body could get lost in this place, let alone a pocket knife. I don't suppose you got a receipt?"

"From a damn yard sale?" Donny stomped his way to a shoulder-high white refrigerator planted next to the office door. He yanked open the door and pulled out an energy drink. He popped the top and gulped it down, tossing the empty can in a black plastic bag-lined trashbin.

He burped, wiped his lip with a dirty finger. "So, what do you want?"

"I want you to account for your whereabouts between Friday night and Monday morning."

"I was working."

"Everyday? All day? You don't strike me as the workaholic type." Maybe the alcoholic type.

"What's that supposed to mean?"

"It means let's break this down." I stuck my head in the window of a Ford Taurus missing its front fender. "Friday night. Where did you go? What did you do?"

"Worked till about six. Hit the bar. Went home. Watched TV. Went to bed. That clear enough for you?"

"What bar was this?"

"Buster's."

"In Point Harbor?"

"That's right."

I knew the place. Buster's was located right next to a popular strip club. I wondered if it was popular with Donny Clark.

"Are we done now? I've got work to get done. Unlike you, I've got to work for my money. I don't finish the job, I don't get paid."

"You left the bar at what time?"

"About eight."

"Then you went straight home?"

"That's right. Talk to Ariadne. She'll tell you."

I waded through an oil slick and admired a dusty El Camino parked against the far wall. "My dad had one of these back in the seventies. Tell me about Saturday."

A dented and rusty gallon-sized can of turpentine rested against the right front wheel, balancing a half-roll of blue paper towels.

"I was here at the shop."

I smiled. "Don't tell me, working?"

"Lucky guess. And before you ask, I was working the next day too."

"On a Sunday?"

"Yeah, so? You got something against hard work? Maybe you ought to try it yourself sometime."

"The sign outside says you're closed on Sundays. Only open half the day on Saturdays too."

"Fuck the sign. This is my shop. I work whenever the hell I want to." Donny didn't lose much time replying. "Saturday I had some jobs to catch up on. Sunday I had a customer. Emergency kind of thing."

"What kind of emergency does a body and paint shop have?"

"Somebody hit this guy's front fender. Didn't leave a note. The fender was rubbing against the tire. I banged it out for him."

"Who was this guy?"

Donny shrugged. "Hell, I don't remember. Just

some guy."

"What say we go check your invoices and you give me this emergency customer's name?"

"I can't."

"Why is that?"

"I don't have any paperwork."

"Why not?"

"He was a tourist. On his way home. I got a call from him that he needed to get his car fixed so he could get the hell on his way. I came by, fixed him up. He paid me and left."

"What a Good Samaritan you are, Donny. You give him a receipt?"

"He paid cash."

"Which I'm sure you plan on reporting on your taxes."

Donny looked at me like I was the dumbest man on the planet.

A telephone rang in the office. He ignored it.

"No, secretary?" I asked.

"It's only me and a couple of part-timers for when the workload gets heavy."

"So you have no real alibis for Saturday or Sunday."

Donny picked up a dirty red rag off a workbench and began polishing a large crescent wrench. "Paul Massengill. He works for me now and again. He was in the morning. You check with him."

"I will. What's his number?"

Donny threw the shiny wrench into a drawer, slammed the drawer so hard it bounced back open. He reached into his pocket and pulled out a thick black leather wallet. He dug around and came up with a mangled business card. He flipped the card over and read the phone number scrawled on the back.

I made a note of it. "And Saturday night?"

"Me and Ariadne hung out. Ordered pizza."

"What time?"

"Around seven thirty, eight."

"Where'd you order from?"

"Crusty's, right by the house."

"Is it any good?"

"It's pizza."

"Not much of a recommendation. Can anybody vouch for you on Sunday? Besides, this so-called mystery client of yours?"

"It's all true, Sheriff. Everything I told you is the truth."

"How well did you know Ryan?"

"That asshole?" Donny threw his head around. Somehow it managed to stay attached to his neck. "I barely knew the guy."

"And yet you seem to have developed quite a strong opinion of him." I toyed with a chrome-plated steering wheel lying on a shelf near a grungy sink holding a handful of rusty bolts bathing in an inch of brown soapy water.

Donny yanked the steering wheel out of my hands. "You mind? This is a custom piece. Belongs to a customer."

He rubbed my fingerprints away with the bottom of his T-shirt and carefully set the wheel back down. "Yeah, I didn't like the guy. So what? He's Ariadne's ex—"

"Soon to be ex."

"Yeah, soon to be ex. Why should I like the guy? Besides, like I said, I barely knew him."

"Did he ever come to your house?"

"Not while I was there." Donny Clark's fists tightened at his sides.

I nodded. I could imagine Ryan wouldn't dare visit if Donny was around. Not if he valued his hide.

"Were any of these part-time employees of yours here Sunday?"

"Nope. Didn't need them." The telephone in the office started calling for attention again. Once again, Donny ignored its plea.

"What time did you get home Sunday?" I had a hunch Ryan had been dead before Sunday night but it was too early to be certain. Only the official autopsy could confirm or refute that.

"I dunno. Six or so. Me and Ariadne ate. I watched the game and then we screwed. That enough detail for you or do you need to know what position we took and how many times I came?"

"Tell me, Mr. Clark, did you ever get the impression that Ariadne wanted to go back to the way things were?" I walked over to the hydraulic car lift. Donny dogged me. I pushed the green button on the box on the side. With a hiss of breath, the machinery sprang to life. The hotrod shivered and shot upward a couple inches.

"Watch what you're doing!" Donny hit the red button, stopping the ride. "What do you mean back to the way things were?"

"I mean, did she ever hint that she might want to get back together with her husband?"

Donny snorted. "Not on your life. She has plenty to say about Ryan and none of it good. She hated the wimp."

"Enough to murder him?"

Donny stepped back, pulling his lower teeth over his lip. "I never said that, Sheriff."

"Did she ever say it?"

Silence hung between us for a minute.

"If you're thinking I'm gonna say anything bad about Ariadne, you can think again."

"That's admirable, Mr. Clark. The thing is, I wonder if she feels the same sense of loyalty when it comes to you?"

20

Donny's countenance moved further to the dark side. Something which I didn't think possible considering how dark it had been up until this point.

Figuring I'd gotten all I could and would get from him for now, I ambled to the front of the shop and jiggled the Yale lock on the garage door. "Cute. Like to play games do you, Donny?" I grinned at him. "I like to play games too. In fact, I've got a nice one we can play right now. In my game, I give you a choice. Want to hear how it works?"

Donny shot me a sort of half-smirk, half-smug look.

"No? Let me tell you anyway. You see," I unsnapped my weapon, "in my game, you get three choices." I rested my hand on my weapon. "First choice, you unlock this door." I slid the weapon from its holster. "Second choice, I take this Glock and shoot this lock off." I aimed at the door.

"Third choice." I aimed my weapon at Donny. He made a big soft, slow-moving target. My favorite kind. "I shoot you, take the key to this lock out of your pocket while you roll around the greasy floor in pain because I blew your fucking knee all to hell."

Donny jerked. "Hell, are you crazy? Can't you take a joke, Sheriff?" He quickly closed the distance between us, unlocked the garage door. He yanked on the chain, hoisting the door upward. The sun had disappeared, to be replaced by a wall of gray.

And I'd made the mistake of leaving my coat at the office. Even though I was relatively new to this part of the country, I should have known better.

"I can take a joke but I've got no patience for jokers. You remember that, Donny." My Glock fell back into its holster.

Donny followed me outside to the empty lot. Traffic flew by on the road, paying us no mind. Donny and I were no more than specks in the peripheral vision of any passing birds.

"I hear you're new," Donny said it like it was a slur. "Don't know your way around, do you?"

"Is there a point here someplace, Donny?" He was sort of right. I'd been on the job a short time. After nearly two decades in the Coast Guard and half of those in the Intelligence Service, I'd taken an early retirement. Truth is, I should have retired earlier. Those past few years had taken their toll on me. And my marriage.

I crossed the country, moving from Washington to North Carolina, three years ago. Leaving behind an ex-wife, and an ex-life, and a boatload of memories I'd just as soon forget. Unfortunately, most of those memories seemed to have tagged along.

I moved into Grandpa Pierce Edge's house, did nothing for over a year, then ran for sheriff. I never thought I'd win. Running was just something to do. The ex always said I was good at running, away from things.

And I never would have stood a chance of winning except that everybody who'd known Pierce Edge sang his praises. He'd been Sheriff of Currituck

County back in the day. The old-timers still remembered him. And idolized him.

And maybe they thought my living in Pierce Edge's house made me somehow more capable of the job, like the way some say the uniform makes the man.

I knew I was going to be an acquired taste.

Case in point, Donny Clark.

"The point is we don't like outsiders—even if their grandpappy leaves them a house."

"Even if they're the Sheriff?"

A sneer turned his ugly face even uglier. "Especially if they're the Sheriff."

"That your boat there?" I pointed to the only boat on the lot. The one on the trailer.

"Belongs to a buddy."

"Right. I remember seeing a boat out at the dock at Ariadne's house."

"Yeah. It belongs to the guy we rent the house from but he lets us use it whenever we want. In fact, we took it out a couple hours this weekend."

"Saturday or Sunday? You told me you were working both days."

"Huh?" Donny's face reddened. He scratched the top of his head. "That's right. I must be mixing up my weekends. Must've been last weekend."

"Which was it?"

Donny huffed. The phone inside begged for attention. "We took the boat out Sunday afternoon."

"Where did you go?"

He shrugged. "Nowhere. Tooled around a couple of hours. Drank a few beers."

"Did you happen to be out by Carova Beach?"

"I've never been to Carova Beach."

"Anybody see you on this little outing?"

"Plenty of people. I mean, it's not like we were the only two fuckin' boaters out on the water."

"But nobody to vouch for you?"

"What are you trying to get at, Sheriff? You accusing me of something? A man can't go out on his own boat and have a little fun?"

"I don't suppose Ryan Deering joined this little pleasure cruise of yours?"

"Fuck no. Why the hell would we do that?" Donny spat a wad of phlegm into the wind. "The wimp did try to borrow the boat once. Ariadne told me about it."

"Did he now? When was this?"

"I don't remember." He adjusted his doo-rag.

"Did she let him?"

"Hell no. Told him to drop dead."

"Looks like he took her advice." I climbed into my truck and cranked up the heater to the accompaniment of Donny Clark's scorching eyes.

Did Ariadne get tired of waiting for the slow-moving legal system to officially separate her from Ryan once and for all?

Would Donny do whatever he could to make Ariadne happy? Would he kill for her?

I rolled down my window. My face met a blast of cold air and a hot look from Donny Clark. "By the way, I talked to Joe."

"Who the hell's Joe?"

"Joelene?"

Donny fumed, reminding me of that bull in the old Bugs Bunny cartoons I used to watch as a kid on Saturday mornings before all the news shows and infomercials took over the airwaves.

"Your ex claims you knew Ryan quite well. She says you frequently came by the Slowater to talk to him. Not in a good way, I might add. So," I said, my hand fidgeting with the heater, trying to coax a little extra heat out of the engine, "all that crap you were telling me in there?" I pointed towards the bowels of the body shop. "It seems to me, you're quite the storyteller."

"You calling me a liar?"

"Why would I do that? No, I think you've done a good job proving yourself a liar all on your own."

"You done?" Donny's fists were tight as drums and looked big as baked hams.

"For now. I have a hunch we'll be talking again, Mr. Clark." I let the window slide up, cutting off Donny Clark's foul curses.

Donny put on quite a show in my rearview mirror. He kicked the shed with the toe of his work boot. Next, he picked up a loose cinderblock lying against the side of the Quonset hut and hurled it through the windshield of some customer's Chevy.

Was he going to add that to their work order?

21

I found a prime spot for the Bronco at the small waterfront park overlooking the recreated lighthouse in downtown Manteo. The town skirts the edge of Roanoke Island. It's only a few minutes' walk from here to Sonia's condo. The one she shared with her cat. Where I was heading for dinner.

Hopefully a dinner for two and not two and a furball. No offense to furballs, I just prefer not sharing a dinner table with them.

The Roanoke Marshes Lighthouse juts eastward into the Roanoke Sound at the end of a forty-foot pier. It's tiny and not what most folks would picture a lighthouse to look like at all—towering conical shapes painted black and white.

At a mere thirty-seven feet, this replica of the original light station built in 1877 looks more like a quaint coastal cottage than an aide to navigation, especially with its white-clad sides and red roof.

Nonetheless, the lighthouse boasts an original fourth-order Fresnel lens. Sonia told me the Coast Guard had permanently loaned the lens to the NC Maritime Museum, which was in charge of the lighthouse, so I felt a certain pride of ownership whenever I laid eyes on it.

Like now. At night, the fixed light shines out

into the Roanoke Sound guiding boats to and from Shallowbag Bay, the name given to the protected waters nearest Manteo.

The town of Manteo took its name from the Native American Indian chieftain who'd befriended the early English settlers who'd first landed here in the late sixteenth century. The island is the home of the Lost Colony and birthplace of the first English child born in America, a girl named Virginia Dare. I dare say Virginia wouldn't recognize the place now.

She might also wonder why it was located in a state named North Carolina and not Virginia.

I glanced at my wristwatch, a gift from Sonia, and tugged at the collar of my thick wool sweater, another of her gifts. The dark blue sweater never did fit me right. It was too tight in the neck and pinched me in the armpits. I once tried to tell her that. She got mad and we fought for three days. Now I wear it even though it did leave me feeling lightheaded and numb armed.

Sonia told me it fit perfectly and diagnosed my complaints as being psychosomatic in nature. Something about our relationship and feeling strangled or some crap.

Regardless, I only wore it on special occasions. Like this one where I was going to see her.

I know a tight sweater when I wear one and this was one. I gave it one last tug at the neck and one at each arm, praying it would stretch enough to get me through our dinner date. If Sonia saw me tugging at it at the table, we'd fight about it all over again.

The smells of french fries and fried fish wafted from the exhaust stack of a seafood restaurant on the corner, and carried on the wind, increasing my hunger.

This was not what we'd be having for supper. Knowing Sonia, she'd be cooking up something exotic. That worked for me. As long as there's a good bread to go with it and a good drink to wash it down with, I don't ask for much else.

Walking along the few picturesque streets comprising downtown Manteo was practically like stepping back through time to a quintessential cozy waterfront town in a quieter, more laid-back existence. Of course, the downtown shops and eateries catered mostly to the tourists today. Despite this, it had managed to retain a certain downhome charm.

Reaching Sonia's building, I pulled open the street-level glass door leading up from the parking garage to the residential units occupying the top floors of the harborside structure.

I avoided the elevator and climbed the two flights of steps to Sonia's door, third on the right. I tugged my sweater one last time before knocking.

I remembered too late that I should have stopped somewhere and picked up a bottle of wine or a bouquet of flowers. Something, anything.

The door opened silently. Sonia appeared in a peacock blue silk dress that fell to her ankles. Black hair hung loose behind her ears. Diamond earrings danced like stars at the tips of her earlobes.

My mouth went dry.

"Tom. Don't you look handsome." Sonia smiled and opened her arms.

I walked into them.

"Evening," I said, enjoying the warmth and scent of her.

Sonia pulled me inside. Her tuxedo cat, Dawon,

watched me disinterestedly from her perch near the window.

She'd named him Dawon in honor of some sacred tigress of Hindu mythology. A gift to the goddess Durgan. The tigress attacked her enemies fiercely with tooth and claw, while the goddess rode her like a horse into battle, herself wielding ten weapons—one held in each of her ten arms.

A fearsome duo.

The way cat Dawon had attacked me the first couple times we'd crossed paths left me no doubt that she truly was directly descended from the sacred tigress.

I still had the scars on my left calf to prove my theory.

Sonia and I kissed. She took my coat and hung it from the brass tree inside the door.

"There's a bottle of merlot on the table. Would you mind opening it while I check on dinner?"

"No problem." Her two-bed condo offered a terrific view of the Roanoke Sound. The round table nestled in the corner caught the view on both sides. The wraparound patio was great when the weather was right. Tonight was not one of those nights.

I opened the wine and poured two generous glassfuls into the stemware provided. Sonia had set the table for two. "Sorry, Dawon, looks like it's kibble for one tonight."

Dawon looked at me with one dour eye then returned her attention to the darkness. Probably on the lookout for potential enemies. Pirates maybe. Some folks claim Blackbeard's headless ghost still prowls these waters.

A tapered lotus blossom-scented candle flickered in a silver base in the middle of the dining table.

"I hope you're hungry!" Sonia called from the kitchen.

"Hungry enough." I took a sip of merlot. Sonia always bought the good stuff. I stuck with whatever was on sale. "Can I help?"

"No, have a seat. Put on some music if you like."

"I'm good."

Sonia surprised me with a platter holding homemade spaghetti, garlic rolls and spinach. So much for exotic. Then again, being Indian, this probably seemed exotic to her.

Everything was homemade. And delicious. With so much great food to eat, we didn't waste much time making small talk.

Dinner finished, plates cleared, we settled on the leather sofa facing a fancy steel and glass ethanol-burning fireplace mounted on the opposite wall.

Sonia leaned into me and I rested a hand on her knee. The other held my wine.

Sonia's free hand gently caressed Dawon who'd made herself at home on my girlfriend's lap.

In my next life, I might just come back as a cat.

"Geraldine called," I said.

"Jerry? How is she?"

"Good, I guess. I didn't talk to her. Frenchie took the message."

"How is Frenchie?"

"Always the same." That was pretty much all I could say about Frenchie. "He's my rock."

"You need one. Tell him hi for me," Sonia added quickly—before I could bite into that last comment of hers and ask her what she was trying to imply by it.

"What was Jerry calling about? Anything special?"

I noticed that Sonia's hand, the one she was stroking the cat with instead of me, had come to a stop. Jerry and I had dated a few times. Nothing serious. Those couple of times had been while Switch and I were in the Off position.

Still, bad blood runs deep.

"No." I drank some wine to give myself time to consider my words. "She's hosting a party, a working party really for this year's Creepy Carolina."

"Ah, right." Sonia smiled. It was a small smile but I'd take it. "And you're involved?"

"In the event, yeah. Have you ever seen Jenkins made up like Frankenstein's monster? Now that's creepy."

This earning me an actual chuckle.

"I was hoping you'd come with me."

"Did you mention that to her?"

"To Jerry?" A tiny alarm blinked on in my cerebral cortex. It might have been the one connected to my fight-or-flight response mechanism. "No."

"Do you think she'll mind?"

"If you come? Of course, not."

"But you didn't bring it up with her?"

"Well…"

"No, of course, not."

"Sonia, I never even spoke with her." Why did I always feel like I was on the defense with this woman? This. This was why.

"Fine. When is it?"

"I'm not sure. I'll check." I blew out a shallow

breathe. I'd dodged a bullet there.

22

Sonia nodded, turned and kissed me on the jaw. Dawon, unseated in the process, shot me a dirty look. The furball got up and disappeared towards the kitchen and her food and water setup.

"Let's talk about something else."

"Okay. Have you figured out who murdered that man yet?"

"Ryan Deering? No. Plenty of suspects to go around but plenty about this case that doesn't make sense yet too."

"Such as?"

"Are you sure you want to talk about this? We went over all this before."

"I don't mind. Maybe it will help." Sonia ran a finger along the rim of her glass. "I spoke with Nat today. He had some interesting things to say."

"About the case?"

"That's right."

"And you talked to him today?" I felt myself getting hot and it wasn't because of the fireplace because that thing gave off next to no heat. All style and no substance.

My index finger tugged at my collar. I didn't think Sonia noticed.

"That's right. He also told me Ryan's stepbrother

and stepfather were quite upset."

"He has a stepbrother? And a stepfather?"

"Yes. The brother is up north some place. His stepfather lives in Okracoke."

"I see." I figured the less words I uttered the less likely it would be that I'd say something I'd regret and she'd sink her teeth into. "So my chief deputy told you what he learned instead of reporting to me, his superior?"

Sometimes a person just can't keep things bottled inside no matter how much they know better. I was one such person.

"It's not like Nat was reporting to me. I called him. It merely came up in conversation. I'm sure you'll be getting a written report from him, filling you in on everything.

"No doubt." Nat Midgett wasn't much for words when it came to talking—leastwise not with me. But when it came to the written word, he could turn a routine traffic stop into a Lord of the Rings-sized trilogy. He was a big reason I was always knee deep in paperwork. "Why did you call him?"

"Do you have to do this?" Sonia planted a fist under her chin. "It was a social call, that's all. You're getting upset over nothing."

"I'm getting upset because my chief deputy is first reporting new evidence concerning a murder investigation to my girlfriend instead of me."

"Can we drop this, please, Tom?"

"Yeah." I said yes but we both know I wasn't dropping anything. I was just internalizing it. "Did I tell you about the markings on the body?"

"Yes, Nat mentioned that." Seeing the fire in my

eyes, Sonia quickly added, "Sorry. Nothing else?"

"Nothing Nat hasn't already shared with you."

"You said we were dropping it."

"Right. It's dropped. I searched his room and came up empty."

"Nothing?"

"A box of unopened condoms and a how to get rich book."

"Maybe he was trying to better himself?"

"Or trying to get laid."

"Tell me about this wife." She rubbed the back of my hand.

"Not much to tell. I don't think her or her boyfriend would know the truth if it bit them."

"Let's go back to the beginning. When you found the body." Sonia's voice was soft, soothing. Professional.

"Is this how you talk to your patients?"

"Tom."

I recognized the signal. It was a plea and a warning.

"Okay." I rolled my neck side to side to release the kinks. "We got a call about a body washed up on the beach. Reported by a family of day trippers. Mom, Dad and two rug rats. Lizzie was first on the scene." I narrowed my eyes, reviewed the scene in my mind.

"Everything seemed reasonably straightforward until Tracy examined the body. That's when the waters got muddied."

"Such as how?"

"Such as how come somebody sticks a knife in a man's back when he's already dead? Such as why dump him in the ocean after he's been struck on the back of the head and drowned somewhere else? Such as who disliked such an apparently unremarkable man as Ryan Deering enough to go to all that trouble?"

I quickly downed the rest of my wine and rose for a refill. "You want some?"

Sonia lifted her glass and I poured her some from the dwindling contents of the bottle on the table.

I resumed my seat on the corner of the couch. Dawon resumed her sentry duty atop the carpeted perch at the window. Sonia scooched closer to me and took my hand.

"Who's your number one suspect? Or do you have one?"

"The wife, of course. Separated but still married to the victim. Ariadne Deering. And her live-in boyfriend, Donny Clark."

"You think one of them did it?"

"Separately or together, maybe, yeah."

"What's their motive?"

"For the wife? A fast track to DivorceLand. For Donny, I don't think he needs a motive. He'd slice a man's throat for kicks."

"Sounds delightful." Sonia sipped pensively. "Will she inherit?"

I shrugged. "Maybe, but I can't imagine what. He didn't own a house and his car is a piece of crap."

Sonia looked at me over the rim of her wineglass. "Insurance?"

"That's a thought. I'll look into it. Money is always a good motivation. For good or bad." I tugged at my collar.

Sonia's eyebrow edged up.

This time she'd definitely seen it.

I blushed like a schoolboy caught with his pants

down.

"Any other suspects?"

"We're looking into his past. Pasts can be real treasure chests. Deering has a couple of prior arrests for gambling."

"Gambling?"

I explained about the poker machines.

"Any other family or friends with a grudge?"

"As you already know, I've asked Nat to look into that. Any family's got some relationships where bad blood turns to spilled blood."

"That's rather cynical."

I set my wineglass on the little table in front of the sofa and discreetly tugged at my left armpit. Not discreetly enough.

"Is there a problem?" Little lines formed between Sonia's brows. And they weren't love lines.

I patted my belly. "That was a really great meal. I didn't know you cooked Italian."

"Thanks." The word came out but it came out on the cool side.

Desperate to get this boat back on course, I decided to stroke her ego. Subtly, of course. "As a trained psychologist, what do you think? Who murdered Ryan Deering?"

"I have no idea." She'd long removed her sandals and wriggled her bare toes, feet planted on the low table.

"Care to hazard a profile?"

"No. Nor do I need you humoring me."

A subtle shock of electricity ran up and down my body and out each extremity. "Who's humoring you? I'm asking for your professional opinion."

"And if my sweater is making you uncomfortable, why don't you just take it off? Why do you even wear it?"

Horrified, I pulled my fingers from beneath my collar. I hadn't even realized they were in there pulling. "What? I had an itch."

Sonia blew out a breath.

For a minute, we watched in silence the ethanol flames burning behind the glass rather like alien goldfish composed of orange plasma. That fireplace of hers drove me bananas. Where was the crackling wood? The smoke? Where were the cinders and ash?

And the smell of burning pine or hickory? Any smell at all?

The next thing I knew, Sonia stood at the window. One hand on Dawon. Like the cat, her eyes on the darkness.

I slowly creaked to my feet. "It's getting late. Maybe I should be going."

Sonia didn't try to dissuade me.

In some small corner of my reptilian brain, I heard the distinct sound of a light switch as it moved from On to Off again.

23

I waited until I'd made my way back around the Sound, up Highway 12, over the dark beach, parked the Bronco in the carport, stepped inside the house, let the dog out for a pee, let the dog back inside, fed the dog, kicked off my boots sitting in my grandpa's rocker in the main room before dialing Nat Midgett's number.

By the time I'd done all that, it was good and late. Nat might be sleeping.

I could only hope.

I checked my wristwatch—that special US Coast Guard edition diving watch Sonia gave me on the anniversary of the day we'd met—before punching in his number.

If Sonia were here observing me now, she'd claim this was some sort of displaced aggression behavior on my part for not punching him in the nose.

She wouldn't exactly have been wrong.

Ring. Ring. Ring.

The ringing stopped.

"Hello?"

"You tell my fucking girlfriend what's going on in an open murder case before you tell me?!"

"Who is this?" came a groggy voice on a midnight dreary.

"Me. You're supposed to tell me. Not a

psychologist. Although I'm beginning to think you might need one!"

"Sheriff?" A massive yawn filled the air. "Is that you?"

"Not your hairdresser. Not your fucking mechanic. And not *my* fucking girlfriend."

"But, Sheriff—"

"I don't care if Sonia is your friend or how long you've known her, you have something worth telling that concerns one of my cases, you tell it to me!"

"Listen, Sheriff, I didn't—"

"You got that?"

I punched the life out of my mobile phone and threw it—proving it was as mobile as the manufacturer claimed—at the defenseless wing-backed chair—which up until that moment had been minding its own business in the corner of the sitting room near the fireplace. My phone took a big bounce and hit the hardwood floor. A death rattle erupted from the phone and then the phone stilled.

Leaning forward, hands clasping my upper thighs, I pulled in a couple lungfuls of air.

I didn't know how Nat was feeling right then, but I felt better. A whole hell of a lot better.

I clapped my hands. Bladder Boy sprang to his feet from his spot in front of the fireplace. The hearth was cold but BB was, if anything and like most dogs, an optimist. "Come on, Boy, wanna take a walk?"

I grinned as he shook himself, barked, and pawed the air. Of course he did. He was a dog.

Bladder Boy at my heels, I grabbed a strong flashlight from under the kitchen sink and a cold beer from the fridge.

I changed out of my uniform and into a pair of jeans and a denim shirt, grabbed a coat, and put my boots back on. "Let's hit the beach."

I opened the door. Bladder Boy took the lead. No need for a leash in these parts. Unless we ran into Nat, in which case, I'd be the one needing restraining, not the dog.

I like to walk the beach at night. So does Bladder Boy. Less riffraff. More soul seekers.

The sky hangs like a starry blanket and there's nothing but space and infinity, above and beyond.

Out here I could breathe.

And this was one of those nights. The kind of night Vincent Van Gogh would've loved to paint. I could picture running into him out here, in the midnight hour, easel balanced precariously in the sand. Red hair dancing, eyes focused, hand moving with an impassioned focus, painting the heavens above with the wind swirling all around.

I'd bring him a beer. We'd chat.

Maybe about women. From what I'd read, he'd had more than his fair share of woman trouble.

What man hadn't?

We walked down the sandy road to the beach. The wind was mild and the sea relatively quiet. Over my shoulder sparkled the lights in the windows of the beach houses rising up from the dunes.

I approached a fire burning close to the slope of the dunes. A group comprised of three young men and two young ladies huddled around the fire. The sounds of laughter broke the solitude. I waved and kept walking, not wanting to spoil their good time. Being an old guy sometimes causes kids that age to tighten up.

Bladder Boy and I were headed south when a couple strolling hand-in-hand at the surf's edge veered in our direction further up the shoreline.

"Nice dog. May I?" Hand extended, the young woman looked at me.

She wore a jacket and he'd cloaked himself in a tie-string hoodie. Something about her, both of them, seemed familiar. Then again, none of us were much more than shadows.

"Be my guest," I said. If Bladder Boy peed, and he would, what would it matter? We were standing in nature's litterbox.

"What a good boy you are." She ruffled him behind the ears and he dutiful wagged his tail and marked his spot in the sand.

Her companion laughed. "Hey, man. You looking for some action?"

I put up my hand. "Before you go any further, I should tell you that I'm the county sheriff." I watched his face pale, not an easy thing to do under these dim conditions. "So if you're about to offer me any illegal substances—"

"Peter!" said the young woman.

He threw up his arms. "No, man, nothing like that. Nothing like that at all. I just thought, I mean, I won over a thousand bucks tonight." He thrust his hands in his pockets and pulled them back out. "See?"

"Congratulations."

"Thanks. I won most of it playing poker."

"Lucky man," I said.

"Yeah," he grabbed the woman. "I'm on my honeymoon and I win a fortune. Luckiest guy in the world!" He kissed her as she giggled.

"I only thought you might be interested in checking it out."

"Maybe some other time." I stuffed my hands in my coat. "You're the couple from the beach, aren't you?"

Out of the edge of my vision, I watched Bladder Boy pounce at ghost crabs in the sand. The beach is crawling with them at night. With squarish translucent bodies and big eyes stuck on top their heads that can swivel in three-hundred and sixty degrees, the three-inch crabs are a tourist attraction in their own right. Several tour operators run folks out to the beach at night to take a gander.

Ghost crabs are yellow-gray in color. The golf-ball sized holes they excavate are easy to spot during the day. They are shy and fast. Bladder Boy's never caught one. It's all about the chase.

"The ones that were out for a stroll the morning the body was found?" I asked.

"Oh, hey." The young lady punched her companion in the shoulder. "You *are* the Sheriff." Turning to her husband, she said, "He really *is* the Sheriff, Peter."

"Oh, shit." The poor kid looked troubled. "Maybe I shouldn't have said anything, about the money, I mean. It's not illegal, is it?"

"I won't tell, if you won't," I answered with a wink.

"Thanks, Sheriff."

"No trouble. What were your names again?"

"I'm Peter. This is Chloe."

"Right, Peter and Chloe Goslin, yes?"

Both nodded.

"Did you find the killer yet?" Chloe asked, her

hand draped over her husband's shoulder.

"I'm afraid not."

"Gee, maybe we shouldn't be wandering around out here." She peered into the distance. "Especially after dark."

"I wouldn't worry too much. I probably shouldn't be saying this but I don't believe he was killed here on the beach."

"That's good," said Peter. "I mean, well, you know what I mean."

"Yeah." I did. Murder was bad enough but when it came to your neighborhood, it got a little too personal, even if it was only your temporary neighborhood while you were enjoying your honeymoon.

"I tell you, Sheriff. That was crazy. One of the wildest things I'll remember from our honeymoon. Right, babe?"

"Yes. That and that awful woman."

"What woman?"

"The one that yelled at us."

I grinned. "That's Captain Gutierrez. Don't let her scare you. She's mostly bark, very little bite."

"I don't know that I'd want to run into her out here after midnight," Peter said with a little laugh.

"I don't suppose either of you have heard anything else? About the murder, I mean?"

"Such as?" asked Chloe.

"Such as any rumors or anybody mentioning to either of you that they'd seen or heard something that morning?"

Both shook their heads. Peter answered. "Sorry, Sheriff. Except for hitting a few restaurants and bars, me and Chloe have kept pretty much to ourselves except for a little poker tonight. It is our honeymoon, if you know what I mean."

"I believe I do."

"Peter," admonished Chloe. "The Sheriff doesn't need to hear about our love life."

She didn't know how right she was considering how my date with Sonia had gone that night. What about the planning party concerning Creepy Carolina? Would she cancel on me?

"What? What'd I say?"

"You two have a nice night." I whistled for Bladder Boy. "And if you hear anything you think might even be of remote interest to my investigation, you give me a call." I handed the young lady my business card and she tucked it into a pocket of her denim jacket.

Bladder Boy shook himself, sending sand and water over my lower half. I swiped at my pants as the spaniel pawed the beach and scooped something up in his mouth.

"What's that you've got, Boy?" I flicked on the flashlight and wrestled it from between his teeth. He thought it was a game, so it took some doing, and me tossing a piece of driftwood, to get him to release the damn thing.

The spaniel dropped his now old treasure and went racing after the newly discovered, ulna-sized, water-soaked scrap of timber I'd lobbed fifteen yards off. Who says there's no new treasure to be found yet in these parts?

I shined the flashlight on what Bladder Boy had dropped. A blue and white poker chip. I wiped it clean with my fingers and slid it into my pants pocket for good luck.

Maybe some of Peter Goslin's luck at poker would rub off on my love life.

24

Chief Deputy Nat Midgett rapped on my office door casing. Bits of spackle—my poor attempt to mitigate some of the damage done to the frame when the space cadet had ripped the door off—crumbled to the ground. "Sheriff?"

"What is it?" I looked at him from over my computer screen. There he stood. Uniform freshly pressed, manilla folder in hand. The object of my midnight fury.

I was tackling the budget report. Again. Numbers swam before my eyes. Another fury, this one early morning but I wanted to get this out of the way to leave myself plenty of time for the investigation into the death of Ryan Deering. I don't like cases to go too long, get too cold.

I was on my third cup of coffee and my fourth aspirin. I hadn't had five hours sleep what with the murder and Sonia on my mind.

I didn't need a mirror to tell me that I looked like shit.

"I've got that report for you."

"Sit." I swiveled the monitor out of my line of vision so I could see him. He looked tired. Like he'd had a rough night. I suppressed a smile. "How did court go?" I figured I'd start easy. We'd work our way into the crap.

Nat sat at attention in the wooden chair, planted his polished shoes and looked me in the eye. "It was a clean sweep, sir."

I nodded. "Good." A clean sweep meant that everybody who'd tried to weasel their way out of their ticket had lost their appeal to the judge and had to pay up. That meant my officers were doing their jobs correctly. Giving tickets where needed, warnings where warnings would suffice. We weren't a ticket mill, designed to fill the county coffers, and never would be under my command.

Nat cleared his throat. "Seeing how everything went so smoothly at court yesterday, I had some extra time and thought I would do a further background check on Mr. Deering and his wife." His eyes met mine and I nodded. He continued. "I drove down to Dare and made some inquiries."

"So I hear."

Nat's cheeks heated bright pink.

I didn't push him any further. That was enough. "Is that the report?" I nudged my chin toward the folder on his lap.

"Yes, sir." Nat opened the crisp manilla folder and extracted a thick typed report.

I weighed it in my hand. Impressive. Nat rarely printed anything. He said it was a waste of resources and sent me every report and bulletin in electronic format, which I found hard to read. I always had to squint at the computer screen. I'd reached that point where reading glasses helped but hadn't reached that point where I felt comfortable wearing them.

I set the file on my desk and thumbed through. "Give me the Cliff Notes' version."

"Mr. Deering's family, if you could call it that, mostly include a stepfather—who isn't really his father at all, not biologically or legally, ever, and a brother who —"

I leaned back into my chair, lacing my fingers behind my neck. "Let me guess," I said, interrupting my chief deputy who'd suddenly become Mr. Blabby. Maybe my late-night phone call had broken something loose. "Isn't really his brother?"

The corner of Nat's mouth turned down. "Yes, sir. That's right. Hank Norton and his son, a man about Ryan's age named Jack. Ryan's mom, Gloria, and Hank had a relationship after Ryan Deering's father died."

"But our boy Ryan was never legally adopted."

"Correct."

"What about Ryan's mother?"

"Mr. Norton says she ran out on him years ago. He hasn't seen or heard from her since."

"How did Hank and Jack get along with Ryan?"

"Not great. Not terrible. Neither had anything negative to say about him."

"In other words, a typical American family." I'd lived through one myself. Two, actually.

"Yes, sir."

"Didn't I hear that this Jack Norton lives up north someplace?" A frigid breeze blew between us. We both knew damn well where I'd heard it.

"Yes, sir." Nat suddenly found the tops of his shoes terribly interesting. "He resides in St. Paul. I spoke with him by phone. Hank Norton has a place in Nags Head."

"Nags Head?"

"That's right, sir."

So Sonia had gotten that part wrong. She'd said Okracoke. Not that I was going to remind her of that fact, let alone rub her nose in it. I valued my own hide too much.

I thumbed some more through the written report. He'd developed full histories on the two men. All that was missing was the names of their elementary school teachers and the weather reports for the days they were born.

"When was the last time either of the pair claim to have seen Ryan?"

"Jack says it's been over a year. That was the last time he visited his dad. Hank Norton says Ryan visited him about ten days ago. He claims that was the first time he'd seen him since the three of them got together during Jack's last visit. They took him out for a fish dinner."

"Interesting." I grabbed a pen and jotted down a few notes on a pad. Several items in Nat's report proved useful. Not that I was going to tell him that. Not now, anyway. "Any particular reason?"

"According to Mr. Norton, Ryan asked to borrow his boat."

"Did he now?" Hadn't Donny Clark told me the same thing?

I rubbed my chin and tapped the nib of the pen against my desk. I did that a lot. Hence, the desktop's pointillist finish.

Nat cleared his throat. "About Sonia, sir—"

"Forget it." I handed him back the report. I had enough papers cluttering up my office already. Besides, the entire file would be living inside my PC the minute he got to his PC and hit Send. "Water under the bridge."

"Yes, sir." Nat rose. "If there's nothing else, I'll be getting back to work now." Shoulders square, he marched to the door.

"Oh, and Nat?"

"Sheriff?"

"The next time you share confidential police business with a civilian, I'll be tossing you off that bridge."

"Yes, sir." Nat shot Lizzie Gutierrez a troubled and embarrassed look as she shoved past him and barged to my desk.

"What was that all about?" she demanded, as Nat disappeared to his desk in the front corner.

"Let's call it a male bonding exercise."

Lizzie chuckled. "Judging by the look on Nat's puss, I'd say you bonded him pretty good."

25

"Want to take a drive?" I slid my notebook into my pocket.

"And keep my feet dry for a change?" Lizzie sat on the edge of the desk, legs dangling. "Sure, what's up, Tom?"

"Nat did some digging. It seems the widow Deering could be in line to receive twenty-seven-thousand dollars' worth of life insurance money to help her get over her loss." I'd read that juicy item in the chief deputy's report. Whether she was his beneficiary remained to be discovered.

"You mean if she didn't kill him to get it."

"There is that caveat. I want you to run down to the Food King in Grandy. Ariadne Deering is a cashier there. She says she worked all last weekend but that doesn't exactly jibe with what her boyfriend, Donny Clark, told me. Though with those two, the truth seems to be more slippery than an oiled blacksnake."

I explained about Donny's own shaky alibi and their alleged boating trip on the Sunday.

"Maybe the two of them decided to cash in her husband's chips." Lizzie helped herself to the rest of my coffee. I didn't care. It had gone cold. "By the way, what was a poor working stiff like Ryan Deering doing with a twenty-seven-thousand-dollar life insurance policy?"

"It was a hotel job benefit."

"Must be nice." She handed me back my empty mug.

"We provide you with life insurance. More than twenty-seven too."

"Sure but I've got to be dead to collect."

"What can I say? There's always a catch, isn't there?" I stood and strapped on my holster. "Talk to the manager at Food King. See if you can verify that Ariadne Deering was working that weekend and what hours."

"Will do." Lizzie's feet slapped the floor. "By the way, you look like crap."

"Thanks." I rubbed my palms over my stubble. "Nat's fault."

"I'll bet. I'm ready to roll."

"Me, too." Hanging out in the office was the last place I wanted to be even at the best of times. And this wasn't the best of times. I stuffed my fist in my mouth to squelch a yawn.

"What are you going to be doing?" Lizzie beat me to the door.

"Digging into Ryan Deering's past. Nat made a good start. Now it's time to dig a little deeper. We need to build a profile on our murder victim and our suspects. Sooner or later, the pieces will start fitting together. In one of his past lives, Ryan Deering was involved in operating a video poker scheme."

"So I heard."

"Ryan did a little jail time. His partner was one Charles Harker. Harker did five plus years in Bertie." The Bertie Correctional Institution in Windsor was one of the state's largest and meanest. "I'm running up to Moyock to have a word with him."

"What's this Mr. Harker up to these days?"

"Can you believe it? He runs some sort of video arcade sales and restoration business."

"Now isn't that a hoot," Lizzie said. "Tell me, Sherlock, what strategy are you going to try on Harker?"

"How's that?"

"You know." She socked me in the arm. The woman packed a punch. "Some of your famous adduction, deduction or seduction?"

"I guess I'll have to play it by ear. First see if he's my type."

Lizzie laughed and went one way. I went the other.

26

In the 1700s, Moyock existed as a small coastal community situated along the Currituck Inlet. That inlet, like many along the OBX, was gone now. The only proximate waters of significance these days were those bordering Tulls Bay and the Northwest River that meanders through the Northwest River game lands and nature preserves.

Inlets have a way of disappearing along the Banks. That was what made traversing these waters so fun and challenging—and deadly. They didn't call this the Graveyard of the Atlantic for nothing. One day you're safely navigating a channel, the next day you're stranded and listing on a sandbar that Mother Nature has shoved in your path unannounced.

It was rather like one of those shell games the con artists play on the streets of any big city in America, except here it wasn't little orange rubber balls getting moved around, it was the land itself.

Try winning that game.

With a resident population of approximately four thousand, Moyock's big by county standards. Pushed up against the Virginia state line, the burg was the last place you'd see when leaving and the first place you'd see when entering Currituck.

That made Moyock the perfect pitstop for

highway travelers. Barbeque, chicken, ice cream, knickknacks, beachballs, T-shirts, gas stations and fastfood galore. And enough restrooms, some of them clean, for when you've got other business to attend to.

We get our share of criminal activity here too. Burglaries, robberies, a daughter-father business feud that turned real ugly when daddy found out his daughter had embezzled nearly a million dollars from the tourist biz he'd put her in charge of running.

He'd gone after her with a handgun. He claimed the gun wasn't loaded and he only wanted to put a scare into her, not a bullet. She claimed she wasn't stealing his money, only reallocating resources. The new Cadillac Escalade in her garage and new bass boat tied to her slip were merely two examples of her ability to creatively reallocate Daddy's resources.

Both were serving prison sentences. Not in the same place. Smart move on the state's part.

Moyock also has something of a reputation for gambling and I was gambling that that might've been something that drew Charles Harker here.

Greyhound racing was big in Norfolk, Virginia in the 1930s, with its home being the Cavalier Kennel Club. Then Virginia shut the track down and the operation moved across the border to Moyock.

Popular with locals and the thousands of service men and women doing time at one of the many military bases in the region, dog racing continued to flourish until North Carolina also decided to shut down the dubious sport.

In the early 1960s, entrepreneurs paved over the old dirt dog track. The location sprang back to life as the Dog Track Speedway hosting another form of gambling

—this one where NASCAR race drivers and their sponsors gambled their money and their lives travelling at high speeds around a banked oval track. That track was long gone now too.

I drove past plenty of farmland. At various times of the year, this sprawling region sprouts acre after acre of cereal crops like wheat and corn, sweet potatoes, and an assortment of fruits and vegetables.

A group of Amish Mennonites settled in an area known as Puddin' Ridge, west of Moyock, back in the early 1900s.

Their roots went back to the sixteenth century Anabaptists and the Protestant Reformation. Simple living and plain dress was their thing. There was something to be said for that.

This particular branch of the Swiss Mennonite tree came to be known as hook-and-eye Mennonites because they eschewed buttons on their clothing. It wasn't that they were making a fashion statement. This was a statement on taxation. In long-ago Switzerland, the government levied a tax on buttons.

Here in Puddin' Ridge, they farmed peanuts, soybeans, corn and potatoes. Their big cash crop, however, had been peppermint and, to a lesser extent, spearmint. They built and ran a peppermint mill, crushing the mint and extracting the oil that they then bottled and sold to pharmaceutical companies and candy makers.

But life was hard. The peaty swampy soil, when it dried, became highly flammable. All those carbon-rich dead and decaying lifeforms. When the earth smoldered and went up in flames, as it occasionally did—due to careless hunters tossing their cigarettes, more so than the occasional lightning strike—there was nothing these buttonless Mennonites could do but helplessly look on while their precious farmland burned—not *to* the ground because ironically it *was* the ground—and wait for the rains to come and douse the flames.

And being swampy, if their land wasn't on fire, it was boiling over with mosquitoes. Like I said, hard.

So it's no wonder that, like the ever-shifting sands of the Outer Banks, the community eventually eroded away and all traces of their lives gone with it.

My destination in this storied country was an industrial park on the outskirts. I found it tucked behind a Duckees Drive-In and a converted convenience store/gas station now home to a dental practice boasting affordable dentures.

Comprised of three long and low, single-story structures, the industrial park served as home to various small businesses and one of those self-storage facilities that seem to be popping up everywhere in America. The ones where folks pay month after month, year after year, to store all the crap they don't want to keep and/or don't have room to keep in their homes, garages and backyards.

Triple-A Video Works occupied a spot towards the rear. I parked beside a pair of dusty pickup trucks blocking entry to a rollup steel door. Not that it mattered, the overhead door was in lockdown mode. The beige, windowless building itself looked about as inviting as a visit to the dentist up the street for a root canal.

A door the same dull shade of beige—what, the owner wouldn't shell out a few extra bucks for an accent color?—bore the name of the company along with Charles Harker's own name and number.

I grabbed my uniform hat from the passenger seat and stepped down from my truck. The delicious aroma of authentic Mexican cooking wafted over from the commercial taqueria kitchen in the building across the lot, making my mouth water and my stomach get down on its knees and beg.

I had a sudden craving for green chili tamales or a couple of tacos smothered in queso. But now was not the time.

I dropped the Sheriff hat on my head and gave it a tap. The hat wasn't necessary but I'd found that it gave me a more intimidating appearance. Gravitas. Not that the weapon strapped to my waist shouldn't have been enough. But I really wanted to get Charles Harker's attention and hold it.

I tried the doorknob, hoping to catch whoever was inside by surprise. No doing. The door was locked. As I raised my fist to knock, the mobile phone in my pocket sprang to life.

My hand went from the door to my pocket. I pulled out my mobile and checked to see who was calling.

Switch.

27

I backed away from the door, took a second to try to figure out how to handle myself, then answered.

"Hi," I said, striving for happy-to-hear-from-you but not overly obsequious nor angry. After all, Sonia probably wanted to apologize for last night. I could be gracious.

"What the hell were you thinking calling Nat up in the middle of the night and yelling at the poor man?"

"What?" I looked at the phone like it was a handful of angry bees.

"He's not your lackey or your toad. If you have a problem with me, yell at me, Tom. Don't you dare take your frustrations and insecurities out on somebody else."

"Who said I had a problem with you?" I pinched the loose skin along the underside of my neck until my eyes watered. "I don't have a problem with you—"

"Ha! What about last night, Tom? You were barely civil."

"I was fine. You were the one who was making too much of things."

"You're blaming last night on *me*?"

I froze. Literally. My brain seized up and the blood in my veins chilled to minus thirty Fahrenheit. No, Celsius.

I had walked into a trap. And I was a cop too. I should have known better.

"Well?" Sonia prodded.

"Sonia," I whispered into the phone, "I'm on duty. I'm working now. Can we talk about this later?"

"Everything always has to be at your convenience, doesn't it?"

"What's that supposed to mean?"

"It means you hide behind that badge of yours. You throw it up as an excuse to do what you want when you want and to avoid anything and everything whenever you want. Like I said, convenient."

"What? That's not true!"

"No? You wake Nat up in the middle of the night to bust his balls all because you're too immature to handle the fact that he talked to me!"

"I didn't bust anybody's balls." An outright lie. That was exactly what I'd done. "I merely pointed out to him that there is a chain of command, operating procedures in place that we as police officers are sworn to—"

"Cut the bullshit, Tom. You're jealous. Admit it. Jealous that Nat is my friend. It's not my fault the two of you can't be friends. Give him a chance. Nat's a nice guy."

The metal door creaked open and a gnarly red face glared at me. "Can I help you?"

I groaned and mashed the phone's speaker against my lips. This was not the first impression I wanted to make on my suspect. "Listen, Sonia. We can talk about all this later."

"We're talking now."

"I know but now is really not a good time."

"You want somethin', mister?" the gnarly-faced

man in loose dirty blue jeans wiped his runny nose.

"I'll be with you in a second," I told him. He slammed the door shut on me. "Look, Sonia. Do I call you at your job and give you a hard time when you're trying to do your work?"

I retreated across the blacktop toward the building opposite. The insidious smells of Mexican cuisine infiltrated my soul. My empty stomach begged to be fed. My throbbing, under-attack head begged for some comfort food. I really needed that taco.

"No!" she yelled, vibrating my ear like her lips were pressed to it rather than attached to her face a county away. "You only call people up in the middle of the night and give them a hard time merely for being somebody's friend."

"Look, maybe I should have waited till morning," I used my Coast Guard and sheriff voice. The one I'd been trained to use to keep potentially dangerous situations from escalating.

It wasn't working. Apparently, it had not been rigorously designed and tested for special circumstances—such as these of the boyfriend and, dare I say it, crazy girlfriend variety.

Still...I was not going to apologize for my behavior. That was a slippery slope that I knew I could never climb up from. "I'm sorry." Damn, I apologized. Oh well.

"Can't we talk about this later?" How many times had I said that now? "How about dinner? Tonight? Anyplace you like."

I was talking to dead air. Sonia had hung up on me.

Resisting my dire need for Mexican food—hell, at

this point, I felt like hopping in my truck and driving to fucking Mexico City—I stomped back to the Triple-A Video Works door and tugged at the knob. It was locked again. "What the hell!"

I rattled the knob, pounded my fist against the door, and kicked the bottom panel hard enough to put a dent in it. I didn't stop kicking and denting until somebody came and opened the door.

I was in a bad mood and somebody was going to pay the price for it.

And that would be the man I was about to interview.

28

The door inched open. From the narrow gap, my gnarly-faced friend looked me over through a pair of angry, bloodshot green eyes. He coughed and I practically tasted the beer and nicotine spewing out his mouth. "Want something?" He hitched up his floppy Wranglers.

"A tetanus shot would be nice," I brushed his spittle off my shirt. "Charles Harker?"

A frown turned his pumpkin face into a downer. "Hey, Slot." Cough. Cough.

"Yeah?"

"There's some cop here to see you."

"What the hell does he want?"

"Invite me in and find out for yourself," I hollered. Not waiting for the invitation, I nudged my greeter aside and moved into the workplace.

A plywood countertop ran six feet out from the wall and extended for about fifteen feet further back. An assortment of tools, empty beer, soda, and Red Bull cans, crumpled packs of Marlboro and Kool cigarettes, and food wrappers from every fastfood joint in Moyock provided ambience. And stench.

Then again, that odor could have been emanating from the fellow tailing me inside.

The overhead fluorescents were dim but no so

dim that I couldn't make out that the thousand square foot or so space beyond was filled with pinball machines and other arcade games in various stages of life and death. Rows of gray metal shelving, holding what could only be the guts and wiring for these and most any other video arcade game ever built, flanked the bare sheetrock walls.

My shadow coughed, leaned his hip against the counter, and rubbed his nose. Though he was a bantamweight, the counter tilted and threatened to topple.

Short of stature, long in the neck and with a fowl-like hitch in his step, he could've been fifty-percent bantam chicken. Somebody should DNA test him. I placed him in his late forties and that was being generous to a fault.

Funny how parts of the mind work even when the rest of you isn't even trying. Had it been my thinking of the Mennonites that lead me to comparing him to a bantam?

A Dutch novelist named Eduard Douwes Dekker, writing under the name Multatuli, had been born into a Mennonite family. While working at various government postings throughout Indonesia, he'd written a satirical novel, titled Max Havelaar, as a criticism of Dutch colonial policies as seen through the eyes of a coffee merchant.

Dekker had been posted to Bantam, a small port town on the western edge of Java around the time he would have been writing his most famous novel.

Thus completed the Mennonite-bantam link.

Thinking of Java, I now had a craving for coffee. A nice Java blend. Hot, dark and rich.

"Speak your mind and get out. I'm busy here." The silhouette of a man on his knees gave me my first image of Charles Harker.

I wended my way between the elephant's graveyard of pinball machines and tapped my fingernails against the glass top of the machine behind which Charles "Slot" Harker toiled.

Hands on the back of the machine, Charles Harker hauled himself up and coughed. Whatever disease the two men shared, I hoped it wasn't contagious.

Charles Harker was big, soft and black-bearded. Like the pirate. Unlike the Outer Banks' most popular, if infamous, pirate, he showed to the world a pudgy baby face.

Maybe it was the beard that made him look fat. Six years older than his one-time partner, Ryan Deering, Harker looked double that. Maybe it was all that fastfood he scarfed down. Maybe it was prison. Maybe it was his DNA.

The black T-shirt and black jeans held up with a wide black leather belt and silver Budweiser belt buckle gave him the appearance of an overweight cat burglar. Although I couldn't picture this man climbing in through any second story windows.

I could picture him behind bars and wondered if he'd find his way back inside state accommodations once again.

I could also picture him as a murderer.

Harker scratched his thick forearm with the slotted screwdriver held in his right fist. The assorted technicolor tattoos running up both arms gave him some much-needed color. NASCAR, Uncle Sam and Jack

Daniels appeared to be a few of his favorite things. I wondered what Julie Andrews might have to say about that.

Glancing at the motley characters featured on the face of the Addams Family pinball machine Harker was either disemboweling or reassembling, I couldn't help wonder which branch of the Addams family tree he'd sprung from. He had Gomez's sallow complexion, hollow eyes and piggy nose but Morticia's long neck and high cheekbones.

"Well, you come here to watch me work or to talk, Sheriff?"

"Let's talk." I glanced at his coworker. "You want to go someplace private?"

"This place is private. Jeter knows to keep his mouth shut." Harker jabbed the screwdriver in his coworker's direction.

"Fine. Let's talk about Ryan Deering." I finally figured it out. Harker looked the way I pictured Uncle Fester would look if he'd had hair.

"If that's why you've come, you've wasted your time." Harker spat and disappeared behind the pinball machine.

I slapped the surface of the machine. Hard.

The glass rattled.

Harker shot up like the clown in an old-fashioned jack-in-the-box. "What's your problem?"

"My problem, Mr. Harker, is that Ryan Deering is dead. Murdered in my county." I folded my arms over my chest.

"Yeah, I heard about that."

Off to the side, Jeter chuckled. Something he apparently had the skill to do whilst keeping his mouth shut.

"I'll be you did. Want to tell me about it? I hear confession is good for the soul."

"I said I heard about it. I didn't say I was the one that done it." Harker bent over, plunged the screwdriver into a foot-long cardboard box. He slit the box open and extracted a small electric motor with wires dangling from its ends.

"You handle that screwdriver like it was a knife."

"You got a point, Sheriff?"

"When we found Ryan, he had a knife sticking in his back."

"Yeah, a knife. Not a fuckin' screwdriver." Harker slammed the electronic gizmo into the back of the pinball machine.

Nothing happened.

"Having a bad day?" I asked.

"I wasn't until you came along." Harker ran his arm under his nose and Jeter sneezed.

"You two putting together a vaudeville act?" I asked.

Nobody in the room thought that was funny— including me.

"I hear an itchy nose is a sign of guilt." Complete bullshit but Harker and Jeter looked like the gullible types and I'd seen the power of suggestion do powerful things to people.

"I keep my nose clean," hissed Harker.

"Too bad your friend can't say the same thing."

"He's got allergies."

"Yeah, allergies." Jeter smirked.

My dislike for the pair was growing by the minute. "Right. About Ryan Deering."

"What about him?" Harker settled his butt on a cardboard box and tapped his screwdriver against his knee.

"You two got involved in some criminal activity. And like most criminals you got caught."

"Pure luck."

"Yeah," I said with a smirk. After all, it was my turn. "All bad. The thing is, Ryan Deering hardly did time and you did hard time."

"So?"

"Hardly seems fair, does it?"

"Yeah, that's right. Tell it to the judge next time you see her, Sheriff. That prick was more guilty than me. It should have been him locked up for five years." Harker blew out a long breath and rolled his neck. "But that's a long time ago. I did my time and now I run a legitimate business."

"No hard feelings?"

"Towards Deering? Nope. Besides he's dead now. I'd say he got what was coming to him."

"Any idea who was responsible?"

"Not a clue and I don't care." Charles Harker stood. "Look, I don't have to answer your questions. I didn't kill him."

"Why not answer anyway? If you've got nothing to hide, and you're innocent as you say?"

"A man's got a right to his privacy. Ain't that right Jeter?"

"That's right, Slot."

I turned my attention to Harker's pal. "What about you, Jeter? How did you spend your weekend? By the way, have you got a first name or is that it?"

"Paul." Jeter glanced nervously at Harker for

guidance. "I wasn't anywhere."

"That's interesting. We've all got to be somewhere."

"I-I was working."

"Here?"

"That's right."

"All weekend?"

"Most."

"How well did you know Ryan Deering?"

"Never meet him."

"You're wasting your time, Sheriff," said Harker. "And ours."

"When was the last time you saw Deering, Harker?"

Harker appeared to think the question over for a minute. "About a month ago."

"What was that about?"

"Nothing. You could say we just sort of ran into each other."

Jeter laughed. "Yeah, he just sorta ran into your fist."

"You fought?" Finally, we might be getting somewhere. These two didn't have the brains of a pinball machine between them.

"No," Harker told me, although he was glaring at Jeter. "We tap danced."

"Like you're tap dancing around the truth?"

"The guy was a loser. Losers lose. End of story."

"Not quite. You still haven't provided an alibi for the weekend."

"And I don't intend to. You gonna arrest me?"

"Not yet but don't plan any long vacations, except maybe at state expense, that is. If you and your little buddy here have got anything to hide, we'll find it."

Harker pointed. "There's the door, Sheriff."

Jeter grabbed my right arm to help me out.

Big mistake.

I spun, putting my weight into my left leg, bent his arm behind his back, and pivoted against his hip. Before he could scream like a little girl, I threw him into a reconditioned Super Mario Bros. pinball machine circa 1992.

I could practically hear the bells going off between his ears.

Too bad the damn thing wasn't plugged in, I might have racked up some big points.

Harker proved himself to be the smarter of the pair, looking on as Jeter pulled himself together, cursed, lowered his head and rammed me in the crotch.

At least, that had been his intention. What kind of idiot lowers their head and makes a run at a guy?

I locked my fingers, stepped to the side, and slammed both fists in unison down on the back of Jeter's neck.

Jeter's jaw made a funny sound as it connected with the floor.

"I'll let you clean that up," I said to Harker, as I stepped over the sprawled shape.

I heard a groan, so I knew the moron wasn't dead. Thankfully. I'd have been filling out paperwork by the ream.

Harker stood there a moment. I could feel the fury emitting from him like heat from a bed of hot coals. He struck out his hand to help Jeter to his feet. Jeter swiped at the blood oozing from his nostrils. His lips were purple and swelling.

"You two have a nice day." I scooped my hat up from the floor.

I could have hauled Jeter in on a charge of assault but he wasn't worth even that amount of paperwork. And if I'd killed him—which would have been way too easy—it would just be more work for Tracy. She was busy enough as things stood. The woman was pregnant too.

Lucky for Jeter, I'm the compassionate type.

29

I had to give Jeter credit for one thing—I was in a better mood exiting Triple-A Video Works than I had been going in.

I was heading to my Bronco when the smell of tacos forced me to angle across the lot to Taqueria Mexicali. The door stood open. I took that for an invitation.

"Olá," I plucked my hat from my head in deference to the young senorita toiling beside a well-used commercial oven. "Can I get some tacos to go? Por favor?"

I waited expectantly, having used up pretty much my entire Spanish lexicon in just those three words.

"You want tacos?" Lines creased her forehead as she tucked a lock of shoulder-length hair behind one ear. A hair clip the color of a cherry pepper kept her locks from tumbling over her eyes. "For you?"

Her hair mimicked the shade of Aztec xocolatl, a spicy Mexican chocolate drink I had acquired a taste for while stationed down in San Diego near the Mexico border. Xocolatl is the Nahuatl word from which the English word chocolate derives.

Traditional Aztec xocolatl is a bitter and spicy chocolate drink made from cacao beans, green chiles and water. The Maya and Aztec considered this the food of the gods. They used it extensively in their rituals. I had been a habitual drinker for as long as I'd been stationed in southern California—which was, as it turns out, too long.

The Aztec also considered the beverage an aphrodisiac, so I'd heard but never noticed personally.

I used to frequent a small family-owned Mexican restaurant on the southern fringe of Old Town San Diego every chance I got. They added cayenne to their version of the beverage.

The proprietor mixed a damn good mojito too. Those had also been a habit.

I nodded to the dark-eyed young lady. "Yes. Any kind you've got. I'm not picky." I threw in a smile. They're free and can be quite effective. I'll never understand why more people don't employ them more commonly.

She wiped her hands on a splotchy apron tied at the waist. "I'm sorry. We do not sell to public here. We only prepare the foods."

"Couldn't you make an exception? I mean, everything smells great. I'd love to try some of your food."

Several Mexicans, three male and one female, watched me from further back as they toiled over stoves and fryers. Under furrowed brows, suspicious eyes snuck looks at me.

The young woman shook her head vigorously. "I'm sorry. Is against the law. We have no license to do this." Her eyes seemed fixed on my uniform and I understood.

"Oh. No. Look. I'm really just hungry. I do not want to get anybody in trouble. I promise, I won't tell, if you won't."

She turned her head slightly to one side and chewed her lip. "I do not know…"

"Por favor?"

A smile broke out on her pretty face. "You want chips and salsa with that, Sheriff?"

I smiled back. "Chips and salsa would be awesome."

She shouted some words way beyond my handful of street Spanish at the workers in back. The man who appeared to be the oldest and in charge hollered some words back at her.

This went on for another thirty seconds or so during which I thought I heard about ten thousand words being slung across the room.

Finally, he barked at one of the other men who wiped the sweat from his brow with the back of his arm before yanking open a commercial-sized stainless refrigerator and tossing out some ingredients on a prep table. I recognized lettuce, taco shells, cheddar, chicken and beef.

The senorita turned to me. "Your food will be ready in a minute or two."

"Thanks. I hope I didn't get you in trouble."

"No, Papa likes to yell. It makes him happy."

"In that case, glad I could help." I whipped out my wallet. "What do I owe you?"

She waved her hand. "Nothing. Is free for you."

"No, I insist." I laid a ten-dollar bill on the stainless-steel table beside her.

While waiting for my food, I stared out the open door at Triple-A Video Works. Nobody went in or out.

"Señor Sheriff."

I turned to see Papa holding a large brown paper bag extended in his right hand.

"Yes, gracias. Muchas gracias." I took the food sack and inhaled. "Smells delicious."

Papa smiled. "Perhaps, if you have some special occasion or event, you might consider us. We cater many events. All sizes." He spread his arms to show just how big, then reached into his front pocket and pulled out a business card and thrust it into my empty palm.

Papa was more like Papa Bear, with the bushy black eyes, hair and sideburns and enough paunch to see him through winter. All packed into a five-foot six frame.

"I'd be happy to. In fact, there may be an event coming up." I could suggest his services for this little get-together Commissioner Jewel was hosting regarding Creepy Halloween. Who doesn't like a little Mexican food? It would sure help make the meeting go down better. Better still if he delivered a couple kegs' worth of mojitos. I'd be willing to cover the cost of that myself.

Papa growled.

I swiveled to see what had caught his attention. Harker was departing, climbing into his truck. No sign of Jeter, probably nursing his wounds.

"You know him?" I asked.

Papa growled once more, deep, from the chest. "Not a nice man."

"I agree." I tried to ignore the overpowering smell of fresh, warm tacos and taco chips, and the fact that lunch was literally within my grasp. This was more important. "I don't suppose you can remember whether or not the truck that just pulled out or the truck sitting there were parked here anytime this past weekend?"

Papa rubbed his knuckles up and down his stomach. He was always going to be Papa to me although the name on the business card he'd handed me told me his real name was Julio Sevilla. "They not here."

"You sure?"

"Friday? Maybe." He scratched the thicket atop his head. "But Saturday? No way, José."

"Sí, Papa," called his daughter. "Don't you remember? Saturday night, both trucks were parked out front."

"Sí, sí. Gracias, Camila. Saturday night. She is right. The men were here for an hour or so. Loading a truck. Then they drive off." He motioned with his right arm.

"Any idea what they were loading?"

Papa shrugged. "Machines. Games. I do not see good."

"What time was this?"

"Maybe eleven, twelve o'clock."

"They left a little before twelve," added Camila. "Maybe fifteen minutes before us."

"That's pretty late. What were you all doing working at such an hour?"

"That's easy." Camila laid a hand on her father's shoulder. "We were hired to cater a meal Sunday for St. Iglesias. There was much to do."

"And there is much to do now." Papa clapped his hands. "Trabajo!"

Camila shot me a wink and went back to her ovens.

"Tell me, Sheriff," Papa said, his voice low. "These men are bad?"

I pulled in a deep breath, sucking up acres of taco smells. "They aren't good. Do me a favor." It was my turn to hand out a business card. He took it and took his time reading it over. "If you notice anything suspicious, any suspicious activity at all, you give me a call."

"Sí, I do that." Papa bobbed his head energetically.

"I'd stay away from them."

I wanted to add: "And lock up your daughter." But he just might have taken me literally and that didn't seem fair to Camila. Papa had that old school look about him.

30

I inhaled my tacos—some of the best I'd ever eaten— along the edge of the road, with the Bronco's windows rolled down, elbow resting on the door, watching the cars and trucks whiz by, and realized this was becoming a habit. All that was missing was that mojito. I settled for a stale, half-empty plastic bottle of water I discovered under the passenger seat. How long it had been rolling around under there I had no idea.

Spaniel hairs clung to the bottlecap and the water itself had a telltale flavor of dog as it splashed over my tongue, reminding me that I'd last given Bladder Boy a chug from this very same bottle.

So it goes.

My phone rang. I plucked it from the dashboard. "Yeah, what's up, Lizzie?"

"Switch called me."

My nerves tightened reflexively. "Why would Switch call you?"

"Because we're BFFs and we tell each other everything—from spilling about our sex parts to our sex lives."

"You do?" I chilled. This was news to me. Big news. Did I want Lizzie, an officer I had to work with every day, knowing everything there was to know about my sex life and my sex part?

"No, Tom. Switch called me because she said that whenever she calls you, you yell at her." Lizzie sounded more than a little annoyed.

"Is that what she told you? I didn't yell at her. Besides, I was in the middle of something."

"Yeah, well I'm in the middle of something too. A couple of dumbass tanked-up fishermen in a stalled boat that I've got to tow in. I'd arrest them for drunk and disorderly but I think they'd only get a kick out of it if I did. They've both made passes at me. Shut up back there!"

I could hear noises in the background, the thrum of a boat, probably ours, and a drunken male chorus.

Lizzie could have gone on and would have if I didn't put a stop to her rant. "What did Switch want, Lizzie?" I rolled up my windows, turned on the engine and cranked up the heater.

"She said meet her tonight, seven-thirty. Ducks On The Waterfront."

"Fine. I'll talk to you later. By the way, did you get a chance to check on Ariadne Jones' alibi like I asked you?"

"Sorry, Tom. Between working as your and your girlfriend's personal answering service and rescuing drunken boaters, I've kind of been busy. But, hey, I've got an idea." She didn't give me time to ask what that idea was. Not that I'd been intending to. "You want to trade jobs?"

"No, thanks."

"I didn't think so."

"Thanks for the message. I'll see you back at the office."

"Wait. Switch wanted me to tell you one more

thing."

"Shoot." I hoped Lizzie understood that I didn't mean that literally.

"She said 'don't be late'."

Lizzie hung up.

I glanced at my watch. I had hours.

I now had time to follow up on one more lead. Plenty of time.

31

From the file Nat put together, I knew that Ryan Deering had held a large number and a wide variety of jobs in his short tour of duty on Planet Earth.

Far different from me. Beyond a couple of minimum wage jobs in my high school years, I'd had a grand total of two jobs now—the Coast Guard and the Currituck County Sheriff's Office.

Outside his life of crime, Ryan Deering clerked in a grocery store for a number of years. Perhaps that was where he'd met the lovely Ariadne. He'd worked as an assistant property manager for a firm overseeing over one hundred properties, and he'd worked for a cleaning service, emptying wastebaskets and dusting desktops for approximately an equal number of years.

He'd also tooled about the county working as an auto parts deliveryman. That was the job that interested me at the moment. While Donny Clark claimed to have never met Ryan Deering prior to sleeping with the man's wife, according to Nat's never-wrong information, Deering would have been schlepping auto parts throughout Dare and Currituck counties during the years that Clark had been, and still was, operating his body and paint shop.

Maybe there was more to their relationship than a shared bedmate. Or maybe that was enough and the two men had quarreled over her. Crazier things have been known to happen.

Ariadne claimed Ryan wanted her back. How did Donny feel about that?

Axle Auto Parts world headquarters, such as it was, occupied a large two-story warehouse standing in a sea of asphalt a couple hundred feet back from the Caratoke Highway on the north side of Grandy.

I'd been in myself a time or two in search of parts and supplies for my personal vehicle. The county also has a contract with Axle for car and truck parts for its fleet. The left front side of the building was open to the public and served as a storefront. The rest of the building stored the parts and supplies that came in from across the country.

From here, Axle's drivers delivered these parts and merchandise to their own stores throughout the county as well as to individual commercial customers— like Clark's Body & Paint.

Three pickup trucks and two vans, all painted blue and gold with the name and website for Axle Auto Parts, sat in the lot mingling with the vehicles of employees and customers alike.

I parked and stepped inside.

"Afternoon, Sheriff," greeted a middle-aged clerk with prematurely gray hair standing behind the front counter. "What can I getcha today?"

"How are you, Oliver? I'd like one case of oil and one Bernard Basnight." I unzipped my coat. One thing about Axle Auto Parts, they keep it toasty inside. All the stores provide free coffee and danish too. That's what kept me coming in.

"Another case of motor oil?" exclaimed Oliver.

"I'm telling you, you need new valve seals."

"You're probably right. But right now, I'll settle for the oil." For months now, the Bronco had been burning more oil than a funnel cake fryer at the annual county carnival on a busy Saturday afternoon.

"Fine. It's your money."

"Only until you bring me the oil. Then it's your money."

While Oliver fetched the oil, I strolled over to the coffee pot set up on a tabletop glued to an old diesel engine along the side wall, and filled a paper to-go cup. I poured some sugar from a jar that looked as old as the Model T image gracing its side and pushed down the plastic lid.

From the black rubber floor mat serving as a plate, I picked up a warm pecan danish that was practically screaming at me to eat it and did just that—if only to put the poor thing out of its misery.

Oliver banged the case of 5W-30 down on the sales counter. "On sale this week too. Anything else, Sheriff?"

"Mr. Basnight?"

"Mr. B?" Oliver's silver brows shot up. "You serious about that, Sheriff?"

"Yep. Dead serious."

Oliver leaned over the counter and stage-whispered. "He do something wrong?"

"Besides hiring you?"

"Very funny." Oliver's hands worked the cash register. He pointed to the credit card scanner. I slid my card in and out. "He's in his office. Go on back. I'll have the kid drop the oil in the bed of your truck."

"Thanks, Oliver." I swiped a second pecan danish

and carried it and my coffee through the door marked Employees Only.

A couple dozen employees scooted around the cavernous warehouse. The loading dock doors along the back stood open. Two big rigs rumbled at the doors, much like a pair of fat queen ants waiting to be serviced by their obsequious workers.

A blue forklift emptied one truck while its mate busily loaded up a second truck of equal size.

All this buzzing and running around seemed a big waste of effort to me but what did I know about the auto supply business?

Nothing.

I noticed a big pond in back with a patch of trees on the far side.

Inside the warehouse, boxes of all sizes bounced along a waist-high snaking stainless roller conveyor that branched out in several directions across the floor. Men and women in Axle uniforms kept a close eye on the moving merchandise, comparing each box's label with a list hanging at eye level, grabbing and stacking the boxes on pallet jacks ready at their sides.

I found the combined noise, an eardrum-irritating mix of trucks, forklifts, ventilation fans, people and machinery, unbearable compared to the quiet of the store. So did many of the employees judging by the number who wore earplugs or earbuds.

Their jobs seemed to me a terrible way to spend the day but it beat the unemployment line.

I stuffed the danish in my mouth and stepped in front of a beefy employee pushing a handcart. "Mr. Basnight?" I chewed hard. The pastry went down fast but not with anywhere near its proper savor.

"Mr. B?" The employee plucked an earbud from his left ear. The sounds of Pink Floyd's The Wall spilled out. "Over there! Behind the tires! Can't miss it!"

"Thanks." I certainly couldn't miss the dozens of stacks of brand-new tires climbing like black rubber stalagmites from the polished concrete floor to the ceiling.

Circling through the noxious tires, I discovered three doors. Mens Room, Ladies Room and No Admittance.

Mr. Basnight did not seem to be the sort of boss who calls his employees friends. I bet they felt the same about him and I hadn't even met him yet.

A sheet of nailed up plywood kept me from peeking in the four-foot window. So I had no idea what he was up to or if I'd be interrupting something.

I didn't care.

I wasn't in the mood to knock either, so I didn't.

32

Throwing open the door, I discovered Bernard Basnight seated in a high-backed apricot leather chair that looked like it was in the act of swallowing him whole.

The massive desk came practically to his weak chin. His blue eyes, way too close to his nose, came even closer as he laid eyes on me.

Climbing from a chair fit for a king—or a petty lord—which did nothing to increase his height, Bernard Basnight demanded, "What are the police doing here?"

"I'm Sheriff Edge. I'd like to ask you a few questions about Ryan Deering. Excuse me." I set my coffee on a bookcase to my left and wiped my sugar-sticky fingers off on the inside lining of my jacket pockets.

"That piece of shit? He's not worth my time." Bernard Basnight dropped back into his chair and tugged at a poorly chosen chartreuse bowtie. He was the only person within a mile of the warehouse whom I'd seen wearing a suit. His was boring brown.

He picked up an expensive gold pen, with fingers that didn't appear to have ever picked up a car part, let alone worked a part on or off an engine, and tapped it against his shiny mahogany desk. Did he rub it down daily with motor oil or have one of his minions do it?

"Well, he's worth my time seeing how he was murdered in my county." I grabbed my coffee and helped myself to a surprisingly comfortable leather guest chair, a pared down version of his own. Didn't he know it was always better to keep the guests as uncomfortable as possible? "So I would appreciate it if you'd give me a few minutes of your time, Mr. Basnight."

I puzzled over a list of long numbers, followed by strings of accompanying zeros, on his computer monitor, before he turned it away from me. Apparently, he wasn't the sharing type.

"What do you want to know?" Bernard Basnight sighed to let me know how put out he was with my being here in his lair. "Please, make it quick. I've got trucks at the loading dock coming and going."

"So I noticed." I didn't think this was the time to share with him my theory of leaving everything on the trucks as they were now, and simply sending the vehicles off in different directions and with new marching orders. I was pretty sure he wouldn't appreciate the advice, no matter how friendly and helpful.

"Ryan Deering was an employee of yours."

"Was is the key word." Basnight rested his elbows on his desk and his chin on his fists. "That was more than two years ago."

"And that's the last time you saw him?"

I watched as Basnight glanced at the papers piled on his desk. He seemed to be making his mind up about something. In my experience, that meant trying to figure out whether it was safe to lie to me or not. And, if so, how big a whopper he might figure he could get away with.

Basnight slapped his arms down on a stack of invoices. "He was by on Thursday."

"You mean here at the warehouse?"

"That's right."

No wonder Basnight decided against lying to me. Too many witnesses. And I had a hunch most of them hated his guts.

"And it wasn't pleasant."

"No?"

"No." Anger spread across his weaselly face. "You may as well hear it from me. We argued."

"What about?"

"Look, Ryan Deering is a thief. I've got no solid proof but, if you ask me, he was stealing parts out of my warehouse and selling them under the table for cash. Cost me a bundle."

"But you had no proof?"

"No, but the minute I fired his ass, the shrinkage stopped. Good riddance." Basnight ignored the ringing of his desk phone.

"If you were on such bad terms with the guy, what was he doing here? Why did he come to see you, of all people?"

"He wanted to talk to me about a business arrangement."

"What sort of business arrangement?"

"He wanted Axle to contract with the Slowater as a preferred vendor."

"For what?" What could auto parts and beach hotels have in common?

"The go-to place to house our visiting reps, drivers, what have you, when we need to put them up overnight. Offered me a hell of a good rate too."

"What did you tell him?"

"I told him to get lost. I wouldn't give that bum our business if his was the only motel within a hundred miles."

I nodded, tucking his answers away, intending to sift through the words later and see what stood out. Maybe it was all part of Ryan Deering's get-rich plan, like in the book he'd been reading. "Where were you this weekend?"

"Here, at the office. Like I am most weekends."

"Have you got an alibi?"

"For when?"

That was the problem. I had no definite time of death. A family found him Monday morning. "We believe he was murdered sometime between Friday night and Sunday." That was a big stretch of time, but until the complete autopsy, it was all we had to work with.

"As I explained, I was at my desk working throughout most of the weekend."

"Did anybody see you?"

Basnight smiled smugly. "We've got a weekend crew, Sheriff. This place never completely shuts down. Ask anyone. They all saw me."

"Even after hours?"

"I was home. My wife will back me up."

After spending five minutes with him, if I was his wife, I wouldn't be backing him up. I'd be backing over him with my truck. If I didn't own a truck, I'd go out and buy one, a big one, purpose-built to the task.

"And you never saw or spoke with Deering after Thursday?"

"Aren't you listening, Sheriff?" Bernard Basnight

stood and pressed his hands against the desktop. "Deering came by around two-thirty Thursday afternoon. He came into my office here uninvited— much like you did," he said with a frown.

I pictured him ordering an early warning system in the near future.

"Only in his case, we quarreled. I threw him out."

Seeing that Basnight came up to about my bellybutton, that seemed hard to believe unless he'd been wielding a loaded shotgun. "Was there any physical violence?"

"No. I told him to get the hell out of here before I crushed his thick skull with a four-barrel carburetor. But I never laid a hand on him." Basnight chewed on his thumbnail before continuing. "I might've thrown a bronze paperweight through the window."

That explained the fresh plywood. And the statuette of a headless cowboy struggling to hold the reins on a bucking bronco rising from a black marble base that occupied the far corner of his desk.

I waited. Sometimes, interviewing suspects was like going fishing. You had to be very patient and wait for the fish to come to you.

"You may as well hear everything."

"I'm listening."

"Like I said, the loser stole from me. What I didn't tell you was that he once dated my kid sister. Got her pregnant."

"Ryan Deering has a child?"

"No." Basnight shook his head. "There were complications."

"I'm sorry to hear that."

"I'm not. She's better off without him or his kid.

The asshole was married at the time too. The point is, yeah, I hated the guy. And I fired his ass. And you know what? The fucker sued me! Can you believe it?"

Basnight paced back and forth. "For firing him for stealing from me. It took me six months to so-call win the lawsuit he filed against me." He shot me a pair of air quotes. "You call that winning? The lawyer cost me nineteen thousand dollars. Nineteen fucking thousand dollars. Some win, right?" He fell back into his desk chair, deflated and defeated.

I gave him a moment to reinflate, regain his composure, watched him tug at the tufts of brown hair above his ears.

"Do you own a boat, Mr. Basnight?"

"Yes. A thirty-two-foot sloop. What the hell does that have to do with anything?"

"When is the last time you went sailing?"

"Summer before last."

"That's a long dry spell."

"Like I told you, I'm a busy man. Besides, she's got a hole in the forward hull. She's sitting in drydock. One of these days, I'll get her repaired."

"One of the marinas?"

"Banks Marine in Bethtown. If you're interested, check it out. Make me an offer."

"I might just do that." But not for the reason he mentioned. I stood and walked halfway to the door. "One more thing."

"Promise?"

"How deep is the pond out back?"

"The pond? How the hell would I know?"

"Just wondering."

"If you're that curious, why not wade in and find

out for yourself, Sheriff." Basnight's hands hovered over his keyboard, showing me again what a busy man he was. "By the way, when are you up for reelection?"

"Does your asking mean I can count on your vote?"

His pink mouth dropped open but no words fell out.

I knew what he wanted to say next. And I gave him plenty of time for a comeback.

But he didn't have the balls to verbalize it.

33

If I'd learned one thing about Bernard Basnight, it was that he wasn't the sentimental type. Okay, I'd learned two things. The second was that he had a temper and he knew how to use it.

The question remained. Was he the killer type?

I was still pondering that question when Frenchie, smelling like a warm chocolate éclair, dropped into my office with a single sheet of paper in hand. "What have you got?"

"I did some deeging into Monsieur Basnight, as you ask me, Chief."

"And?" I uncrossed my ankles and dropped my boots to the ground. The truth was, I'd been on the verge of dozing off.

"And Ryan Deering had a restraining order against Monsieur Basnight."

"Are you sure? Don't you mean vice versa?"

"Vice verse of what?"

"Let me see that." I pointed to the paper before we went into another verse of Frenchie speak. "So Ryan Deering had a restraining order on Bernard Basnight."

"Oui. Monsieur Deering claimed that Monsieur Basnight threatened him with physical violence, even the death, on multiple occasions."

I tapped my fingernail against the printout. "In

front of witnesses, too. That was dumb." Not that Basnight struck me as particular smart. "This is back about the time that Basnight fired him."

Frenchie nodded. "This restraining order never officially expired, Chief."

"No." I crumpled the paper and tossed it into the corner of the room to join six or seven of its mates on the industrial gray carpet. "Now that Deering is expired, I believe we can officially consider this order expired, too."

"You think perhaps Monsieur Basnight is your killer?"

"I tell you, Frenchie, there was no love lost between those two. And Monsieur Basnight might be small in stature but he's got a big mouth and a big temper."

"Oui, like Napoleon Bonaparte."

"Exactly."

"Ah, if only we could all get along," Frenchie sighed. "Such a world it could be."

"A world in which we'd all be out of work."

"There is that." Frenchie frowned. "My wife would not like this so much."

On that interesting tidbit of news and accompanying conundrum à la Frenchie, I drove home.

The case was going to have to remain unsolved for yet another day.

34

I got home, exercised Bladder Boy and myself with a jog on the beach, shaved in the shower, and dressed in my nicest jeans and a long-sleeve blue shirt I remembered Sonia once telling me she liked. I grabbed my charcoal peacoat from the hook by the door.

Ducks On The Waterfront wasn't fancy but it wasn't totally casual. Besides, Sonia would dress up in something nice. She always did. I didn't want to come off looking too bad in the comparison.

Checking my watch for the umpteenth time, I relaxed, said goodbye to Bladder Boy, told him to hold down the fort and not pee all over it, and drove south.

Cold rain came down but my spirits went up. I was looking forward to a good meal and making things right with Sonia.

The popular restaurant sits on the south side of the Duck Town Park and Soundside Boardwalk, a strip of land following the eastern contours of Currituck Sound.

The entire boardwalk is a great place to sit and watch the spectacular sunsets visible over the expansive Currituck Sound. Watching the sun go down from here was a popular pastime for locals and tourists alike. Sunsets were even better with a drink in hand seated at one of the boardwalk's handful of restaurants and bars.

Bookended by the Waterfront Shoppes on the north end and the Scarborough Lane Shoppes on the south end, with Town Park in the middle, the boardwalk covered nearly eight-tenths of a mile.

In that tiny distance, one could stroll through willow swamp, marsh, maritime deciduous forest, and maritime evergreen forest.

Driving past the Slowater Motel's neon sign led me to thinking about the investigation. I forced those thoughts from my mind. Tonight was all about Sonia and me.

As I reached the sign reading Welcome to the Town of Duck, my phone vibrated in my pocket. I'd switched off the ringer when I took a twenty-minute nap earlier. I wanted to be at my best with Sonia tonight.

I pulled over to the shoulder and checked my mobile. "Frenchie? What's up?"

"A Monsieur Miller called for you, Chief. He says he can speak with you now."

"Who the heck is Miller and what does he want to speak to me about, Frenchie? I'm on my way to dinner. With Switch. I'm off duty." Of course, off duty was something of a gray area when it came to sheriffing.

"Ah. This is Isaac Miller. He tells me you were most insistent. You left a business card in the door of his mobile home and left a message on his phone telling him that you must speak to him pronto."

"Sorry, not ringing any bells, Frenchie. Tell him I'll telephone him in the morning."

"Voila, that is exactly it, Chief. Bells."

"Frenchie, now is not the time—"

"Bells Island Life Campground. He manages this

place, he tells me."

I sighed. "Right. I'd forgotten." Manager of the campground where Ryan Deering's Grand Am had been discovered abandoned.

Suddenly this night was about the investigation.

The rain stopped like someone had thrown a switch and I killed the wipers. They'd been clacking noisily and driving me almost as batty as my sergeant. "Thank Mr. Miller for calling and tell him we'll arrange to speak tomorrow."

"No can do, Chief. Mr. Miller tells me he is going out of town first thing in the morning. He will be gone indefinitely. The Bahamas, I think. Traveling by boat."

"Beats traveling there by truck," I quipped.

"Oui, Chief. Absolument."

All my best jokes, and many of my worst, were wasted on Frenchie.

"Okay, then get Nat to go speak with him tonight." I liked the sound of that.

"I can't," said Frenchie.

"Why not?"

"Nat told me he's going to be incommunicado, no cell phone tonight."

I didn't like the sound of that. "You're joking."

"No, Chief."

"Did he say why?" It was against all protocols. Worse, he was throwing a monkey wrench in my love life.

More wrenches it didn't need.

Was that what this incommunicado shit was all about? Was Nat fucking with me? Did he know I had dinner plans with Sonya tonight? Was he trying to get me in trouble? Had he suggested that Miller call and request to see me tonight?

I bit the inside of my cheek. "Tell Mr. Miller I'm en route. I should be there in twenty minutes or so."

"Will do."

I ended the call and did some mental math. No matter how I toted the number up, I came up late for my dinner date. There was nothing for it but to let Sonia know and hope she was in an understanding mood.

I took a minute to compose a long and heartfelt text explaining the bind I was in, slipped in a line about how Nat was supposed to handle the interview but had bailed at the last minute, leaving me to handle the job as always, and sent it off.

I'd have been a fool to call her and try to explain live. Sure, texting was cowardly. But it was also safer and wiser.

As for Nat, I'd get even with his ass.

35

Darkness stuck to the ground like La Brea tarpit goo as the Bronco and I slid to a stop in a shallow pool of muddy water outside the manager's dimly lit mobile home. His red Chevy truck didn't appear to have moved from the side of the structure since my last visit.

I hopped out and found myself standing in a cold puddle of muck. "Shit." I ran to the steps of the mobile home and wiped my feet on the edge of the stairs. I had on my best shoes. They even had shoelaces and none of the strings had been knotted back together again like I'd done with my sneakers.

I cursed Nat some more and hoped that he could hear me wherever the hell he was. I lifted my fist to pound on the door—I needed to pound something— when the door flew open and my knuckles came within a whisker of punching the nose of the man who'd been reckless enough to open the door.

"Sheriff Edge?"

I pulled back my arm. "Yes, sir. Mr. Miller?"

"Call me Isaac." He stepped away from the door. "Come on inside. Warm up."

"Thank you." I puzzled over my muddy shoes. It wouldn't be very sheriffy to interview him in my stocking feet, even if my socks were reasonably clean. "My shoes are—"

"Don't you worry about it. Give 'em a good wipe and climb aboard. That's all I ever do."

I briskly wiped the bottoms of my shoes against a worn and dirty square of blue carpet placed just inside the door and entered the trailer. Warm was right. Space heaters placed at opposite ends of the trailer created a sub-Saharan environment.

"Have a seat."

I joined Isaac Miller at a square wood veneer kitchen table too big for the long and narrow space. The middle of the table held the remains of his dinner. An old desktop PC with a boxy monitor took up another third of the tabletop. Crumbs littered its white keyboard.

The window next to the table was too dirty to see anything out of—not that there was anything worth seeing out there.

Too small to begin with, randomly tossed clothing, boots, and shoes, a case of beer atop which a small flat-screen TV precariously balanced and faced a lumpy brown chair, an assortment of foodstuffs, and a black bowling ball bag with a hole in its side, were but a few of the many things I noticed cluttering the single-wide mobile home from floor to ceiling.

The way he managed his own life, I could only imagine how well he managed an entire campground.

A half dozen fishing rods leaned next to a dingy toilet with its seat up. A red and brown tackle box on the floor held the bathroom door wide open for all to see.

I assumed Isaac Miller lived alone.

"Sorry I couldn't call you sooner, Sheriff."

"I'm sorry you couldn't call me later," I couldn't resist replying.

"How's that?"

"Never mind." I snuck a peek at my watch. Sonia would be arriving at Ducks On The Waterfront about now and quickly notice that I was not to be found.

If she hadn't accepted my text graciously, my duck would be cooked. Face it, even if she had graciously accepted my excuse, my duck was cooked to one degree or another.

Sure, Sonia's a practicing psychologist, but she never seemed to practice any of that psychology on herself. Not that I'd ever dare tell her that. Not even in a text.

Mr. Miller rose and opened a hip-high refrigerator across from the table. "Can I get you something to drink?"

"No, thank you."

"A snack, maybe?" He yanked open a couple of upper cabinets. "I know I've got some pretzels around here. Now where did I put them?"

"No, really, it's okay. I don't want to put you out or take up too much of your time." Or mine.

"If you say so." Isaac Miller sank back into a pine chair with a green vinyl cushion and lit a cigar. "But I really don't mind. Anything I can do for the police, it's the least I can do."

"I appreciate that, sir."

"Isaac."

"Right, Isaac. What can you tell me about the Grand Am that was parked outside this past weekend?"

Isaac Miller ran a trembling hand through a tumble of stringy blond hair. He had a long face and thin pink lips.

I pegged him to be somewhere in his fifties and

not a fitness freak. Moths had made a meal of his blue wool sweater and his jeans had holes at the knees that I was sure he hadn't paid extra for—like the hipsters do.

I could see he didn't care too much about keeping the rugs clean because his steel-toed work boots were nearly as muddy as my shoes.

"It's like this, Sheriff. I can't really tell you much. To tell the truth, I didn't notice it. I'd gone fishing with some friends of mine Saturday morning. In and out all weekend. Mitch says you found the car Monday morning?"

"That's when we received his call. You don't recall seeing it there Friday night?"

"Sorry. Maybe I don't pay so good attention as I ought to. Then again, it's pretty dark out here come night."

"So I noticed." Except for the lights from the guests and the stars, the grounds were unlit.

"Cigar?"

"No, thank you." Sonia would murder me if I showed up for our date smelling of cigar.

I pulled up a mugshot of Ryan Deering on my phone and showed it to Isaac. "I don't suppose you recognize this man?"

The manager shook his head. "No, I don't suppose I do. Sorry." He pushed up from the table once again. "You sure I can't get you something? I hate to see a fella sitting at my kitchen table without a drink or a bite in his hand."

"No, really, that's not necessary."

Isaac balanced his cigar at the edge of the kitchen sink. He grabbed a can of lightly salted mixed nuts from the kitchen counter. He popped the lid, scooped a handful, tipped back his head and swallowed them up, chewing vigorously. True to form, he offered me the can. I declined.

"Can you think of any reason why Ryan Deering might've left his car here at your campground?"

Isaac pondered this a minute or two. I could smell the nuts on his breathe as he inhaled and exhaled. "Visiting somebody?"

I nodded. "You'd think so. But I had a deputy canvass everybody here and no one knew him."

Isaac shrugged. "Sorry."

"Have you noticed any suspicious or unusual activity here at the campground, Isaac?"

Isaac ran his index finger over his salty lips then licked off the salt that had stuck to it. "Mitch is pretty unusual," he said with a smile. "Wouldn't you say, Sheriff? You've met him, I hear."

"I believe colorful is the politically correct term."

That earned me a chuckle and I felt like signing Isaac up as a deputy right then and there. "He's colorful, all right."

The manager leaned against the counter, popped another handful of mixed nuts and chewed quietly before continuing. "But other than him, no, I can't say I've noticed anything. Generally, it's pretty quiet out here on Bells Island. To tell the truth, that's what I like about it."

"I know what you mean."

"We had a young fella about three years back. Come down from Vermont. Dealing pot out of his camper."

"Oh?"

"Yessir, but the police busted his ass. Good

riddance. That was before your time, I believe, Sheriff."

"Yes, it would have been." I stood. "Thank you for your time, Isaac. If you do think of anything, you give me a call."

"Sure thing, Sheriff. But like I told that Frenchman on the telephone, I'm going to be taking a little trip tomorrow."

"So I heard." I noticed a battered red suitcase, open and half-packed blocking the bedroom doorway up the hall. "I hope you have a good time."

"I intend to. I hope you catch your killer."

"I intend to." I bade the manager a goodnight and tumbled out to the Bronco, sinking two inches in the mud. The shoes might be destined for the trash.

Would Ducks On The Water let me in like this? Would Sonia be waiting?

I sank into the driver's seat, feeling the cold seep into my hamstrings, started the motor, put the truck in gear and drove off.

Too bad. Isaac Miller was nice. Almost too nice. Quite a change from the suspects I'd been talking to the last couple of days.

Friendly, yes. But helpful? No. The manager really was no help at all. It was a pleasure talking to him though and I hoped I'd see him again.

36

With the parking lot full, I waited for a Honda to back out before pulling into a space along the perimeter.

I ran into the restaurant, ignoring the hostess. Sonia wasn't at the bar or seated at any of the tables, inside or out. In fact, only three couples braved the outdoors. Sunset long over, everyone else had retreated indoors to the warm air and soft sounds of the jazz trio hired to provide a soundtrack to their meals.

I left the restaurant and walked down to the deserted boardwalk, the moon over my shoulder.

I had two choices left.

Go home or drive to Manteo.

Sonia might not even have read the text until arriving at the restaurant. Seeing how I was nearly two hours late, it wasn't surprising that there was no sign of her or her Land Rover.

My two phone calls to her went unanswered. I didn't leave a message either time. What could I say?

I still didn't know what to say. But the one thing I did know was that whatever I said next would be better said in person. With a bottle of the best wine I could afford.

And a dozen red roses. Long-stemmed.

And a box of chocolate truffles. She loved those.

Probably more than she loved me at the moment.

Maybe even a can of fancy tuna for Dawon the demon cat.

I chose home. Riding to Sonia's condo in Manteo would have meant a long drive, followed by what could be a long argument.

I wasn't up to it, physically or mentally.

Besides, she'd calm down overnight.

So I hoped.

I arrived home, unlocked the door, looking forward to an enthusiastic greeting by Bladder Boy. He never let me down.

Except that he wasn't waiting for me at the door with those big, adoring brown doggy eyes of his.

"Bladder Boy? Hey, Bladder Boy! Let's go outside!" I slapped my thighs. Boy wasn't as young as he used to be and sometimes fell into a deep dog slumber in front of the hearth or curled up in the middle of my bed. "Bladder Boy?"

I kicked off my shoes a little harder than I should've, sending them flying into the wall, leaving scuffs—not the first time I'd done that—and entered the sitting room. No sign of Bladder Boy. Ditto the bedroom —not even a divot in the bedsheets.

"What the hell?" I was sure he'd been here when I left. There was no sign of a break-in or a breakout.

I scratched my head.

I was pouring myself a bourbon as a dinner substitute, my mind running in circles as I tried to figure out where Bladder Boy was hiding himself, when I noticed the handwritten note on the butcher block kitchen counter within reach of the stove.

Tom, Boy is spending the night with me. Since neither the dog nor I had your company, we decided to keep

each other company.
Sonia.
P.S. You need help.

I crumpled up the note and threw it at the window. "Shit!"

She'd stolen my dog and I didn't dare arrest her. How would that look, a sheriff arresting his girlfriend?

It wouldn't look good. That was for damn sure.

What the hell good was being a cop if you couldn't arrest a loved one, girlfriend or family member once in a while?

I spent the next five minutes cursing and searching for my mobile phone before remembering that I'd left it tucked in the inside pocket of my peacoat, which I had dropped at the front door.

I fumbled for the phone, kicked the coat across the floor and dialed Sonia's number. She answered on the first ring. "You stole my dog?"

"Oh, hello, Tom. This is a surprise. How is your evening going?" She sounded so calm, so cool, so collected. I wanted to play that game too but failed miserably in round one.

"Sonia, you stole my dog. I was working. I told you. I had to interview an important witness in a murder investigation. Nat was supposed to—"

"Don't you dare foist this off on Nat, Tom. It's beneath you."

"Fine." Actually, it wasn't beneath me at all. I was pretty sure she knew that as well as I did. I sucked in a deep breath. "When will I be getting Bladder Boy back?"

"You're neglecting him, Tom."

"I'm no psychologist—"

Sonia snorted. Very unladylike.

I pushed on. "But even I know that the one you're telling me I'm neglecting is you."

"Good of you to notice. I didn't think you would."

A sudden burst of anger overran my better judgment. "You want the damn dog? Keep him!"

I hung up.

I knew she wouldn't keep Bladder Boy.

Her demon cat wouldn't let her.

37

The temperature dipped into the forties but I was hot under the collar when I stomped into the Sheriff's office the following day.

In the third grade at the Jefferson Elementary School in Tempe, Arizona, I'd been roped into playing a role in Snow White and the Seven Dwarfs by my teacher, Mrs. Allison. Each year, the third-grade class put on a two-act play for the entire school during the Fall Festival celebration.

For me, it had been no celebration. I'd been forced to dress up in a dorky costume, complete with scratchy fake moustache and beard, bulbous red rubber nose, green frock and brown tights—every eight-year-old boy's worst nightmare.

My friends—those I had left after they'd seen me dressed in public like what my former ex-best friend described as a boy-girl-goat hybrid—tormented me for weeks afterward.

I'd been drafted to play the part of Grumpy. At that time, I was about the height of a dwarf. Other than that, I couldn't relate to the character. I alternately blushed, giggled and stuttered my way through the entire length of rehearsals and the evening's performance.

Ironic that now I could relate to Grumpy on a

whole other level. Not that I was putting on those tights again for anybody.

"Good morning, Chief." From his desk, Frenchie saluted sharply.

"That's Sheriff, Sergeant." I stabbed my jacket down on the peg beside the door and heard the fabric rip.

"Of course, Chief," Frenchie looked surprised by my comment. "Everybody knows that."

I winced and stormed into my office. I swiveled the monitor so I could pull up the overnight report and see what hell I might have missed—besides my own personal hell, that is.

And I hadn't missed that at all.

I missed Bladder Boy though. I wasn't used to waking up and him not being there.

Ignoring a stack of messages and satisfied that my presence in the office wasn't necessary—and probably not wanted—I decided to get some fresh air and some fresh coffee.

I grabbed my jacket, ignoring the ragged gash in the neck. "I'll be at Davie's, Frenchie." I paused, hand on the door. "That's on a need-to-know basis and nobody needs to know except for Gutierrez and Midgett."

"Yes, sir."

"I want Captain Gutierrez and Chief Deputy Midgett there in five, no, make that ten minutes." I could use a few minutes of me and coffee time. Solo. "Got that?"

"Yes, Chief."

I narrowed my eyes at Frenchie. Sometimes I think the homme is messing with me. "Nat is here, isn't he?"

"Yes, sir. He's in the cells, speaking with one of our overnight guests."

We currently hosted two such overnight guests, a DWI and a petty larceny. Neither of whom I was wasting my time with today. Lizzie chose not to lock up that pair of amorous drunken boaters she'd hauled to shore. I couldn't blame her. They probably would have serenaded her all night long and I would have insisted she stay overnight and listen to every drunken verse and chorus as punishment for foisting them on us.

"And Lizzie?"

"She radioed minutes ago to say she was driving up from checking something out for you in Grandy."

"Fine." I shot up five fingers twice. "Ten minutes."

Frenchie nodded.

Davie Jones Diner was reasonably priced, and the fare was reasonably good. It was also more than reasonably close to the office. Walking distance. Sixty-one steps door to door.

Add it all up and that made the diner the best spot to eat in all of downtown Moyock, such as it was. Downtown was nothing more than a short strip of road that the locals jokingly called Main Street, home to, among other things, Jarvis Gas Station, a fifties relic. The Sheriff's office was the gas station's biggest customer.

Up the street, Franklin's Flowers and Gifts received a good percentage of its business from the nearby Immanuel Lutheran Church Cemetery—most of which I believed was on the flower side of the business.

Gifts had to be the tougher sell. What do you get the recently deceased who already has everything? And needs nothing?

A couple of other stores that seemed to change names and inventory every year or two, a lawyer, and a real estate office, filled in the gaps.

Then there was Davie Jones Diner. Built to resemble a pint-sized Spanish galleon, the diner was claimed to be a replica of the Elizabeth II, which was itself a reproduction based on the various Spanish galleons that explored and exploited the Carolina coast, its peoples and resources, toward the tail end of the sixteenth century.

That replica lives as a tourist attraction down in Manteo, floating in Shallowbag Bay. It's visible from Sonia's place.

Frankly, I didn't see much of a resemblance between Davie Jones Diner and the Elizabeth II but the diner was fun to look at and always nabbed its share of tourists rolling through the area unawares. Who wouldn't be surprised to find a landlocked Spanish galleon so far from sea?

Sails once hung from a tall wooden mast from which there now only flapped a North Carolina state flag and the Currituck County flag.

I walked the wide plank ramp serving the dual purposes of evoking the pirate life and meeting ADA compliance ordinances and climbed aboard.

Pulling open the brass-handled door, the mingled aromas of breakfast cooking knocked me over, telling me that the Oreo and glass of tap water I'd nourished my body with this morning was hardly enough to see me through to lunchtime.

Burgundy-and-white vinyl tiles created a checkerboard on the floor. And I was a mere pawn.

Standing on a wooden keg beside the cash

register up front, at child—or dwarf—level, an open treasure chest beckoned. At the end of a meal, kids could dip their hands in the chest and pull out a piece of treasure or two—chocolate candies wrapped in gold foil stamped with Edward Teach's, aka Blackbeard's, profile.

White-topped booths decorated with pirate flag tablecloths filled the floor. De rigeur pirate paraphernalia, like eyepatches, cast iron shackles, wooden legs wrapped in tattered bandages, muskets and cutlasses, littered the walls.

A mermaid the color of a robin's egg swam over the hall leading to the Gents and Damsels rooms. Scalloped white seashells, strategically placed, kept her family friendly.

An authentic brass cannon—a six pounder that would've swallowed a three-and-a-half-inch cannonball— on a wooden gun carriage greeted guests as they entered. So far, no one had died.

But with this new vegetarian cuisine the diner was now serving, I figured it was only a matter of time.

38

Knowing I was going to have company, I skipped the long-and-wide varnished-wood breakfast counter and opted for a somewhat more private booth halfway along the front. I had words to say to my two associates and the locals didn't need to hear all our business.

Fortunately, the view was pretty good, the original builder having decided that while tiny portals might be more true to period, concave four-foot glass circles let in the light—and let everybody on the outside know what they were missing on the inside.

I nodded to the chef/owner behind the counter, Conan the Vegetarian. The original Davie had long ago, long before my time anyway, gone off to that Great Diner In The Sky—or maybe it was that Great Locker In The Sea.

Either way, after Davie had come a nice lady named Lucille Cress. Unfortunately, Lucille, whose lifelong dream it had been to run a diner of her own, didn't live to enjoy much more than three months of that dreamed-for life. But those three months had been heaven for me. Her food was, as they say, to die for.

And she did.

So now we were stuck with Conan.

Conan had a more pedestrian name, something like Sheffield, but he'd always be Conan the Vegetarian to me because the first thing he did when taking over was convert all the menu items to vegetarian versions, in addition to adding some all-new veg-inspired dishes of his own.

Pretty much the only thing that hadn't changed was the oatmeal. Conan pours soymilk in the now-misnamed buttermilk pancake batter. He tops these pancakes with mounds of melting vegan butter he says he whips up out of coconut milk, cashews, and a handful of other ingredients I can't—and don't want to —remember the names of.

To locals, Conan was the prototypical barbarian at the gate—if Moyock had had a gate. Too late did a band of locals wish they'd erected one.

Despite Conan's unfortunate vegetarian bent, I did like his food, especially the fist-sized scratch-made biscuits and soup that came in bowls big enough to dip your mop in.

I ordered the Cowboy Omelet from a young she-pirate in a white blouse with poufy sleeves, black slacks, and a red kerchief knotted in her hair. The omelet's an insult to cowboys everywhere since it contains not a scrap of sausage, bacon or ham—or cholesterol for that matter.

I knew it would be good because I'd eaten plenty of them—after my initial hesitation and self-imposed ban at trying anything that contained a breakfast sausage made from pea protein and walnuts, that is.

The eggs were real though. Conan's a vegetarian, not a one hundred percent vegan. He keeps a henhouse at his farm and harvests the eggs fresh every day. No egg from the supermarket can compare to those fresh eggs. And every Cowboy Omelet is made with four of them.

My waitress dropped a basket of warm biscuits in front of me and left a pot of coffee and three mugs like I'd asked.

I ripped open a flaky buttermilk biscuit that I knew wasn't made with real butter and slathered on some butter that was not real butter.

I shoved half in my mouth, chewing and inhaling. The result was real enough though. Because, in the end, it smelled great and tasted pretty damn good.

I took a sip of sweet hot coffee and was swallowing the second half of my biscuit as Captain Gutierrez and Chief Deputy Midgett sauntered over to the booth. Mouth full, I waved for them to sit.

I waited until they'd slopped coffee into their mugs and ordered their meals before starting.

"Okay, let's get down to business." I wrapped my hands around my mug, letting the heat soak into my cold fingers.

"Murder being the business du jour?" Lizzie drowned her waffles with a quart of real maple syrup and dug in. Nat stuck with the oatmeal and blueberry compote with a side of whole grain toast—a real health freak.

"Yes." I resisted an eye roll. "So what have we got?" I glanced across the table at my two officers. "Frenchie says you've got something for me, Lizzie?"

"Uh-huh." Lizzie swallowed a thick square of dripping waffle and licked her lips. "I checked out the supermarket where Ariadne Deering is employed."

I waited, dipped my whatever-it-was-it-wasn't-sausage around in some house-made ketchup and bit. "And?"

"And she was working Saturday morning. Left

at one o'clock and didn't punch in again until Sunday morning. In at seven, out at one then too."

"Interesting. And doesn't match at all what she told me."

"What did she tell you?" asked Nat, dabbing his chin with his napkin to scrape off the boiled steel-cut oats clinging to him.

"That she worked all day, both days."

"An exaggeration maybe."

"Or an outright lie."

Nat took it upon himself to refill our mugs. "Did I tell you Ariadne Jones collected on a prior twenty-thousand-dollar life insurance policy when her first husband died, Lizzie?"

Nat added unfiltered honey to his coffee from a jar at the end of the table. What kind of lunatic does that?

"Died under rather suspicious circumstances too," Nat added for dramatic effect. He should have been an actor. Had he ever performed in any elementary school plays featuring Snow White?

What role did he play? Dopey? Nothing personal, but with those 24/7 clean-shaven looks of his...Dopey was the only dwarf never to sport a beard.

"No," Lizzie gaped.

"You didn't tell me either," I said rather icily.

"It was in the report I gave you, Sheriff."

"Oh, right. I remember now." I lowered my eyes and focused on my eggs for a minute.

"What was so mysterious about this first husband's death?" asked Lizzie.

Nat balanced his spoon on the edge of his empty bowl. "His name was Raymond. He drowned in a boating accident."

"Here in Carolina?"

Nat shook his head. "Down near Jacksonville, Florida."

"Did he drown with a knife in his back?" I quipped.

"No, sir. But there were questions."

"Such as?"

"Such as how a former high school swim team member could drown in the Intracoastal only a hundred yards from shore."

"And where was Ariadne while he was drowning himself?" Lizzie wanted to know.

"Sleeping belowdecks." Nat explained how they'd been staying overnight on a small sailboat. "She suggested to the police that Raymond got up in the middle of the night to get some air or piss off the rail, fell in and drowned."

Lizzie furrowed her brow. "That does sound a shade suspect."

"Any drugs or alcohol involved?" I wanted to know.

"Some alcohol found in his system. Not enough that you'd think he couldn't find his way back onboard or, failing that, to the nearest dock."

"What do you think, Tom?" Lizzie asked.

"I suppose there are some obvious similarities but it's a little too soon to call it a pattern, and her our chief suspect." I helped myself to the last biscuit and buttered it up—so to speak.

"Do you have any other good suspects?" Nat asked.

"Outside of Ariadne's boyfriend, Donny?" They

both nodded. "I've interviewed Ryan Deering's ex-partner in crime, Charles Harker, and one of his ex-employers, Bernard Basnight. Neither has a good alibi and both have plenty of reasons to hate him."

I slid the menu closer and ran my eyes down the possible dessert choices. "In fact, based on their tempers alone, the three of them would make a great MMA tag team."

I waved for our waitress. "I'll have the black and white cookie." Each cookie was handmade, hand-iced and, better still, hand-sized.

I fluttered the menu in front of Lizzie and Nat's noses. "Anybody?"

They declined. The waitress flipped her ponytail and said she'd be right back.

"I interviewed Mr. Miller last night," I tossed into the conversation.

That got Nat's attention. "I thought you had a date with Sonia?"

"Well, I didn't. I interviewed Mr. Miller." I felt my intestines tightening like steel coils. "Somebody had to." I locked eyes with Nat. He surrendered first, averting his eyes and reaching for his mug.

"Besides, how did you hear about my date with Sonia?"

"Lizzie told me."

"Hey!" Lizzie whirled on him. I saw the look on Nat's face as he realized he maybe shouldn't have said that.

Lizzie slugged him.

Nat bit his lip.

"Sorry." Lizzie rubbed her knuckles. "I didn't know it was supposed to be a state secret, Tom. And, to be clear, I knew about your date before you did."

I let it slide. "You two kids want to hear what Miller had to say?"

They both nodded.

"Nothing."

"Nothing?" Lizzie appeared disappointed.

"He didn't see or hear anything. He didn't notice Ryan Deering's vehicle parked on the property. He isn't aware of any suspicious activity at all." I leaned back, folding my hands over my full stomach. "An utter and complete waste of my time."

I was staring at Nat now. His jaw muscles twitched.

"And you missed your date with Switch," Lizzie added.

"And I missed my dinner date with Swi-Sonia."

My phone decided to ring. I held up a finger to indicate they should wait, dragged the implement of distraction from my inside coat pocket and frowned at the screen.

"It's her."

39

Instead of disappearing so I could have some privacy, both leaned closer, crowding my personal space.

"Hello, Sonia," I began. "We've had a report about a stolen dog. You wouldn't happen to know anything about that, would you?"

"Oh, that's a great way to start," muttered Lizzie.

I glared across the table at her but took the hint. "What, Sonia? You took my dog. Of course I'm angry."

"Put it on speaker," whispered Lizzie.

Figuring I could gain some support for my POV if they could only hear how crazy and unreasonable Switch could be, I did.

"I did not take Bladder Boy, Tom. I merely borrowed him for the night. We had a sleepover. For your information, we had a wonderful time. He's at the station now. I dropped him off a few minutes ago. You weren't there and Frenchie told me he didn't know where you were."

I gestured with my arms at Lizzie and Nat to say "You see what kind of crazy I have to put up with?"

I also made a mental note-to-self to give the sergeant a gold star on his next employee review for having so ably deflected Sonia for me. Better to deal with her on the telephone than in person here at the diner. In front of my officers, civilians, and Conan the Vegetarian.

"What happened, Dawon throw a pussy fit?"

Sonia's heartfelt sigh cut the air. "Admit it, you hate cats, don't you, Tom?"

"No, I do not hate cats. I don't hate cats at all."

"Huh!"

"Can I say something?" whispered Nat.

"Shut up," I hissed.

"What's that? Who's there?"

"Nobody. I-I'm driving." I gave Nat the ugliest face I could conjure. He stuck a triangle of toast in his mouth and chewed morosely.

"I'll turn down the radio," I lied.

"Admit it, Tom. You only like dogs. You hate cats."

"I do not hate cats." Everybody in the diner was listening now. Great. In a pirate-themed, pirate ship diner, I'd become the star attraction. "Sure, I like dogs. That's not to say that I don't like cats."

And then I made mistake number one. "But, I mean, really, what is there to like about them?"

I foolishly ignored the warning signs Lizzie's big eyes were flashing. "I mean, cats are okay but they're just cats." Mistake number two. "They don't actually *do* anything."

Lizzie's open hands flapped in front of my nose like giant stop signs, warning that the end of the road was near and that cliff was coming up fast, to be followed by a calamitous hundred-foot drop into the churning sea below.

I ignored her. I couldn't seem to stop myself. "It's not like they're dogs or anything." Mistake number three.

"Do you hear yourself?" yelled Sonia.

Nat got up, nodded to us both and walked out. Apparently, he'd had enough. I'd had enough too but I wasn't free to leave like that lucky bastard.

I forged ahead. "I don't hate cats. You want to know the truth? Your cat hates me." Mistake number four.

"You're impossible!" Sonia hung up.

Lizzie chuckled. "You really put your foot in it that time, Tom. Or should I saw *paw*?"

"Not funny." I wiped a wall of sweat from my forehead and slid my phone into my pocket. "Damn. I've worked up a bigger sweat arguing with Sonia for five minutes than I did on my last forty-five-minute jog along the beach."

"It was like watching some loser walk the plank. And telling her all that stuff? Comparing cats to dogs? Stoopid." Lizzie grinned, shook her head. "Yep, you are one sick *puppy*, Tom."

"That's insubordination, Captain. Pay the check."

"Hey!"

I shot up from the booth and stamped towards the exit, intercepting our waitress on my way to the door. She held my cookie in a wax paper sleeve in one hand and our check in the other. "I'll take that. Thanks. You can give the bill to the young lady at my booth."

"You mean the one who looks angry enough to shoot somebody?" the waitress inquired, a slight tremor of fear in her voice.

"You have a very keen sense of observation. Have you ever thought about becoming a deputy?"

"No, thanks. I have a feeling it might be less stressful being a pirate."

"You could be right." I slid the cookie upward in its sleeve and took a nibble right down the middle. I'd save the rest of it for later. Once my stomach settled.

Black and white. If only life could be this simple. And sweet.

I made back to the office in fifty-one steps this time. A new personal best.

40

Back at the office, Frenchie scrambled from his chair and waved to me. "Oh, Chief! Switch came by and —"

"I know. Thanks for running interference. You did your best." I marched on past him.

Bladder Boy, curled up in my desk chair, jumped up and came running to greet me.

I petted him fiercely as he licked my face, not minding at all the warm puddle he created on the floor. I was that happy to see him.

I sniffed, gently grabbed his snout. "What's up? You smell so...clean. You haven't had a bath, have you?"

Bladder Boy shook his head. Was that a yes or a no?

Reunion completed, Bladder Boy followed at my heels as I got some paper towels from the supply cabinet. I cleaned up his mess, stuffed the dirty towels in a plastic grocery sack. I knotted the sack and dropped it in the metal trash bin at the side of my desk so it wouldn't stink up the office too bad. The cleaning crew doesn't show up until after 9 p.m.

That was when I noticed the stuff on my desk.

A shiny new stainless steel dog bowl, double-bowled actually, and engraved with Bladder Boy's name. A brand-new glow-in-the-dark Frisbee, and a twenty-pound bag of dogfood—the gourmet stuff too, not the regular food I normally purchased.

I also noticed the paper to-go cup of coffee, a large one, and one of those plastic boxes with the clear snap-on lid. Visible inside, like a treasure—a gooey, golden treasure—sat a pastry. And not just any pastry.

Lying inside the box, waiting to be taken like a bride on her honeymoon, sat a fresh, thick vanilla-cinnamon roll from Annabaker's. My mouth watered up. A purely Pavlovian response. I loved that place. It's in Manteo, around the corner from Sonia's condo.

Sonia.

Crap.

Lizzie was right.

I really had put my paw in it this time.

Forget black and white cookies.

Suddenly, I wanted a pastry.

No, I wanted Sonia.

I fell into my desk chair. Bladder Boy cozied up under the desk. I dialed Sonia's number and got the voicemail saying she was with a client. Client meant patient. This time of day, she probably was with one of her patients too—not simply avoiding me.

I reached down and patted Bladder Boy on the head. "I really screwed up this time, didn't I?"

He rolled over on his side and dribbled.

41

Pastry polished off and coffee downed, I was ready to go. Even the coffee had been deliciously thoughtful—not merely a cup of any old coffee. This was a cup of Annabaker's cinnamon-and-brown sugar blend that I craved. And it paired great with the cinnamon pastry.

I hadn't left Bladder Boy out of the festivities either. We christened his new dog dish with a fresh bottle of water and a full scoop—I used my mug—of the gourmet dog food. To say he loved it would be an understatement. He gobbled up the pricy kibble like it was his first and his last meal. This could set a bad precedent.

"I'll be following up on some leads if anyone is looking for me," I told Frenchie, at his desk. "And if Switch should call or stop by, tell her I've been trying to reach her."

"Sure, Chief. Anything else?"

"Yep. I'd like you to do some digging for me, Frenchie."

"Deeging, Chief?"

"Do your magic. Give me a report detailing everything that happened that we got word of between last Friday night and Sunday night." I tapped my fingers on his desk. "Maybe something else happened that weekend."

"Something that might be connected to zee murder?"

"That's the hope."

Leaving Frenchie in charge of Bladder Boy—or vice versa—I punched the Leftkowitzes address into my mobile phone and took off.

I needed to shake something loose in this case and maybe going back to the first persons to find the body would help.

The Leftkowitzes didn't live too far from that boatyard/marina where Bernard Basnight told me his sailboat was sitting in drydock. That was something I wanted to see for myself because it wouldn't be the first time someone lied to the police in general or me in particular.

Jeff Leftkowitz stood in the driveway of his modest tract house squirting a layer of dried mud off his pickup. A navy Audi wearing a temp tag sat in the open garage. I pulled up behind the truck and killed the engine.

I could see Jeff Leftkowitz puzzling over me for a minute but he smiled when I unfolded myself from the Bronco and ambled over. "Good morning, Mr. Leftkowitz. Sheriff Edge, remember me?"

"Of course, how are you, Sheriff?" Jeff Leftkowitz twisted the brass nozzle screwed to the end of the green hose and the water reduced to a dribble. He tossed the end of the hose onto the lawn.

"Could be better," I said, despite the glow in my stomach from the pastry dissolving in my gut and spreading goodness throughout my veins.

"Catch that killer yet?"

"No." I smiled to hide the frown that wanted to break out. "In fact, that's why I'm here. I hope you don't mind me dropping by unannounced."

"Nah. Not a bit." Jeff Leftkowitz wore baggy jeans, a green flannel shirt, a ribbed black vest and boots.

"Good. Now that some time has gone by, I'm wondering if you or your wife, Jinny, wasn't it?"

"That's right. Good memory."

I continued. "I'm wondering if either of you remember anything else about that morning."

Jeff Leftkowitz pushed out his lip and shrugged. "I don't think so." He eyed the mud drying on the passenger side of his vehicle. "I tell you what. I can finish this later. Let's go inside, ask the wife, and have some coffee."

Walking along the sidewalk, I nodded my chin towards a for sale sign planted in the lawn of the house next door. "One of yours?"

"Huh?"

"The house for sale. I was wondering if it was one of yours."

Deep ridges formed in Jeff Leftkowitz's forehead. "Why, no."

"Not very neighborly."

"Right."

I followed Jeff Leftkowitz indoors to a small living room overcrowded with kids' toys. Many looked brand new and unopened. "Somebody have a birthday?"

Jeff Leftkowitz appeared to eye the toys with disdain. "No, that's Jinny being Jinny. Spoils them."

"I'd say so. Where are they?"

"In school. They attend Munchkin Academy up the road."

"Who are you talking to, Jeff?" Jinny Leftkowitz, in blue jeans and a maroon sweatshirt stepped from the kitchen. "Oh, Sheriff!" Her hand went to her tousled hair, in which I noticed several small brown leaves.

"This is a surprise." She glanced at her husband. "Why didn't you tell me we were going to have company?" A slight reddish glow lit her cheeks. "I've been doing some dead-heading in the yard."

"Dead-heading?" I asked.

"Removing the dead flowers from the bushes. Helps the new buds grow better come spring."

"Gotcha."

"The Sheriff dropped by to ask if we've remembered anything else about that morning, you know..."

Jinny Leftkowitz wrapped her arms around herself and shivered. "Like I could ever forget. Let's go into the kitchen. Have a seat. I started a fresh pot of coffee not five minutes ago."

"Yes, ma'am." No need to ask me twice. Besides, a cozy, homy setting helped folks relax. And that, I'd learned, could not only help gain their cooperation, it often improved their memory.

Police stations and interrogation rooms are great for intimidation. Not so great for cooperation.

Sadly, the coffee was mediocre and their assistance nil. They'd taken the day off for a little fun and sun at the beach, maybe to hope to find a nice seashell or three. Instead, they'd found Ryan Deering.

Why was it all the nicest people were the least helpful in a murder investigation?

I fired up the Bronco, left Jeff Leftkowitz to his truck washing duties, and aimed my sights on Banks

Marine in nearby Bethtown.

42

Three buildings with blue metal roofs sprawled out along the waterfront. Motorboats, sailboats, rowboats, canoes, kayaks and a few houseboats filled the parking lot.

I pulled up to the middle building with an all-glass front and several expensive looking boats visible on the showroom floor. A row of standup paddleboards caught my eye. That was something I might be interested in for myself and Bladder Boy.

Before I was halfway out of my car, a gray-suited salesman greeted me. He was short and stout and wore a big smile on his face. His hair was white as snow, quite a contrast to a face the color of cognac. This was a man who spent a lot of time outdoors.

"Can I help you, officer?"

"Sheriff Edge," I show him my ID.

"Sheriff?" That got the man's attention. It usual did. "In a buying mood? You've come to the right place. We've quite a selection."

"So I can see. But that's not why I'm here. Besides, even if I was in a buying mood, my bank account isn't." Being Sheriff paid okay but the badge did not give me the right to print money or rob banks without their being legal repercussions.

"We can offer excellent terms for folks such as

yourselves. You'd be surprised how affordable a boat can be."

I laughed. "Let me stop you right there. I'm ex-Coast Guard."

"Oh, then you know how hellishly expensive owning and operating a boat can be." This time, he laughed. "Hank Cassel. Proprietor." He slipped me a business card.

"Lucky you." I slipped the card into my pocket without reading it.

"Some days, yes. Some days, no. If you're not interested in buying, what does bring you, Sheriff?"

"I'd like to take a look at a vessel that belongs to Bernard Basnight. I believe he has a sailboat here in drydock."

"Mr. Basnight, sure. It's got a hole in it. I've given him two different estimates on the repair and I'm just waiting for the authorization to begin work."

"So it's not seaworthy at this time?"

"Not if your definition of seaworthy is keeping the sea out and your ass dry." He extended a hand.

"Can we take a look at her?"

"Sure thing. Follow me." As we wended our way between boats in various stages of seaworthiness, Hank kept up a running monolog, telling me about the virtues and negatives of each boat we passed.

When he pulled off a blue tarp over a sailboat resting on a trailer behind the far building where several workers crawled over boats in for repairs, I could see immediately that Bernard Basnight had told me the truth. Go figure. "This is it, huh?"

"In all her glory. Whatcha wanna see it for?"

"Sorry, I can't say. It's part of an ongoing

investigation." I stepped back, scratched my head.

"Basnight in some sort of trouble?"

"No."

"What is it then, an insurance thing?"

"Sorry, I—"

Hank Cassel held up a hand. "I know, you really can't say." Hank tucked his hands in his trousers. "You know it's a funny coincidence you being here."

"Oh?"

"Yessir, I'd been meaning to call you but my son-in-law thinks I'm being silly. Or losing my mind." Hank Cassel chuckled. "Maybe both. I'll be seventy soon. Thinking of retiring but…"

"But?"

"But it's hard to let go. And I'm not sure the kid is ready to handle it."

"Begging your pardon, Hank, but so far you're saying plenty, however, none of what you're saying explains why you were thinking of calling the Sheriff's Office."

"Yeah, I know." Hank Cassel frowned as he made up his mind. "Okay, it's like this. One of our boats went missing. A Carolina Skiff. Pricey. She was like new."

"Did you report it?"

"No, I was going to but it was back the next day."

"Didn't you find that a little odd?"

"Well, yeah, sort of. Then I got to figuring maybe I'd just misplaced it."

"Misplaced it?"

"Like the kid said, sometimes one of the guys moves a boat around. You know, changing the display or pulling it out to show a customer. Maybe performing some work on the thing. You might not think it, but even on land, boats don't always stay in one place." Hank Cassel waved his arm. "And this is a big place."

"That it is. I suppose it would be easy to lose track of a particular vessel. So this boat was missing and then reappeared. Had there been any damage to it?"

"Nope. She looked the same as ever. Strange, huh?"

"It's one for the books, all right." We walked over to the boat in question, parked in front of the main showroom. "And it's never happened before or since?" I climbed the ladder leading up onto the Carolina Skiff and looked around.

"Not to my knowledge," admitted Hank Cassel.

"She's nice."

"Twenty-six feet long and eight-foot at the beam. Two-hundred horsepower Suzuki engine with less than three hundred hours on her. Underwent a complete overhaul right here. Sure you're not interested?"

"I'm interested in this," I said, bending over the helm and reaching behind the wheel.

"What's that?"

"A pen." I pulled a small plastic bag from my jacket and used it to pick up the pen. I maneuvered it inside and sealed it. "Mind if I keep it?"

"Suit yourself." Hank Cassel stepped away as I climbed down. "Nothing special about a pen."

He didn't know how wrong he was. There was something special about this pen. It was a promotional ink pen bearing the name Slowater Motel on its barrel. But what did it mean, if anything?

"Does the name Ryan Deering mean anything to you?"

"Ryan Deering. That the man I heard about got

himself killed?"

"That's him." I dug out my phone and pulled up the victim's driver's license photo. "Recognize him?"

"Nope."

"Not a customer?"

"Not a customer."

"You sure? A potential customer maybe? Came to look at this boat?"

Hank Cassel was shaking his head no before I'd even finished my asking. "I remember all my potential customers. Like I'm going to remember you. How do you think I've stayed in business all these years?"

"Right. I'm going to need you to do me a favor, Hank."

"What's that?"

"Don't let anybody on or near this boat until I can send a team to look it over."

Not that I held out much hope they'd find anything what with the skiff being outdoors, uncovered and exposed to every element man and nature had to throw at it.

"You mind telling me why?"

"Hank," I sighed. "I'm going to be honest with you. I wish I knew why."

43

I dialed Nat's number, got sent to his voicemail, and left explicit instructions about the skiff. "Send Flo and Eddie," I ordered. "I want that boat checked top to bottom. Stem to stern. ASAP. Any questions, talk to Hank Cassel. He's the proprietor."

Next, I planned to stop at the office to pick up Bladder Boy. He'd be anxious to get home. Afterwards, I'd go revisit some of my favorite suspects, like Ariadne Jones and her boyfriend, Donny Clark.

A telephone call from a certain Frenchman put a stop to those plans as I hauled south down the Caratoke Highway. "Chief, there has been zee fire."

"Since when are we in charge of fires, Frenchie? Did I miss a memo or something? Call the fire department."

"But this is at the Bells Island, Chief. The firemans call me and tell me to call you and tell you to come."

"I'm kind of busy here, Frenchie. A murder investigation, remember?"

"But, Chief, the firemans say you must come. Eez important."

"And what I'm doing isn't?" I sighed. "Look, send Lizzie. Or Nat."

"The Chief Deputy is unavailable. A family matter. Captain Lizzie eez diffusing zee bum."

"What bum?"

"Zee bum that goes boom, Chief."

"What?" That stopped me. "Do you mean bomb?"

"This is what I said, Chief. Bum."

"Are you sure she said bomb?"

"Yes, Chief. Ka-bloomy. Several persons at Corolla beach near zee Duck border report finding this bum washed up on shore. World War Two, maybe, eh? Lizzie goes to see this."

Such occurrences were rare, thank goodness, but had been known to happen. Every once in a while, some unexploded ordnance washes up on our beaches. Most turn out to be harmless.

"At least it's not another dead body." One was enough.

"Oui, this is true, Chief. But what about the other body?"

"You're not making any sense, Frenchie." Nothing new there. "What other body?"

"Zee Bells Island body, Chief. The one firemans want you to see."

"Wait, are you telling me somebody died in this fire of yours?"

"Is not my fire, Chief. Is Monsieur Isaac—Hold on, Chief."

The road passed underneath me as I listened to the rustling of papers on the other end of the line.

"Monsieur Isaac Miller's fire."

I slammed on the brakes. The Bronco slid across the road, earning me the ugly looks of several passing cars and one nearly flattened jogger.

233

44

A gray sky hung over the small Bells Island volunteer fire crew standing around an idling firetruck. An EMS vehicle nosed up alongside it in front of Isaac Miller's mobile home. The door to the home stood open.

Mitch Green, sporting an old green bathrobe over baggy jeans and brown leather boots, hovered nearby with his dog, Mutton.

Tracy Zefferelli roared up in a spray of mud and water. She slammed on the brakes and jumped out of her Range Rover, ignoring the ugly looks of the freshly splattered fire crew. "Where's the body, Tom?"

"Inside, I'd guess. I just got here myself."

Two firemen pointed and in we went.

We found the fire chief in the bedroom, looking at a carton of cigarettes spilled out on the bed and some burnt material. A long-stemmed lighter lay atop the rumpled bedcovers.

So did the manager. And he appeared just as rumpled. And dead. His right hand was charred. The smell of alcohol was impossible to miss. Ditto the smell of smoke.

The room was robed in black grime. An open bottle of whiskey stood on the bedside table, keeping company with a single damp glass.

"Fire started on the bed?"

"On the floor. Edge of the bed. At first, I figured he probably fell asleep." The fire chief pointed. "That hunk of melted plastic is a room heater and the remnants of some bedsheet. Lucky the whole trailer didn't burn to the ground."

The bedroom window hung ajar and it was cold in the trailer. Isaac Miller's crumpled body was cold too by the look of it.

"At least, that's what I first thought."

"And now you don't?"

"Strangled," said Tracy without a trace of doubt in her voice. With a gloved hand, she inspected the victim's mouth and nares. "He sure as hell didn't die of smoke inhalation. I'd say he was dead before the first sign of smoke."

"Yep," said the fire chief. "Besides, a man doesn't get those marks on his neck from smoke inhalation."

"Shit." I peered closer at the body.

Isaac Miller wasn't dead for no reason. This hadn't been an accident. He must have known something. Something to do with the murder of Ryan Deering and he'd died because of it.

I'd let his nice guy vibe fool me. Shame on me.

I'm supposed to know better.

"Well?" I made the mistake of asking Tracy.

"Well, what? He's dead. Wrap him up, I'll take him." Tracy stood, dusted her trousers and stomped out.

The fire chief looked quizzically at me.

"You heard the lady," I said. "But before we haul him off, we're going to have to collect evidence. You guys touch anything?"

"Are you kidding?" The fire chief, a tall man in

235

his fifties with a silver head of hair, who appeared to be built of armor, shot me a wry look. "We touched everything. Until I got the feeling this was a murder, that is."

"Crap."

"Yeah. And it's all yours." The fire chief stomped out after the medical examiner.

When was it going to be my turn to stomp out?

I looked around some more while waiting for some deputies to show up with the crime scene kit and a camera. "Who called it in?" I asked the fire chief, seated along the rear of the fire truck, legs dangling.

"Guy over there in the bathrobe."

"How long ago do you think the fire started?"

"Best guess at this time? Middle of the night." He spat.

Thanks." I picked my way through the muddy minefield to where Mitch and Mutton stood watching. "Morning, Mitch. I hear you called the fire department?"

"Yes, Sheriff. I sure did."

"When exactly did you notice the fire?"

"Well, I didn't exactly notice the fire. I noticed the scorch marks outside the bedroom window this morning."

"Oh?"

"Come on, I'll show you." Mitch waved and Mutton and I dutifully followed him around to the backside of the trailer. "See?"

I saw. Black and brown scorch marks spread out from the open window, marring the sides of the trailer. Isaac Miller's truck hadn't moved from the spot where I'd last seen it.

"Mutton and I were out for a walk this morning.

I noticed the smudges and the smell. Called the fire department."

"You didn't see or hear anything last night?"

"No. Nothing that comes to mind." Mutton rousted a wild rabbit from the tall weeds behind the mobile home and gave chase.

Mitch chuckled. "He never catches them. That dog would probably die of fright if he did. Say, who was that pretty lady just left here in the black Range Rover?"

"Tracy Zefferelli. Medical team."

"She seeing anybody?"

"Didn't you notice how big she was? How pregnant?"

Mitch shrugged, unaffected. "A man can ask, can't he?"

"Let me ask you something, Mitch."

"Sure, Sheriff."

"I spoke with Mr. Miller last night. He told me he was going out of town on an extended fishing trip. He was packing when I saw him."

"And?"

"You know anything about that? Who he was going with, for instance?"

"Nope. I did remember one thing though."

"What's that?"

"I don't know if it means anything to you, but I come to remember seeing a truck here at the campground Friday night."

"Outside the mobile home here?"

"No, sir. Over by the dock."

"What kind of truck?"

Mutton shot between Mitch's legs, sending Mitch careening. He bounced off the side of the mobile home.

I grabbed hold of him to keep him from landing face down in the mud. The ever-present aura of beer clung to him.

"Big box truck. You know, like one of those moving vans. But a little one."

"Did you notice a name on the vehicle? Something to identify it?"

Mitch wiggled his chin. "Now that you mention it…"

"Yes?"

"I'm not sure. It was dark. Something to do with game?"

"Fish and game?" What would the Currituck County Game Commission be doing out here? At night? Or the USFWS for that matter?

"Maybe."

"Was it here long?"

"I didn't look long. It wasn't here the next morning though. That I do know."

Two Sheriff's Office vehicles came splashing up to Isaac Miller's place.

I fondled the pen in my pocket. The one in the evidence bag that I'd collected at Banks Marine.

What the devil was going on? What connected Ryan Deering and Isaac Miller?

I thanked Mitch and went back inside the fire-damaged mobile home in search of the answer to that and other burning questions.

45

Lizzie slammed into a chair across from my desk. She crossed her legs and kicked her feet against the backside of the desk, generating a vibration that snaked its way up and across, into my elbows—which at the moment were holding up my chin—and made my jaw ache.

I lifted my head and looked up from my computer. I was making progress on that budget report —all of it backwards and I couldn't for the life of me figure out how that was possible. Despite the captain's rattling, I was happy for the distraction. "Problem?"

"It turned out to be a dud. Literally." To my furrowed brow, she replied. "The bomb."

"You sound disappointed."

"Do I?" She scratched behind her ear. "I guess I was a little." Her boot stopped kicking my desk. "A girl's entitled to a little excitement."

"Isn't that what spouses are for?"

"Separated, remember?" She wriggled the ringless fingers of her left hand in my face.

"Sorry."

"Don't be. I mean, I like Hector, and the sex is great. I just don't need to see his wet towel hanging in my bathroom. Know what I mean?"

"Can we change the subject to something other

than your sex life if I say yes?"

Her eyes sparkled as she leaned over my desk. "Okay, let's talk about your sex life. How's it going, sport?"

"If you must know, it's going just fine. In fact, Sonia and I are having dinner at my place tonight." I'd been playing telephone tag all afternoon with Sonia and we'd finally connected. Dinner was on for eight o'clock. "I'm cooking."

"Bullshit."

"No, actually I was thinking fish."

The face Lizzie made said it all but she said it anyway. "I hate fish."

"You're not invited."

Lizzie planted her elbows and dipped her chin into her hands. "Flo and Eddie find anything on that skiff over at the marina?"

"Zip. All we got is a pen from the Slowater and there wasn't a fingerprint to be found on it."

"Shit."

"Yep." I ran my hands along my face and squeezed. This case was getting to me.

"Anybody at the marina recognize Ryan Deering?"

"Nope."

"So, nobody remembers him looking at the skiff, you know, like a potential buyer, anything like that?"

"No. Flo and Eddie asked the entire staff. Nobody remembers Ryan Deering. Personally, I'll never forget him."

"Ditto. And now we've got a second murder to contend with."

"Hey!" I shouted as Nat walked past my

nonexistent door.

"Sheriff?"

"Where the hell have you been all day?"

Nat blinked. "Sorry, something came up."

"Yeah, well, next time something comes up, make sure it's job related."

Nat nodded and marched off to wherever it is Nat marches off to.

"Two murders and Nat's off doing god knows what."

"Ah, Tom." Lizzie pulled her lower lip downward with her teeth.

"What?"

"He's got a sick kid."

"Oh. I didn't know. Chickenpox? Measles?"

"Apparently, the pediatrician doesn't know yet. They're running some tests."

"Crap." Running some tests. That never sounded good. "Think I should say something?"

"I don't think he wants to make a big deal of it."

I nodded but I was going to have to say something. Especially given the way I'd been snapping at him the past week or so.

"Call for you, Chief!"

My butt jumped several inches above my chair before falling to earth once more. "Frenchie." The sergeant hovered in the doorway. "Where'd you come from?"

"Been here the whole time, Chief. Okay to put through that call?"

"From?"

"From my phone over there, Chief." Frenchie pointed towards his desk.

"No, I mean, who is calling for me?"

"Carolina."

"North or South?"

Lizzie chuckled. "I'm out of here." She stood, affectionately patted Frenchie on the shoulder and slipped out past him.

"Chief?"

"Just put the call through, Frenchie."

Frenchie saluted, returned to his desk and punched a button. From across the office, he shot me a thumb-to-index finger okay sign.

The next instant, a light blinked on my desk phone and I picked up the receiver. Although I felt a little silly, I said, "Carolina?"

"Sheriff?"

"Yes."

"This is Caroline Frazier. From the Slowater Motel."

"Oh, Ms. Frazier." Frenchie had been so damn close. "How are you? Did you remember who that man was you were telling me about? The one who was asking for Ryan? Have you seen him again?"

If so, this would be the first good news in this case since the beginning. She'd claimed a man had come into the Slowater looking for Ryan Deering a couple of days before his murder and that there was something familiar about him.

"It might not mean anything but I'd still like to talk to him." Maybe he was Ryan Deering's sole friend or another relative.

Or his killer.

"What? No, sorry, Sheriff. This is something else."

"Okay." I tried to mask my disappointment.

"What have you got for me?"

"I think this is something you're going to want to see."

"I'm really quite busy." I didn't want to mention the second murder. The less said about it to the public, the better. "What is it?"

Silence reigned for a moment, making me all the more curious.

"I'd really rather you come see for yourself."

I did some calculations. The Slowater was on my drive home. I could pick up some groceries along the way and still be home with plenty of time to shower and clean up the place. "I'll be there in an hour."

"Great. I'll wait for you."

46

I hung up the telephone as Frenchie came barreling past a six-foot-eight ex-NC State star basketball player whom I knew all too well.

"Chief, Commissioner Foxworthy is here to see you," panted the sergeant.

"He can see me," grumbled Alan Foxworthy, hand moving to adjust the stern knot of his pink necktie. I didn't think it at all matched the brown suit but I was hardly a fashion expert so who was I to judge?

"Everybody can see you, Alan. I'm pretty sure you're the tallest man in the county."

Alan Foxworthy pulled out a guest chair and made himself at home. Although with his size, this was one of those tiny homes. He looked like a grown man being forced to sit in one of those wooden kiddie chairs meant for kindergartners.

In his middle forties, his dark brown eyes stood out starkly against the pale complexion nature, heredity and an aversion to the sun had papered his flesh with. A small mole hung at the edge of his right eyebrow. His long fingers were meant for gripping basketballs.

Frenchie looked like he didn't know what to do with himself.

I took the matter into my own hands. "Thank

you, Sergeant. You can go."

Frenchie did go but he loitered near a filing cabinet within earshot. No matter, if it meant that much to him, let him listen.

"You've caught me at a bad time. I was just on my way out." Either the big guy had taken up baking sugar cookies like my mom used to make or he was trying out a new vanilla-scented cologne. "What can I do for you, Commissioner?"

Commissioner Foxworthy waved away my words like he was swatting at a lazy fly. "Whatever it is can wait, Tom. This is important."

With Commissioner Alan Foxworthy anything to do with him or the county commission was more important than practically anything on earth. If Foxworthy thought it important, it was everybody else's job to think so too.

Alan Foxworthy was Chairman of the Board of Commissioners, but I got the feeling that he felt more like the Chairman of the Joint Chiefs of Staff.

I glanced at my watch. The clock was ticking. Not even the tall and mighty Commissioner Foxworthy was going to screw up my dinner date with Sonia. "What is it, Alan? If it's about the budget—"

More hand waving. It seemed every word I uttered was of no significance to him. "This is bigger than your damn budget report. I'm talking life and death, Tom."

"I am in the middle of a murder investigation. Two, actually."

"Two?" That appeared to nearly scratch the surface of Commissioner Foxworthy's consciousness.

"There's been a second killing." I kept talking

although he hadn't asked for further clarification. "The owner of the campground where the first victim's abandoned car was discovered."

The commissioner grunted. "Let me tell you why I'm here."

No response to my news. It was like talking to a basketball.

I leaned back in my chair, clasped my hands and pressed my extended index fingers together against my chin. This was my listening face, the one I usually put on for company when my mind wandered elsewhere.

I felt stubble under my fingertips. I was going to need a shave before dinner. Speaking of which, I needed to pick up some fresh green veggies. "I'm listening."

Alan Foxworthy rumbled, clearing his throat. It was a big throat and a big rumble. Like an armored tank rolling over rough Afghanistan terrain. "It's like this, Tom. I'm gonna need you to put this little investigation of yours on the backburner."

"On the backburner?"

"The backburner, Tom." I happened to know Alan Foxworthy was born and raised in Connecticut. However, he'd gone to school at North Carolina State University on a full athletic scholarship. He'd left that fine institution four years later with a degree, an ego the size of an over-inflated basketball such that it barely fit within his ribcage, and a distinct Southern drawl.

Go figure.

His parents, both die-hard Northerners, must be so proud.

I struggled to follow the commissioner's meanderings as I also struggled valiantly to fight back the sleep that was suddenly threatening to overtake me like a rogue wave.

Alan Foxworthy dropped his bony elbows on his thighs and leaned towards me. "You paying attention, Tom?"

"I hear you loud and clear." What had he said?

"Good. That's good. Because this public safety initiative is about to begin, Tom. This is a big deal. Very important. We've bought radio and TV spots. TV interviews are already planned and being scheduled. The governor himself is very interested in what we are doing here."

"Right. Important. I can see that." I cleared my throat but it sounded insignificant compared to his, more like a little froggy burping. "However, this murder investigation—"

"Can wait." The commissioner frowned. "My wife was almost killed yesterday. By some lowlife, negligent driver." He punched his right fist into his humongous left palm. Smash! "Broadsided!"

"Broadsided? We didn't get a report about—"

"No, no. Not broadsided, but she might've been. Might've been killed."

"But she wasn't? I mean, there was no accident?"

"No, thank goodness and that's what we, the commissioners, want to avoid here in Currituck. Accidents. Senseless deaths."

"I have two senseless deaths of my own, Commissioner."

Alan Foxworthy frowned even bigger. "I'm talking about innocent people here, Tom. Citizens, tourists. Good folks."

"Ryan Deering worked, paid taxes."

"He's an ex-con."

"Isaac Miller never hurt anybody."

The commissioner pushed his brows together, creating double-V wrinkles across his billboard-sized forehead. "Who the hell is Isaac Miller?"

"Our second victim. And there's more. I believe whoever murdered Deering next murdered Miller."

Alan Foxworthy shrugged, waved his hand yet again, sending a breeze my way. "Then he must've been up to no good too. Innocent people don't go around getting murdered."

"They don't?" I didn't even try to hide the smirk or my scorn. "I'm not sure statistics would back you up on that. Are you saying Deering's murder doesn't matter?"

The commissioner looked like he'd caught himself in the nick of time—almost fell into a nasty bear trap. A bear trap armed with negative publicity rather than sharp steel teeth. "Of course it matters. I'm not suggesting it doesn't matter. It's just not as important. Ryan Deering wasn't exactly one of Currituck's most upstanding citizens."

"No, but he's got as much right to have this murder solved as anybody." I put my face in a one-handed vise lock and pulled at my cheeks to distract myself. Another minute and I'd explode. Frenchie stood still as a statue, listening keenly mere steps away.

Foxworthy plowed on. "This county depends heavily on tourism, Tom. We need safe roads, safe beaches. The tourists, tens of thousands of tourists annually who visit us, depend on us, you and me, to make sure they arrive safe, stay safe, and leave safe."

"This office and my team have an excellent record, commissioner."

These words earned me a two-handed dismissive wave. Wow, I'd really struck a chord. Disdain and dismissal in the key of E-flat minor. A key signature in which both Russian composer Tchaikovsky and Swedish shred guitarist Yngwie Malmsteen had notably composed memorable works of music. Music that stuck with me to this day.

Sadly, that music would now be forever associated in my head with the asshole sitting across from me.

"The commissioners and I are in agreement on this. We've got a lot of dollars tied up in this initiative. I'm counting on your support. We all are. In fact, we're demanding it. We want to see the Sheriff's Office out promoting public safety, making its presence known."

"Babysitting the public?"

"If that's what it takes. I've heard all about your budget issues, Tom. Need I remind you that this sheriff's office and your very job depend on those tourist dollars?"

"How much will your precious budget save if I quit?"

The pregnant pause was bigger than Tracy Zefferelli's belly.

"Not a team player?"

"I'm very much a team player. When that team is this, my police team. This isn't fucking basketball and you're no longer the star. If you want my star," I tugged at the badge on my shirt. "You can have it."

"Now, Tom. No need to go getting upset."

It was too late for that. The USS Upset Ship was under sail.

I stared Alan Foxworthy down. "If not, I've got a

job to do and I can't do it sitting in this fucking chair!"

    I jumped, my chair bucked and hit the wall.

    I hit the road.

47

I was late for my appointment at the Slowater Motel. Lucky for me, Caroline Frazier was waiting.

Unlucky for her, I wasn't in the best of moods when I threw open the door to the Slowater's lobby. The drive over only served to boil my juices.

Bundled up in a white cable knit sweater and black pants, the manager stood refilling postcards in a carousel located next to the check-in counter.

"Sorry, I'm late."

She shoved a handful of Currituck Beach Lighthouse postcards onto the carousel and gave it a creaky spin. "No problem. I've been working extra hours ever since, well, you know."

"Yeah, I know." I warmed my bones beside the fire. "What's so important that you couldn't tell me over the phone?"

"I don't know how important it is or isn't. I guess you'll tell me. Come on. I'll show you."

She lifted a section of the counter and invited me to follow her. We crossed from the lobby to a backroom stuffed with motel supplies such as linen, blankets, soaps and shampoos. Unopened boxes on wood shelves held other surprises. The space smelled of fresh-washed linen, the scent seeping through the AC vent in the wall from the laundry next-door.

"It's through here. This is our breakroom."

I stepped past a coat tree and into a ten-by-twelve-foot windowless room with a brown vinyl-top folding table and three chairs standing against a pine green wall. Photographs of the Slowater over the years peppered the wall. A microwave and fridge stood opposite. Next to the appliances, a row of built-in wood lockers painted blue extended to the corner.

Caroline Frazier faced me, her hand on one of the locker doors. "Let me explain. One of the owners called and asked me to clear out Ryan's room and locker. They've hired a replacement, you see. And wanted me to get everything ready for him."

I frowned. "I didn't even know Deering had a locker."

"I'm sorry. I should have told you."

"Not your fault. It was dumb of me not to ask." Very dumb. I'd kick myself later in the privacy of my own cabin.

She nodded. Always nice to see a woman agree with me when I say how dumb I am. "Anyway, I was clearing out Ryan's locker and that's when I found this." Caroline Frazier sucked in a deep breath and pulled on the handle.

I noticed I was holding my breath.

A brown jacket, a blue sweater, a pair of worn-out Levis, and a black vest clung to hangers on a wood pole running across the top of the narrow locker. A toiletry kit, a cloth like you might use for polishing shoes and a black pair of leather lace-ups looking liked they'd been recently polished sat at the bottom along with a bottle of green aftershave, some lint, hairs, dust, and sixty-two cents worth of loose change.

So far, I wasn't impressed. Or interested. "You know, I've got loose change of my own rolling around in the Bronco."

"Wait." Carolina Frazier picked up the pair of dress shoes. A black sock had been thrust in each. She tugged at the sock in the left shoe and set it down on the bottom of the locker. "See?"

She tipped the empty shoe my way. I found myself holding my breath again. Who wants to smell somebody's stinky shoe?

Except this shoe wasn't empty and it didn't stink. At least, not in that way.

This shoe smelled like money. And that was what it was filled with.

"What the hell. Sorry."

Caroline Frazier laughed. "No need to apologize. I said something much stronger."

She dropped the shoe in my hand and I peered at the rubber-banded wad inside. "Do you know how much is in here?"

Caroline made a face. "I'm afraid I do. I mean, I wasn't thinking. I just pulled it out and looked at it. Counted it."

"And?"

"Seven thousand two hundred and fifty dollars. Believe, me, I had no idea, Sheriff. If I had thought it was important or related to Ryan's murder in any way at all, I would have—"

"It's okay." I put a hand on her arm to stop her. "You did just fine." I set the money shoe on the break table and studied the locker inside and out. "I don't see a lock on any of these lockers."

"No. We've never had locks. Not while I've been

working here anyway. Never had a need. At least, I never thought so. It's just someplace to stash our personal things, like purses and coats, lunch bags, whatever, during our shifts. As far as I know, there have never been any problems."

"I guess Ryan Deering felt the same way. He clearly felt it safe to keep his cash here." I counted the money, verifying the amount. "Have you already cleared out his room?"

Caroline Frazier paled. "I'm afraid so. I mean, that was before I found the money. I had housekeeping move all his personal effects out. Everything is boxed up in the storeroom. I was thinking of donating all his clothes and things to charity. Unless you think his wife would like them."

I made an executive decision. "I'm sure she'd be very happy if you donated everything to your favorite charity."

I pulled a plastic bag free from a box on the counter and stuck Ryan Deering's shoes inside, knotted it shut. "That reminds me, you wouldn't happen to know who Ryan Deering's beneficiary is?"

"Beneficiary?"

"I've been told that the Slowater's owners provide you both with life insurance. Is that not correct?"

"Oh, no, that is correct. Not something I like to think about." She scratched the nape of her neck. "I'm not sure who Ryan designated but it'll only take me a minute to find out."

I glanced at my ever-ticking watch—Sonia was probably getting ready right now for our date, standing in front of her bathroom mirror, applying just the right amount of makeup and I still had some grocery shopping to do.

I smiled and said, "I can give you two."

48

Dinner was a success. Screw Lizzie and her snarky comments. And her dislike of fried fish.

Sonia was happy, warm and snuggled up against my shoulder watching the logs blaze in the stone fireplace. Bladder Boy was stuffed, snoring and happy beside the hearth.

And Dawon the demon cat was home alone at Sonia's condo. Far from here. Probably brewing up some sort of revenge upon me for monopolizing her mistress, but I'd deal with that later.

Now was good.

Damn good.

My eyelids fluttered, drooped, fluttered some more. The red wine and warm fire had settled me. A delicious meal free of argument had been as tasty as any dessert. A good thing too, because I'd forgotten to pick up a dessert.

No matter. Sonia and I shared the remains of the black and white cookie I'd somehow managed not to eat over the course of yet another long day.

Life seemed to be filled with long days and short nights. Over dinner, Sonia had suggested we take a week's vacation somewhere, down in the islands maybe, and I liked the sound of that. No murders, no commissioners, no budgets.

No judgmental cats.

The doorbell rang and I ignored it.

Sonia rustled, her hand resting on my heart. "Aren't you going to get that?"

A sigh ran through me. "No. Probably one of my neighbors wanting to borrow something from me or ask me to fix something for them. Those seem to be the only times I hear from any of the lot."

"Which you like." Sonia grinned at me.

"Which I like."

She patted my heart once again. "Still…"

"It only rang once. Probably nothing."

"Probably," she whispered. "But still…"

"Fine." I kissed her hard. "Don't even think about going anywhere."

"Promise."

"Unless it's the bedroom," I added.

"I guess you'll just have to wait and see."

She pulled back her arms, lifted her legs from my lap and gave me a push towards the door. Bladder Boy, way lost in Dreamville, gave me a desultory look then resumed his position, head on paws, eyes firmly shut against the outside world and all it contained.

"C'mon, Boy. Let's go outside." Why should I suffer alone?

A brief wag of the tail was all I got. I was on my own.

I pushed open the door, braced myself against the cold wind shooting past me, seeking the warmth of my cabin.

"Nobody," I called to Sonia. "Wait." A ghostly flutter of white caught my eye. A pushpin held a sheet of paper to my door. I plucked it free and carried it inside.

"What is it?" asked Sonia, legs tucked under herself on the sofa.

"It looks like a note."

"Somebody left you a note? Why?"

I shrugged. "Maybe they don't like the way I keep my yard." Which was nothing more than sand and scrub but what yard around here wasn't? If I so much as tried to plant a flower or a shrub, Mother Nature laughed in my face.

I unfolded the unlined sheet and read the handwritten note by the light of the fire.

"Well?"

"Must be from one of my nosy neighbors."

"What do they want?" Sonia reached for her wine glass on the table at the end of the sofa and sipped.

"Whoever it is wants me to check out this address." I rattled off the number.

"Because?"

"Because they claim there's some gambling going on." I tossed the paper in the fire, watched it bloom orange one minute, disappear in flakes of black ash the next.

"Aren't you going to check it out?"

"No."

"Why not?"

"I already heard about it. It's nothing. I ran into a couple of young newlyweds on the beach the other night. They happened to mention it. A few dollars change hands. Big deal. A little harmless fun."

"Isn't that a crime?"

"Practically everything is if you look close enough."

"Are you sure about this?" Sonia's feet hit the

floor. "If someone took the time to write you a note, don't you think it might be more important?"

I sat beside her. "Not tonight it isn't."

Sonia strapped on her shoes. "Come on, let's go check it out."

"Now?"

"It will be fun."

"Your idea of fun and mine seem to be miles apart tonight." I gazed at the open bedroom door.

"That can wait." She planted a kiss on the bridge of my nose. "Come on, Tom. Let's go snoop. I've never had a chance to do anything like this before."

"You snoop into people's heads every day."

"This is different. Grab your coat." Sonia had already grabbed hers.

What choice did I have?

49

The house mentioned in the note sat a quarter mile north and wasn't hard to find. Number one, there aren't that many places out this way. Number two, this one was lit up like the electricity was free for the taking. A number of 4x4s crowded the driveway.

The home itself was a sprawling number that probably slept a dozen or more. I'd seen this house in the daylight, with its Olympic-sized pool on the opposite side and a full outdoor kitchen.

"Nice house,' commented Sonia, holding me close —that was one benefit of walking the quarter mile through the wind and sand on this cold fall night.

"In season, this place rents for something in the neighborhood of eighteen-grand per week."

"Seriously?"

"Yep. That's far out of my neighborhood."

"Maybe you should consider renting your cabin out during season."

"And where would I stay?"

"Good point."

I couldn't help noticing that she didn't suggest I stay at her condo. But it was better that she didn't. Neither of us were ready for that.

A black Jeep rolled up and two couples left the vehicle. They went around to the side of the house, the side with the pool, and disappeared.

"Let's see where they went," urged Sonia.

"That's trespassing."

"You're not on duty. Besides, we're just a couple out for a stroll."

We strolled around to a paver-stone patio large enough to land a single-engine plane on. As well-lit as the patio was, circling planes would have no trouble sticking their landings.

Thick drapes covered a wall of sliding glass doors. Twin underwater lights at the deep end of the pool went from red to blue to green and back again.

One of the sliders opened silently but the two burly young men who spilled out—each clutching a beer bottle—talked loudly, rather like they were speaking from the center of a Coast Guard cutter's engine room.

"They must've had a good night," I whispered in Sonia's ear.

"I'll say." Sonia gave my hand a tug. "Let's go inside."

"We haven't been invited."

"Do you think it matters? Where's your spirit of adventure?" She punched my upper arm. "Chicken?"

"Sheriff, remember?"

Sonia frowned. "You're right. Besides, I don't think this looks like our crowd. Plus, I'm getting cold." She ran her hands up and down her arms. The light jacket she'd worn for the evening was of little use against the wind.

"You're in luck. I have a recipe for getting warm."

"Oh?"

I lifted her chin delicately and kissed her hard.

"Trust me."

Sonia giggled and pushed her hand up under my shirt.

I stiffened. But that wasn't why. And Sonia realized it.

"What's the matter, Tom?"

"That man who just stepped inside. I know him."

"So?" whispered Sonia.

I pulled her into the shadows of the patio. "His name's Paul Jeter."

"How do you know him? Do you want to go say hi?"

I shook my head. "No. He works for Charles Harker, one of my main suspects in the murder or Ryan Deering. He's got a record."

"You mean he's a convicted criminal?"

"Yep. The question is, what is he doing here?" I'd been thinking this was only some friendly gambling amongst the tourist crowd. Was it something bigger? I was going to have to be careful here. Commissioner Foxworthy was already pissed with me. How would he take it if the Sheriff's Office busted a tourist over a friendly poker game?

I knew exactly how he'd take it. The media would explode with bad publicity. I didn't care so much for me, but the entire team would pay the price.

I took Sonia's hands in mine. Her fingers were ice cold. "I want you to do me a favor."

"Okay." She didn't sound too sure.

"I want you to go in. Take a look around."

"In there?"

"A minute ago you were dying to go inside."

"That was before I knew there were criminals in

there!"

"I understand. Take a quick look. Then leave. Don't linger. Don't talk to anyone. If anyone asks you who you are or why you're there, say you're a friend of Toby Tillet."

"Who is Toby Tillet?"

"Tillet is the surname of the family that rents out a big percentage of these houses. Including this one. Toby took over the business from his father."

"You think he knows what's going on out here?"

"I don't even know what's going on out here. That's why I'm asking you to go inside there." I pointed to the door.

"Fine." Sonia pushed back her hair. A useless gesture because the wind simply pushed it back the opposite way once more.

Sonia took three steps then turned towards me. "Don't you dare leave before I get back."

"I'm not moving from this spot." I scuffed my feet against the concrete pavers.

"And if you hear me scream—"

"I'll come running, guns ablazin'." Not that I was carrying a gun or even a pocketknife.

She nodded. I held my breath as Sonia disappeared inside the house.

50

I must have done so but I didn't remember letting my breath out again until I saw Sonia reappear some five minutes later. She ran to my side at the end of the patio.

"Well?"

"You won't believe it, Tom!" Sonia whispered, hands stuffed in the pockets of her jacket. "It's like a Vegas casino in there!"

"Seriously?"

She nodded.

"Did you see Jeter?"

"No. I mean, I never really saw him the first time. He must be inside though. You should see, there are poker tables, video poker machines, and slot machines everywhere. The entire downstairs is practically stuffed with them. There must be fifty people inside too. I even spotted a busy baccarat table."

"This is a lot bigger than a few tourists getting together to drink and play cards."

"Definitely." Sonia looked back over her shoulder at the three-story house. "What are you going to do?"

If I went in there alone, everybody—including whoever had organized this operation—would flee like cockroaches when you turn on the kitchen light.

"I'll call for backup. You go wait at the cabin."

"Why do I have to go?"

"Because you don't wear a badge and carry a gun."
I patted her arm. "Go. I'll call you as soon as I can."

I waited until Sonia's dark shape disappeared down the sandy road before making the call. "Hello, Nat?"

"Sheriff? What's up? Kind of late, isn't it?"

"Yeah, I know it's late. So what? Anybody ever promise you being in law enforcement would be an eight to—"

I heard a kid crying in the background. Shit.

"Listen, I wouldn't be phoning if this wasn't urgent."

"I'm listening."

"I need you to get a team together. You, Frenchie, Lizzie, Flo and Eddie."

"What for?" I heard his wife comforting the kid in the background. I heard the sounds of a TV too.

"One of my neighbors decided to open Vegas East. Here's the address." I read him the house number. "Try not to make any noise when you get here. I'll meet you outside. Tell the others."

"Will do." Nat promised to get everybody here within the hour.

One thing about Nat, his word was always good.

It wasn't long before two Sheriff's Office 4x4s sat a couple hundred feet away from the house. The clouds overhead helped to keep them shrouded in darkness.

Flo, Eddie, Lizzie, Nat, Frenchie and I huddled. I'd had plenty of time to think while waiting for my team. "Let me explain what I'm thinking."

"I'm all ears," quipped Lizzie. "And I know that because they're frozen and about to fucking fall off." She rubbed her ears for my benefit as much as hers.

Nat silenced her further grousing with a stern look. "Go ahead, Sheriff." Nat loved all this SWAT team crap. Me, I'd rather be home with Sonia. In bed.

"There are only three points of entry, discounting the windows and if we don't get everybody all worked up, keep things quiet and calm, we shouldn't have any jumpers. Eddie, you and Flo take the front door. Nat, you and Lizzie go in through the garage. There's a door in the back that leads inside. It's unlocked."

"And the third entry, Chief?" Frenchie wanted to know.

"That's the sliding glass doors poolside. You'll stand outside. I'm going in."

"Alone?" Nat sounded surprised and not real happy about that.

"Yep. Like I said, we don't want any trouble." While waiting for the team, I'd considered returning to my place and throwing on my uniform and grabbing a weapon. In the end, I had decided against it. "My going in alone will help keep the situation from escalating."

I hoped.

"I don't like it," replied Lizzie.

"You're going to like it less when I tell you who's inside."

"Who?"

"Paul Jeter and Charles Harker. Jeter arrived first. Harker arrived some minutes after his buddy. I followed Jeter down to the boat ramp. He picked up Harker from his boat and drove him back here in a golfcart."

Lizzie rubbed her knuckles. "Well, well, this might get interesting after all."

"Let's not get carried away, guys." No need to point out that I was spotlighting Lizzie. Everybody knew her thirst for a good gunfight. "There are only three people that I want in there for sure. Harker, Jeter and Lipori."

"Who is Lipori?" demanded Nat.

"Lawrence Lipori. He's the one who signed for the rental on this property. I called Toby Tillet, rousting him from a good night's sleep, to gather that information. He also gave us permission to enter the house, should anybody question our legal right to enter."

"Sweet," said Lizzie.

"Everybody here knows what Harker and Jeter look like. Here's a photo of Lipori." I scrolled through my phone pics. Toby had shot me over the driver's license picture that had been affixed to Lipori's vacation rental application.

"Geez, he's got more hair on his face than my dog has on his ass," Lizzie said. She wasn't wrong. I'd seen her dog and this older gentleman's thick curly beard could be used to scrub pots.

"To be clear, I go in. Find this Mr. Lipori. Let him know quietly that we are shutting him down. We ask everyone to leave."

"We do, Chief?"

"Yes, we check their IDs, make a note of their names and addresses in case we need them and send them home."

"And grab Harker and Jeter on their way out?" Lizzie asked.

"That's the idea."

"Wait," said Nat. "Sheriff, you really want to let everybody else go? What they're doing is illegal."

"You want to drag fifty tourists down to the Sheriff's Office? You want to explain to the Board of

Commissioners why?"

"No," replied Nat, looking unhappy.

I clapped my hands. "Let's do this then." I sent Flo and Eddie, and Lizzie and Nat on their way after telling them to give me five minutes to get inside the house before making their presence known.

Frenchie and I walked down to the patio. The sounds of laughter seeped out into the night.

"There's the door. Ready, Frenchie?"

"Born to run, Chief."

"Since when are you quoting The Boss?"

"Pardon? You are zee boss, Chief, oui? You want me to call you Boss? I can do this."

I couldn't believe I was going to say this, but I did. "Let's stick to Chief."

Wondering how I'd ended up with Sgt. Depardieu as my partner, and realizing I had only myself to blame, I stepped into the lion's den.

51

With all the card shuffling, wheel spinning, machine whirring and chiming, excited and nervous chit-chat, and lights blinking, nobody paid me any attention. Except for the two plump gentlemen puffing cigars from the comfort of a couple of gold-studded black leather chairs, everybody else crowded the games and the bar.

Perfect.

So was this setup.

Banks of video poker machines on one side, slots opposite. A number of crowded poker and blackjack tables and a baccarat table resting atop a billiard table further back. Large-screen TVs hosted sports.

A man in black tended a fully-stocked bar. The crowd was mostly younger but Lipori didn't discriminate against the senior crowd. A number of elderly gamblers appeared to be enjoying the games if not their odds of winning.

I spotted Jeter before he spotted me, leaned against a video poker machine with its lights out and power off. The blue-jeaned butt sticking out behind it I recognized as belonging to Charles Harker.

On seeing me, Jeter tensed up and pounded on Harker's back.

I smiled and waved to the two of them, then

turned and mingled through the crowd. The young couple from the other night, the honeymooners, sat at a blackjack table.

I eased my way over to their table and squeezed in between Peter Goslin and his wife, Chloe. I laid a friendly hand on his shoulder. "On a winning streak?"

"Up two hundred bucks!" Peter said excitedly, keeping his eyes on the dealer, a young thing who barely looked twenty-one herself.

"Ah, Peter." Chloe pointed a finger at me.

Peter turned. "Oh, ah, hello, Sh—" The young man paled, dropped his playing cards. "Oh. Shit."

"Relax." I kept smiling. "Maybe you should cash in now. Call it a night."

Peter gulped. Chloe tossed in her cards and Peter did the same. They leapt from the table under the surprised gaze of the croupier.

"Don't forget your chips," I said.

Peter bobbed his head and scooped up a handful of red and blue chips.

They were nice kids. I'd give them a couple of minutes to cash in and check out before shutting everything down.

I walked over to the bar and caught the barman's attention. "Some night, eh?"

"What can I get you?"

"Is it like this every night?"

"It's ten bucks. You want vodka rocks? Ten bucks. Jim Beam? Ten bucks." He pressed his hands against the edge of the counter. His eyes were hard blue, cold and uncaring. "What's it going to be?"

"How much for a beer?"

"What'd I say? Ten bucks. No plastic. So what are

you thinking?"

Over the heads of the crowd, I watched Peter and Chloe slip out through sliding door. Hopefully, Frenchie wouldn't hassle them. Turning my attention back to my friendly barkeep, I said, "I'm thinking I'll have to get back to you on that."

Lipori had a lot of nerve charging New York prices for Outer Banks booze.

I squeezed around a hot roulette table and angled into the corner to the baccarat table gently bathed in the glow of the overhanging billiard light. The table was doing its job— sucking the money out of several gamblers' bank accounts.

"Hello, Larry." Even though it seemed like a lifetime ago since I'd seen the man fishing out at the Milepost 21 Carova Beach Park boat launch— a mere hop, skip and a golfcart from this house— and his driver's license picture looked nothing like this clean-shaven and well-groomed man, I had no trouble recognizing Lawrence Lipori, aka Larry.

Larry Lipori's eyes bulged with recognition. He turned and took a hasty step. My hand clamping down on the back of his scrawny neck put a quick stop to his flight.

"What's your hurry? We're just getting started."

Larry Lipori reached for a black aluminum cue stick hanging on a rack with several of its friends.

"You don't want to do that," I cautioned. "You'd be surprised how many people get hurt with those things in the wrong hands." I raised my hands, wiggled my fingers. "Do these hands look wrong to you?"

Larry Lipori dropped his hand. "It's not what you think."

"No? I think you're looking at some serious prison time." I was keeping my voice low. The paying customers still had no idea what was going on or about to go down. "Have you ever been to prison, Larry? I hear the fishing's not so good there."

"Listen, Sheriff. I'm sure we can make some sort of accommodation."

"You mean money?"

Larry Lipori shrugged, smiled an alligator smile, the one the beast makes right before it swallows your toy poodle and then spits out the pink ribbon in its hair. "Everybody needs money, Sheriff. It's what makes the world go round, right?"

I was pretty sure even your run-of-the-mill astrophysicist would disagree with his statement but now was not the time for a physical cosmology discussion of money versus cosmological forces and their impacts on making the world go round. So I kept my reply succinct.

"Right. And you're going to need lots of it. Lawyers aren't cheap and you're going to want a good one." I pulled Larry Lipori away from the table. "I want you to tell all your customers that the party's over. You and your buddies Harker and Jeter are under arrest."

"Those men are not my buddies, as you say. I hired them to do some work for me."

I had a sudden inspired thought. It happened once every blue moon or three. "Like you hired Ryan Deering?"

Larry could keep his mouth shut but his face betrayed the fact that I'd hit on something. What it was and how deep it went remained to be seen.

My eyes swept over the room. "On second

thought, the barman stays too."

"Why?"

"I don't like how much he charges for beer. Ten bucks? That's extortion." My eyes slid across the room. "Anybody else here special? As in owns a rap sheet?"

"No."

I wasn't sure if I believed him or not, but short of holding and questioning everyone, I didn't have much choice other than to take him at his word. Besides, we were taking the names of everybody as they left. If anybody interesting popped up, I'd learn about them soon enough. "Where's your wife? Upstairs?"

"She passed away some years ago," mumbled Larry Lipori. He suddenly appeared half as big as he had five minutes ago when I'd first noticed him.

"You mean you lied to me? Shame on you, Larry. The other day, you told me you were married. Shame on you." Frenchie waved to me from the slider. "Here I thought we were going to be fishing buddies."

Larry's eyes filled with hope. "It's not too late."

"It is for you. It appears my team has let your customers know we're here and is herding them outside."

I clamped my fingers over his upper arm. "Let's go."

52

Settled at my desk the next morning, I carefully reviewed the overnight reports, of which there were more than usual. Most of the team had been up half the night. Nat had remained all night.

Despite the night's excitement, we were all exhausted and moving slowly. Lizzie ran computer checks on everybody we'd let go. They were all clean. And would remain so since I'd made the decision to release them without charges.

Our remaining guests chilled in the cells.

Except for the barman. It turned out he was a local, an out-of-work plumber with a wife and kids. We'd cut him loose first thing this morning. He didn't know much anyway, except how to fix a leaky toilet by day and pour an overpriced drink by night.

Memories stirred like embers in a drafty fireplace. After last night's raid and bust, I hadn't been in a hurry to interview our suspects, so much as I had been in a hurry to get home. I didn't think my relationship with Sonia could have withstood another incident. Not so soon after all the others, anyway.

Returning to the cabin after the raid, I told my tale to Sonia because she was dying to know what happened and refusing to go any further until I explained.

Tale told and Sonia's curiosity satisfied, I grabbed a bottle of wine, invited her to inspect how well an ex-Coast Guard man can make up his bed, and we went further. In the end, I believe we were both satisfied.

And the bed needed making up again.

I hoped Larry Lipori, Charles Harker and Paul Jeter had had memorable nights too, but for entirely different reasons.

I also calculated that it would do the trio good to spend a night behind bars before we got down to business. Bring back old memories. Get them used to the idea of some time in prison once again. The two of them at least.

Mr. Lipori had had some previous charges brought against him, like receiving stolen goods, operating a gambling den—no surprise there—and even a hint of having been involved in a prostitution ring.

I'd get the rest of Larry Lipori's history this morning when the out-of-state reports came in.

I signed some papers Frenchie had left on my chair for my signature. Some of which I'd actually skimmed. "Frenchie!"

Frenchie stepped into my office, unshaven but in uniform.

"Thanks, Frenchie." I accepted another cup of unrequested but much appreciated coffee. I think it was cup number fifty-two. My brain thanked me. My bladder, on the other hand, was about to burst and cursed me loudly. "Let's bring in Lipori."

"Sure, Chief." The sergeant cleared his throat, tugged at his collar. He raised a foot then lowered it without having covered any new ground.

"Something on your mind?"

"Something I need to tell you."

"About the case?"

"About the commissioner." Frenchie fiddled with the back of my computer monitor. The screen went dark.

"Oops." Frenchie held up the end of the power cable. "Sorry." He shoved it back and the monitor came back to life with a crackle of electricity. "Sorry, Chief."

"What's this about a commissioner, Frenchie?"

"Well, you know how Commissioner Foxworthy told you he wanted ziss public safety initiation."

"Initiative, yeah." I sipped my coffee, enjoying the burn as it ate into my tongue. "Kind of hard to forget. Though I wish I could."

"I give him zee ticket, Chief."

"What ticket?"

"Zee speeding ticket. I know this is not my usual job." Frenchie held out his citation book and flipped the pages. "But I see him when I am driving to work this morning. He eez speeding. Fifteen miles over the limit! Zoom!"

Frenchie made a plane of his hand and sent it flying across the room—at least as far as his arm could reach. "Zoom!"

I felt a smile sprouting from the inside out. "And you wrote him a ticket?"

"Oui, Chief." Frenchie sniffed. He stopped shuffling the pages of his book and showed me a copy of the citation. "Voilà. The commissioner, he eez very, very angry. He wants me to tear theez up." The sergeant made exaggerated tearing motions with his hands. "What shall I do, Chief?"

"Nothing. You already did your job."

"I did zee right thing?"

"Absolutely. In fact," I tore the copy from his book, "I wish you'd added reckless endangerment with a moving motor vehicle to the charges." I waved the ticket in the air. "I'm thinking we should have it framed and hang it on the wall."

I swiveled my chair around to face the wall I had in mind and pointed. "Maybe right there, next to the photo of the governor." I placed the ticket in my drawer for safe keeping.

"When's Woody getting his ass back to work?"

"Another week or so, according to Nat. He spoke with him on the phone yesterday." Woody Jefferson was Mainland Patrol Captain, Lizzie's terrestrial counterpart.

"How are his folks doing?"

"Better, I guess. Otherwise, would he still be coming home?" Woody's folks lived in the Atlanta suburbs and suffered a litany of ailments.

Being an only child, Woody sometimes had his hands full.

"Thanks, Chief. Need me for anything else?"

"Mr. Lipori?"

"Right, Monsieur Lipori. I'll bring heem right away, Chief."

"On second thought, let's start with Mr. Jeter." I'd start with the little fish and work my way up. Let the big fish stew a little longer. The longer they stewed, the more they softened.

"Oui, Chief."

53

Two minutes later, the sergeant led Paul Jeter, disheveled and disgruntled, to the seat across from my desk.

I ignored him and he ignored me. I let the air tingle with tension and apprehension a minute, then opened another drawer. "Time for show and tell, Mr. Jeter. I show, you tell."

Jeter sniffed, rubbed his nose.

I pulled out a plastic evidence bag and laid it on my desk. Jeter stared at the bag. Inside, a gray-handled Benchmade Griptilian stared back at him.

"Where did you get the knife?" Last night, Lizzie had spied the knife sheathed to Jeter's belt and confiscated it.

"Somebody gave it to me."

"Who?"

"The lady that sold me the boat."

I sat up straighter. "What lady?"

"The sales lady over at Banks Marine."

"She gave you that knife?"

"Yeah, so? They were giving everybody that bought a boat that week a free knife. It was a whatchamacallit, a free gift with purchase."

"You bought a boat recently at Banks Marine?" The very same marina where I'd found an ink pen from the Slowater Motel on a Carolina Skiff that had seemingly disappeared and reappeared. Coincidence?

"That's right. A shad boat. Nothing illegal about that and I didn't stab anybody with that knife."

"True." Although he did look like he wanted to stab somebody right now and I knew who. In fact, I was intimately acquainted with him. "Shad boats are rare. Pricey."

A local carpenter and builder by the name of George Washington Creef, whose historic-designated house still stands in Manteo, dreamed up the shad boat in the 1870s. Combining conventional plank-on-frame construction with traditional split-log techniques, the unique style vessel suited the surrounding waters and their oft-changing weather conditions.

Among fishermen, the vessel became as well-known and popular as today's pickup truck. Original shad boats are scarce, production having ceased in the 1930s. In 1987, North Carolina designated it the state's official boat.

"It's a replica. And used at that." Jeter pulled his arms tighter across his chest. "When can I get out of here?"

"What were you doing at Lipori's place?"

"You saw what we was doing. Fixing a lousy machine."

"You supply those machines?"

Please say yes, I was thinking.

"No. The man asked us to service them. That's what we done."

"The machines and tables are illegal. What you were doing is illegal."

Jeter stuck out his chin. "I want a lawyer."

I lifted my coffee and took a lingering drink. "Have breakfast yet?"

"They gave us some crap from Duckees."

I smiled. A Duckees breakfast was all our budget could bear. When I got the chance, I was heading to Davie Jones for an early lunch. Sonia and I had shared a frozen poppy seed bagel earlier before splitting for the day.

Nat Midgett and the sergeant huddled over Frenchie's computer. "Nat!"

The Chief Deputy came hurrying over. He looked like hell. No sleep, no workout, maybe no Wheaties. But every hair was in place and he was clean-shaven. How had he managed that? I didn't even keep a toothbrush in the office.

"Yes, Sheriff?"

"I'd like you to call Hank Cassel."

"The owner of Banks Marine?"

"That's right. Ask him if he can verify that they were giving these Griptilians away recently." I turned to Jeter. "When did you say you bought this shad boat?"

"A couple of weeks ago."

"Right." Addressing Nat, I said, "See what Mr. Cassel tells you."

"Yes, sir."

"Wait. If Mr. Cassel confirms what Jeter is claiming, then ask if he has a record of everyone that received one of these. Such as Harker, Lipori, Clark, Basnight—I'm not ruling anybody out yet—Ryan Deering's wife, Ariadne, in particular."

The day manager at the Slowater had confirmed that Ariadne was in line to collect on her husband's death. Again. "Even Ryan himself."

"Will do. Now that it has come up, there is something new I wanted to make you aware of, Sheriff. Concerning Banks Marine."

"What's that?"

Nat cut his eyes to Jeter.

"Go ahead, Jeter and I have no secrets, do we, Jeter?"

That earned me a scowl from Jeter. And not the playful, coy type Sonia sometimes threw at me. No, this was one of those real bitter I'd-slit-you-ear-to-ear-if-I-thought-I-had-half-a-chance-of-getting-away-with-it scowls.

"I was curious, so I checked Isaac Miller's telephone records."

A quick glance in Jeter's direction told me he was either a Peter O'Toole level actor or he'd never heard of Isaac Miller.

"Mr. Miller made a number of recent calls to Banks Marine up until the time of his murder, that is."

"Hey, now." Jeter slid back his chair. "Don't look at me for that!" A bead of sweat popped up along his hairline.

"Do we know who he talked to there?"

"No, sir. Calls go into two main number. One for sales, the other for service and marina operations. Lots of extensions and no receptionist to channel the calls. Whoever is around and wants to, picks up the call."

"What does it mean? Might Miller have been interested in buying a new boat maybe?"

"From what you say about his upcoming trip and his interest in boats and fishing, it isn't out of the question," answered Nat, still looking uneasy about us talking in Jeter's presence. Jeter didn't seem too happy about it either.

Nat continued anyway. "Like I said, Sheriff, nobody at Banks remembers talking to him."

I chewed on that interesting tidbit a minute. "Thanks, Nat. Good job. Follow up with Mr. Cassel and let me know what he tells you."

Nat yessired and turned on his heels.

"Nat," I called.

The Chief Deputy spun back around. I got a kick out of getting him to dance like that. "Sheriff?"

"Take Mr. Jeter out back and shoot him."

"Sir?"

"Hey, wait a minute—" Jeter flew from his chair as fast as the blood drained from his face, leaving a wobbly-eyed ghost staring at me.

"Didn't you hear me? I said please escort Mr. Jeter to his cell and see that he gets a lawyer."

"Yes, sir."

As Nat escorted Paul Jeter from my office, I checked the floor.

Clean as a whistle.

For a second there, I feared our Mr. Jeter was going to pull a Bladder Boy on me and the office was running low on paper towels, budgets being what they were.

54

Charles Harker was a big disappointment. He hadn't been in a chatty mood. The only thing he was willing to confirm—because it would have been senseless to try to deny it—was that he kept a boat at Banks Marine for which he paid a monthly fee. Marina records showed that the vessel had gone out on the day of the murder with only two men aboard, Charles Harker and Paul Jeter.

After squeezing nothing further new or relevant from him, I asked Frenchie to escort Larry Lipori to my office.

Nat popped in while I waited.

"Sheriff, I just got off the phone with Mr. Cassel. He confirmed they gave away dozens of these knives but none to Ryan Deering or any of the other names of interest. Except for Jeter, of course."

"Of course." I spread my hands across my desk. "Yeah, I guess that would have made things too easy." And when had the universe ever tried to do that?

A bustle arose at the front entrance. Nat hustled off to address it. I turned to address Larry Lipori. "Have a seat, Mr. Lipori."

Larry Lipori lowered himself into one of my horrendous chairs. He crossed his legs and folded his arms on his lap. "My lawyer is on his way."

"Great. Let's chat about Ryan Deering."

"Let's not."

"Now, is that anyway to renew our once-budding friendship, Larry?"

"I cannot talk to you without my lawyer."

I stood and paced behind him. "I know that, Larry. I can understand you don't want to incriminate yourself. I get that." I stopped and peeked out at the bustling office. "I tell you what. I'll speak and you can sit there and nod for yes and shake your head for no. How would that be?"

"I'm not saying a word without—"

"Without your lawyer. Right. That's why I'm talking and you're listening and, should you feel like nodding or shaking, you go right ahead." I paced some more. "Okay, Ryan Deering."

"Never heard of him."

"Well, look at that. You're talking after all."

Larry Lipori clamped his jaw tight. His entire body stiffened.

"Did you kill him? Was he supplying those machines? Like he used to in the old days? Where did you meet him? Did you kill him because he tried to cheat you?"

"I'm going to say this one last time. I did not know Ryan Deering."

Frenchie stuck his head in. "Call for you, Chief!"

"It can wait."

"She says eez important. Very important."

"She who?"

"She who is on the telephone."

"Who is on the telephone?"

"Carolina Freezer."

I couldn't blame Larry Lipori for looked confused and amused—he didn't know Frenchie like I did, didn't speak the lingo—but I would have liked to kick his ass for making his amusement at my expense so obvious.

"You stay here and keep an eye on this one. I'll take the call at your desk."

"My desk is unavailable, Chief."

I glanced out. "So I see." A pack of kids swarmed around the sergeant's desk. "Are they doing something with your computer?"

"I couldn't stop them."

"But that's against the rules. Never mind. Just patch the call through here."

"Yes, Chief." Frenchie moved to Lizzie's empty desk, worked some magic and a moment later a light blinked on my desk phone.

I sat and answered. "Ms. Frazier, good morning. I appreciate you calling but now is not a good time. We've had a busy night."

"So I heard. And I know you are probably quite busy. But it's about last night that I'm calling."

"Oh? You weren't there, were you? I didn't notice your name on our list. If so, I wouldn't sweat it. You're not in any trouble."

"No, no. That's not it. I wanted to tell you that I recognize him."

"Him who?" Was she taking communications lessons from Frenchie?

"The man whose picture was on the Currituck Times website this morning. I read it every morning. The Slowater is a subscriber."

The Currituck Times was a local county paper. I'd heard a reporter had been in during the wee hours.

"Umm, you'll have to help me out here. I haven't seen any—"

"Lawrence Lipori?"

"Mr. Lipori. I see." I put the phone on speaker, turned and smiled at Larry as he idled in my Torquemada design-inspired torture chair. "And you say you recognize him?"

Lipori squirmed.

"That's right, Sheriff," said Caroline Frazier. "He's the man I said was here Saturday, after Ryan's disappearance, looking for him."

"You're sure?"

"Absolutely."

"Thank you, Ms. Frazier. You have no idea how helpful you've been."

"Wait, there's more."

"More? Do tell."

"I did some checking on the office computer. Mr. Lipori has been a guest here at the Slowater on multiple occasions."

"You say a Mr. Lipori has been a guest of the Slowater Motel on multiple occasions? Well, well. Would that be in the past year? You know, during the time that Ryan Deering was employed there?"

"Yes, Sheriff. I can show you the records, if you like."

Larry Lipori's tan was fading fast. He scratched the back of his left hand as if obsessed.

"That would be great, Ms. Frazier. I tell you what. Can you make copies of those records for me?"

"I'll be happy too."

"Thanks. I'll send a deputy over to pick them up and to take your statement sometime today. Goodbye."

"This is ridiculous, Sheriff. I'm no murderer. And I am not saying another word without my attorney present. In fact, I insist that you—"

"You insist? You insist?" I bellowed, jumping from my chair. "I don't like being lied to, Larry! I don't like being played!"

"I'm not—"

I loomed over him, leaned in close to his right ear. "What did the two of you argue about, Larry?"

Larry turned on me. "We didn't argue, Sheriff. And I did not murder him. In fact, I didn't know he was dead until Harker told me. Till then, I only thought he'd disappeared. I'd like to return to my cell now, Sheriff."

"Of course." I snapped my fingers and Deputy Eddie Wu appeared. "Mr. Lipori would like to return to his room now. When his lawyer arrives, send him to me first."

"Yes, Sheriff."

As Deputy Wu laid a hand on Lipori's arm, Lipori turned to me and asked, "Is it true what I hear?"

"That depends on what you hear."

"That Ryan Deering died Friday night."

"That's the going theory."

Larry Lipori's smile made me uneasy.

"In that case, for the record, Sheriff, I have an alibi for the crime. So do Harker and Jeter for that matter."

"And what might that alibi be, Larry?"

"The club was open. Full of guests. Ryan Deering was supposed to come by. We had an appointment."

"For what?"

"Let's just say we had some common business interests."

"Like video gambling?"

"My point is, Deering never showed. Ask Jeter and Harker, if you don't believe me."

Sadly, I did.

"They were performing some maintenance. They'll tell you. I was busy playing host the entire time."

"Define entire time."

"We didn't shut down till nearly three a.m."

"And Ryan Deering never showed?"

"No. His partner said—"

"What partner?"

Larry Lipori shrugged. "He didn't give me a name. He simply made a delivery. I paid him and you left."

"What did he deliver?"

"Merchandise."

"Such as?"

"Such as I'd rather not say anything more at this time."

The children at Frenchie's desk were getting louder. Hitting and calling each other names. Almost as bad as dealing with prisoners. Worse, maybe.

"Let me guess, you paid him in cash."

Lipori nodded once.

"How much money are we talking?"

"I can be a very generous man, Sheriff."

Larry Lipori let that sink in but I wasn't in a mood to be bought.

"Would you recognize this guy, if you saw him again?"

"Absolutely not."

Meaning definitely but he wasn't going to admit to it.

Larry Lipori interrupted my thoughts. "That phone call you got, from the Slowater? I did drive to the motel Saturday looking for Ryan Deering. I wanted to find out what had happened to him the night before. I also wanted to make sure that everything was set for our next delivery. Of course, little did I know the man was already dead. Not by my hand, of course."

"Of course. And you've got somebody who can verify all this? Somebody without a criminal record and who isn't on your payroll?"

Lipori's smile broadened. "I shouldn't be saying this, I did say I wouldn't but, if you must know…"

"Let's say I must."

"Then I'd say that Alan Foxworthy might make a nice witness. In fact, I'd say he'd make a great witness."

"Are you telling me Commissioner Foxworthy was gambling at your place?"

"Not so much at the tables or machines but he does like to bet on the televised sports. Especially basketball. Give him a call. In the meantime, if you want anything further from me, you're going to have to wait on my lawyer and talk to him."

Watching Wu escort Lipori to the cells, I had to admit, Larry Lipori had thrown me for a loop.

In more ways than one.

If what he claimed was true, and I was betting it all was, then three of my main suspects were no longer suspects. In trouble yes, but not for two murders. Because if they hadn't murdered Ryan Deering, I doubted they'd murdered Isaac Miller. I was sure the two murders were connected, even if I didn't know what that precise connection was yet.

Damn, damn and damn.

Who was this mysterious partner? The wife? The wife's boyfriend? Or somebody new to the game?

Speaking of game, I was going to have to think long and hard before my next conversation with Alan Foxworthy.

55

The party at Frenchie's desk was growing by leaps and bounds.

Literally.

Three children—sounding and seeming to take up the space of thirty—of varying ages, heights and sexes huddled around his computer.

Upon the screen, fat and ugly aliens in some dark future cityscape were being gleefully slaughtered left and right by some improbably complicated looking silver weapon spewing lime-green death at the hands of an otherwise demure seeming girl who deftly wielded the weapon via her onscreen avatar, herself dressed provocatively and to kill in a skintight purple and black outfit that barely contained her breasts. The avatar jumped and spun in the low gravity world, with a fireworks sky, spitting death with every move, every turn.

Loudly.

Worse, several of my deputies had been sucked into the madness and whooped it up whenever the girl currently controlling the PC keyboard made another kill.

I grabbed Frenchie as he ran past me, his arms loaded up with snack-sized packs of chips, pretzels and cheese puffs. A six-pack of soda dangled from the index finger of his right hand, looking like it might snap off any second—the finger, not the soda.

Great. Just what the Junior Wild Bunch needed, junk food and sugar-laced soda. What was Frenchie thinking?

"What the hell, Frenchie. Can't you control those three kids?"

"But, Chief—" A bag of BBQ potato chips slipped from his arms. He bent to retrieve it, dropping the soda in the process.

"And whose kids are they anyway? What are they doing here?" How could a mere three children cause such a ruckus? "Are they truants?" That would explain a lot.

"Well, you zee, Chief—" Frenchie managed to pick up the pack of soda and the bag of chips using a hand and foot, only to lose three bags of pretzel twists in the process. He wobbled unsteadily to his feet.

"Shouldn't they be in school?" I picked up the pretzels and shoved them into the cradle of his arms.

"I don't know, Chief, but Mitch Green eez here to zee you." The sergeant gestured across the room with his chin, which was the only body part available at the moment for the task. His accent always grew stronger the more agitated he became.

"What's he want?" Mitch Green, plus a small stranger in rumpled clothes and a fishing hat, sat at two chairs near the door. Mitch's dog, Mutton, occupied the space between them.

"Come to zee you, Chief."

"Where's our snacks?" A young boy with sharp brown eyes demanded.

"Yeah, I'm thirsty!" yelled the blond girl as she

sliced the head off a three-eyed brute with spiked obsidian teeth coming at her avatar on Frenchie's computer.

"Go," I told Frenchie. "Before there's an insurrection."

"Oui, Chief."

"Wait."

"Chief?"

"Who did you say these kids belong to? And when are they leaving?"

"Dr. Zefferelli's children, Chief."

"Tracy's?" I scratched the back of my neck. "And she just dumped them here? What? Is this payback for something I did?"

"Payback? No, Tracy stops by to zee you."

I looked around the office. "I admit this place is a zoo, but I don't see a pathologist among the exhibits."

"She went to the restroom!" Frenchie hollered and ran to his desk as the restless natives shouted, "Snacks! Snacks! Snacks!"

If she went to the restroom, it was probably to escape her demon spawn. She'd probably never come out.

"Mr. Green!" I hollered and waved to get his attention. "Come on back."

He and his friend and Mutton stepped into my office. Now, more than ever, I wished I had a damn door. Maybe, with what I now had on Commissioner Foxworthy, there'd be funds for it in next year's budget.

"Have a seat." I took mine, leaned back and crossed my legs, squeezed my eyes shut for a moment to block out the commotion outside, was unsuccessful and opened them to stare at my visitors. "What can I do for you, gentlemen?"

"Sheriff, this is Archie Knapp." Mitch wore a puffy black coat and a multicolored knit cap.

"Hiya, Sheriff." Archie Knapp was somewhere between his fifties and sixties and had the look of a man the world weighed heavy on. His brown hair was clipped short and he wore gold-rimmed eyeglasses that seemed to be having a hard time standing still.

"Say," Mitch interrupted. "I don't see that deputy, Lizzie, anywhere. Which is her office?"

"Captain Gutierrez's desk is in the main room, by the window. She's out at the moment, Mitch."

"Pity." Mitch did indeed look crestfallen.

"That the pretty lady you were telling me about?" Archie Knapp asked.

"Yeah." Mitch rubbed Mutton behind the ear. "You be sure and tell her I said hello, will you, Sheriff?"

"You can bet on it. Now." I folded my hands on the desktop. "As you might notice, it's rather busy here. What's up?"

"What's up is that Archie has something to tell you."

"And what's that?"

"I was talking to Archie. He saw somebody pick up your dead guy and—"

"Whoa, hold it there, Mitch. If you don't mind, let's let Mr. Knapp tell me himself."

Archie Knapp shrugged. The brightly feathered fishing lures on his fishing hat danced. "It's like Mitch says. I was out by the pier looking for Isaac—Lord rest his soul—when I saw this boat come up to the dock. This man of yours—"

"You mean Deering?" I interrupted.

"Huh? Oh, right, Deering helps some fella load the boat. Truck drives away."

"Truck?"

"Truck," repeated Archie Knapp. "Then he gets on the boat and off she goes."

"What about the truck? Did you recognize it?"

"Sure, a big box truck. I've seen plenty of 'em." Archie Knapp scrambled to catch his eyeglasses as they slid down his nose.

"What about this particular truck? Ever see it before?"

"I don't pay much attention to trucks so I'm afraid I couldn't say."

"And the man driving the truck? He helped load the boat?"

"Pushed the dolly out on the pier, helped load 'em, yessir, Sheriff." Giving up on his glasses, Archie Knapp stuffed them down the front pocket of his coat.

"But you didn't recognize him?"

"You got that right."

"But you are sure it was Ryan Deering you saw?"

"Oh, yeah. I seen him pretty good. It was him, all right."

"Please don't take this the wrong way, Mr. Knapp, but I notice you wear glasses." It was impossible not to notice, what with the way his fingers kept moving them around, trying to center them between his nose and his eyes.

"These?" He pushed on the frame and the glasses twisted to one side. "I only really need them for up close for like when I want to read or use my phone."

"And did you get a look at who was driving the boat?"

"No, just some fella. I don't believe I ever saw him before. Not a friend of mine, anyway."

"He saw Ryan Deering's car parked there, too, Sheriff. Tell him, Archie."

"I believe you just did," Archie told Mitch.

Bored with the conversation, Mutton wandered out. Probably more fun to watch the Junior Wild Bunch play their online video game. Did they even call them video games anymore? Was I that old?

"Were there two men, by chance?"

"On the boat? No, not that I could see."

"What sort of boat was this? Did you notice the make and model?"

"Sure, she was a Carolina Skiff. Nice one, too. I wouldn't say no to a fine boat like that."

A Carolina Skiff, the same kind I'd found the pen on at Banks Marine. The pen from the Slowater Motel.

"Are you sure there wasn't a second man onboard?"

"There might've been but I only saw the one."

"Bearded or cleanshaven?"

"Hmm." Archie Knapp rubbed his chin. "Cleanshaven, I'd say."

That let Harker out, further cementing his alibi.

"There are several men in the cells, Mr. Knapp. I wonder if you'd do me a favor and see if you recognize any of them as being—"

"Too late," cut in Mitch. "Been there, done that."

"Oh?"

"Your chief deputy already took us back. We both had a good look. I didn't recognize any of the bunch."

"Me neither," Archie Knapp said.

"Do you suppose you'd recognize this person on

the boat if you saw them again?"

"I couldn't say," Archie Knapp replied. "I won't know until I see him, if you get my drift."

I sort of did. And I was sort of drifting myself. Drifting further from the answers I sought.

"Let's talk about Isaac Miller. He was a friend of yours."

"Oh, yeah. A good friend."

"What about this fishing trip he was supposed to be leaving on? You know anything about that?"

"I don't know nothing about that. It wasn't with me."

"I'm sorry. Do you have any idea who might have wanted him dead? Did he have any enemies?"

"None that I know. He was a good man, a good man." Archie Knapp whipped out a well-worn fishing knife. "You mark my words, Sheriff, I find the bastard that did it, I'll fillet 'em alive!"

Swish! Swish!

The serrated blade slashed the air and came close to removing Mitch's nose.

"Mr. Knapp, I'm going to have to ask you to put your knife away, we wouldn't want—"

Tracy Zefferelli burst into my office, face red and puffy, sweat dripping from her forehead. If I'd had an office door, she would have burst through it.

With ease.

"Tom!"

"Hello, Tracy. Give me a minute. I was just talking to these two witnesses about—"

"Screw your witnesses, Tom!" Tracy clutched her belly, her face bright as a mottled strawberry. "Unless they want to witness me giving birth!"

56

To say Mitch and Archie's exit from my office had exceeded the speed of light might have been an exaggeration but only a slight one.

"You can't have a baby here!" My hands braced the door opening. "This is a Sheriff's office! That's my desk!"

"Oh, no?" Tracy threw herself into my recently vacated office chair and threw her swollen feet up on my desktop, sending papers flying. "Watch me!"

With a swift sweep of her arm, the pathologist cleared practically everything else from my desktop. She breathed in and out, fast and hard. Huffing and puffing like the Big Bad Wolf and I was the object of her howling and fury.

"But, Tracy—"

"But nothing, Tom," she huffed. "Are you going to help or are you going to stand there and gawk?"

"I'm going to get some help. I'll be right back!"

"Tom!"

I ran out looking for somebody, anybody. Through the window, I saw Nat outside. Frenchie was feeding the hoard. "Frenchie!"

"Chief?" Frenchie's head appeared above the heads and shoulders of the Junior Wild Bunch.

"I need your help. Tracy's about to have a baby."

"I don't know anything about that, Chief."

"You've got three of your own!"

"Yeah, but, Chief." Frenchie threw up his hands.

"Where's Lizzie?" She was a woman. She had to be better equipped than me and Frenchie. At least she had the same equipment.

"She radioed five minutes ago. Due any minute, Chief."

"What?"

"I said she comes any minute, Chief!" Rough hands snatched bags of chips from Frenchie's clutches. The biggest boy went for Frenchie's gun belt.

"Hey, don't touch that!" I ran over and pulled the boy away before the situation got ugly.

"What did you do that for?" Sullen, angry eyes pelted me.

"So you don't shoot somebody or yourself. Damn." I yanked the monitor off Frenchie's desk. The cord tautened and broke free from the computer it had been attached to a mere moment ago.

"Hey!" the Junior Wild Bunch screamed.

"Police brutality!" screamed the girl who'd been responsible for most if not all of the alien bloodshed.

"Mon dieu!" Frenchie's hands flew to his cheeks. "My computer!"

"Do you kids have to keep playing that damn video game? Can't you see your mom is giving birth?" I pointed to my open office.

"She told us to keep busy," replied some dark-haired hoodlum who looked a lot like his mother.

"Tooommmm!" shrieked Tracy Zefferelli, sounding like she was birthing a baby elephant. "Get your ass in here!"

"And to stay out of her way," put in the girl,

who had refused to relinquish the keyboard despite her siblings protesting squawks and the dead screen.

"So? Do you always do what your mom tells you?" I slammed the monitor back down on Frenchie's desk.

"Of course."

"Even when she's having a baby?"

"Especially then," answered the dark-haired hoodlum in skinny jeans and a brilliant red T-shirt under a brown leather coat with a Sherpa collar. "Wouldn't you?"

"Who's her doctor?" I demanded. "I need to call him. Or her."

"Tooommmm!"

"She's a doctor, Sheriff. Duh."

"Yeah, but—" Realizing the futility of talking to her demon clutch, I spun away. "Send in Lizzie the second she gets here, Frenchie!"

I stopped at the entrance to my office and yelled over my shoulder. "And call an ambulance or something!" If Tracy didn't need it, I would. My blood pressure soared as blood raced through my veins at twice the rated capacity.

"Help me, Tom." Tracy reached from me from my chair.

"What can I do?"

I felt her forehead. Why, I had no idea.

"Just hold my fucking hand and say some calm shit." Tracy pulled back her lower lip with her teeth and sucked in a sharp breath. "That's what the books say. Have you ever delivered a baby?"

"Not even a puppy!"

"Shit. Well, get ready, because the show's about to start and you've got that look on your face."

"What look?"

"That look of sheer terror rather like the kind you get when the Grim Reaper's come knocking on your door and you realize you just spent the last two minutes of your life—wasted it—brushing your teeth, gums and all.

"Maybe you could hold off a little bit and we can make it to the medical center?"

"I am a damn medical center!" Tracy lurched forward in my chair. Her feet stayed planted on my desktop. I would never look my desktop the same way again. "Hey! One of you kids, call your dad!"

"Lizzie will be here any minute, Tracy. Why don't we wait for her?"

"Arrchh." Tracy's hand clamped down on my forearm. Her long fingernails pierced my shirt, pierced my skin. I think they pierced my radial bone. "Say something soothing, Tom!"

I sucked in a breath, giving myself time to think. "Everything is going to be—Lizzie!"

Lizzie stopped in the entry, eyes wide. I'd never seen her look so scared. I'd never seen her look scared period. "What the hell!"

"Just in time." Sweat gushed from every pore of my body and some places where I didn't even think I had pores.

"Oh, no, not me." Lizzie waved her hands and turned on her heels.

The proverbial rat fleeing the sinking ship.

"Get your ass back here, Captain!"

"Fine." Wearing a frown, Lizzie hurried over. "Help is on the way, Tracy." She laid her hands over Tracy's which were now themselves laced over her swollen belly.

I slipped past. "I'll get some water and towels!" Again, why, I didn't know. But it got me out of there.

"EMT's here!" Frenchie called from the window overlooking the parking lot.

Nat waved them inside. He remained outside. Knowing I'd only be in their way, I joined him.

"Everything okay in there, Sheriff?"

Frenchie, feeling abandoned, joined us.

"Who's watching the children?" I demanded out of fear for my Sheriff's office.

"Who the hell cares, Chief!" Frenchie shouted, much out of character. He leaned over. He clamped his hands onto his knees.

Nat pushed open the door, glanced inside. Shouts and screams funneled outdoors. Was it Tracy, Lizzie, or the Junior Wild Bunch, or all of the above?

I no longer cared. "Who's hungry? I, for one, am heading to Davie's."

"They sell beer Chief?"

"Yep." I started walking fast.

"Need I remind you both that we are on duty, Sheriff?" Nat exclaimed.

"Nope. That's why we're limiting ourselves to two beers apiece."

Nat took the lead.

57

"You wanted to see me, Tom?" Commissioner Foxworthy's impossibly large and well-dressed frame filled my sight.

"Good morning, Commissioner. Close the door and pull up a chair."

Scowling, Alan Foxworthy turned his head. "What door?

"Noticed that, did you?" I quipped. I sat with my sort-of-new chair—a chair I'd swapped my original chair for with a tattered red cloth-covered office chair I found moldering in the storage closet—with its back against the wall.

That was as far as I could reasonably get from my desk and still look like I was behind it. I wasn't all that comfortable seated at the desk after it's being used as a birthing table less than twenty-four hours ago. Ditto the chair, hence, the wobbly set of wheels I now coasted along on.

Fortunately, the baby, named Bella, had arrived without a hitch. Mother and newest addition to the Junior Wild Bunch were where they belonged, home resting.

Coming into the station this morning, I saw some clown had thumbtacked a sign outside my office that read Thomas Edge Maternity Center.

I suspected Lizzie as the culprit and intended to tack it to her butt sometime when she wasn't looking.

"Save your breath, Tom. I already received a call from Mr. Lipori's attorney. They are keeping me out of this." Alan Foxworthy popped the button on his swank blue suit and sat. Manicured fingernails pecked at some imaginary mote of dust on one of his brown wingtip shoes.

"Unfortunately, I'm not sure I can offer you the same deal."

Commissioner Foxworthy's eyes met mine. "I don't suppose you could make all this go away?"

"Not a chance. I've got three men under lockup. Too late for that, Commissioner. But I understand where you're coming from. I spoke with Lipori and his attorney. You're right. Lipori won't say anything about you being at his place. He's too smart for that. He knows he's got you in his back pocket. How's that feel, Commissioner?"

Commissioner Foxworthy paled. "I hadn't really thought of it that way." His hands fluttered, as if seeking a basketball, the same way a normal person would seek a stress ball.

"I've got a back pocket too."

"Meaning?"

"Relax, Alan." Butt planted in my chair, I used my feet to propel myself to the wall to my left. "Lucky for you I don't intend to stick you in it." I pulled a Sharpie from my shirt pocket. "I would like to ask you a favor, however."

"What's that?"

I popped the top on the marker and handed the marker to the commissioner. "If you wouldn't mind?"

"Mind what?" Alan Foxworthy's face wrinkled like a deflated basketball.

"Signing this." I tapped the newly-framed item hanging on my wall. Frenchie had done a nice job. At the local craft store, he'd picked up a sweet walnut frame with a charcoal matte. He insisted on mounting the citation himself.

"What is that?" Alan Foxworthy unfolded himself from the chair and loomed over the frame on the wall. "What the hell is that doing here?"

"Looks nice, don't you think?"

"No, I don't."

"I'm sorry to hear that. I have a sheet of glare-free glass to lay over it once I get your autograph. I'd hate for it to fade or anything else to happen to it." I smiled. "Who knows? It might be worth something someday."

"I sign this and we keep my presence at Lipori's house under wraps?" He rolled the open marker back and forth between his index finger and thumb.

"Plus, I continue prioritizing my murder investigation without any grief from you."

"Yeah, yeah."

"Excellent. See, Commissioner? I'd say our public safety initiative is off to a great start."

"You're an asshole, Edge."

I tapped my chest. "An asshole with a badge. Pay the fine."

"I don't know…" His face contorted in inhuman shapes.

"Go ahead," I said. "Take a gamble."

"Fuck you."

"You'll have to catch me first."

I smiled more broadly as he swirled his name

across the face of the speeding ticket. He shoved the marker at me. I recapped it and slipped it into my pocket. "I'm also thinking it makes a nice backdrop for when the press stop by. You know, for official pictures and stuff."

"Like I said, fuck you." Alan Foxworthy stormed out.

"Don't forget to close the door on your way out!"

That earned me the bird. And quite a bird it was. The man really did have extraordinarily long fingers. No wonder he'd been such a star player at NC State.

58

At the last second before I knew we'd crash and be on our way to a new and, hopefully, better life, Frenchie slammed on the brakes a foot behind Nat's unoccupied 4x4 at the edge of the road. Lizzie's empty truck sat across the road.

The sergeant grinned and shut off the engine. "We make good time, Chief."

"Warp speed." Unbuckling my seatbelt, I realized how badly my hands shook. "In fact, I think we gained a few minutes."

"Thanks, Chief."

Did he really think there was a compliment in there somewhere?

Frenchie begged me to ride with him. He said carpooling was better for the environment.

Maybe, but not the environment I'd been faced with inside his car. Frenchie drives a very unofficial Renault Mégane five-door that he and his wife imported from France. The vehicle, or voiture, as Frenchie would say, had once belonged to his father-in-law. It was painted Cosmos blue. Gray cloth dressed the interior.

It's not a big car or a sporty car, and it doesn't have a lot of horsepower but Frenchie drives like he's at Le Mans. Worse, actually, because even a race car driver has to slow once in a while, especially on those tight corners and chicanes. Frenchie is all gas and no brakes.

The inside of Frenchie's Renault smells like a bakery because he often helps his wife, Madeline, with her deliveries. I could have endured the scent if he'd included a pastry or two for us to nibble on.

"Hi, Mario." Frenchie and I greeted Tracy's husband, busy in the driveway squirting the mud off her Range Rover. She's a stickler for a clean vehicle. Quite the opposite of me.

"Morning, Sheriff, Frenchie." Mario aimed the running water within inches of my boots. "This is all your fault, you know."

"Why's that? I told her when she bought the SUV that black was going to be a hard color to keep looking good."

"You're also the one who sent her over to that campground."

"To be perfectly clear, a corpse sent her to the campground."

"Tracy says it was practically a swamp."

"I wouldn't say that." I tipped my hat. "More a mud pit."

"Funny." Mario is a large Italian with dark brown hair and eyes.

He works from home and is in finance. I wasn't sure exactly what he had to do with finance but, judging by their house, which was the finest waterfront property in the area, he did it very well.

Mario also has one of those weird metabolisms that allow him to stand outdoors in forty-degree weather wearing nothing more than olive cargo shorts, black T-shirt and open-toed leather sandals—washing a car with what had to be ice water straight from the outdoor tap, no less.

Frenchie and I, bundled in our uniforms and fleece-lined duty jackets, were both freezing our butts off.

"How is Meez Tracy?" Frenchie asked, stepping around the Range Rover. "And zee babe?"

"See for yourselves, guys. Everybody's inside. I'll be in after I take care of this mess. If I don't polish the wheels and shine the tires, she makes me start all over again."

"Who you trying to kid, Mario?" I said. "You're out here dragging your ass, thinking up chores to do just so you don't have to deal with everything in there."

Mario twisted off the water nozzle and a torrent became a drip. "Four kids, Tom. Four. And three of them are in there transforming the house from a scene out of Architectural Digest into a scene out of Night of the Living Dead."

"That bad?" Having recently experienced his kids up close, I could empathize.

"I found a pus-oozing zombie occupying my office chair this morning. Scared me half to death. I don't know how I'm ever going to get the coffee out of the Turkish rug."

Frenchie and I entered the house where we found the Junior Wild Bunch turning the once elegant high-ceilinged entry into a cobwebbed dungeon with hyper-realistic plastic implements of torture and severed body parts suspended from the fourteen-foot ceiling.

With tooth-rattling force, the oldest boy hammered nails, in the process of completing work on a tiny gallows constructed next to the guillotine. Next to the guillotine, the severed heads of several startled-face victims filled a wicker basket.

Frenchie and I shared a look.

"Hey, kids. A bit gruesome, don't you think?"

"What's wrong with it?" demanded the youngest boy.

"Yeah, we like it." This from the heartless alien-killing girl.

"You don't think it all be a bit much for your mom and the new baby?"

"She told us to do it," replied the older boy.

"Mom said we could do whatever we want," said the girl.

"As bloody as we want," added the younger boy with pride.

"She says this?" Frenchie pulled off his hat and scratched the top of his head.

"Yup." The boy rolled his eyes to show Frenchie what he thought of his question.

"We do everything Mom tells us," added the girl, who had dressed for Halloween Decorating Day in a gray and white tattered outfit designed to fit in at the next Zombie Junior Prom. A necklace of yellowed plastic skulls and bones roped her slender neck.

"How about testing out the guillotine for us, Mr. Edge?"

"Not on your life. Or mine." Kids today, I couldn't help thinking, as my father and grandfather before me had probably also thought a time or two themselves. But still, could they ever have imagined a bunch like this?

"How about you, Frenchie?"

"Huh?"

The girl snatched Frenchie's hat from his hand

and squashed it down on her head, pushing her hair around her ears. Zombie Prom Cop.

Lovely.

"Come on," said the youngest, hand outstretched, taking a step in my direction. "Don't be a chicken."

I took a step back. I did not like the look in the youngest's eyes. Better to be a chicken than a chicken with its head cut off. "Where is your mom?"

"In her bedroom with your friends."

"Right."

The girl ran off. Frenchie's hat went with her.

"Aren't you going to go after her?" I asked.

Frenchie gaped at me. "Would you, Chief?"

"No. You're right. Better to buy a new hat."

59

Frenchie and I wandered through the house until the sound of voices led us to a magnificent master bedroom overlooking the sound. Nat and Lizzie sat on a couple of blue leather chairs near Tracy's bedside. A table between them held a platter of fruits, cheeses and crackers.

"Hello, Tom, Frenchie." New mom Tracy sounded rather subdued.

I handed Tracy the flower arrangement Frenchie and I had picked up along the way and kissed her cheek. "How's the new mom?"

"Good." Baby Bella rested against Tracy's chest.

The four of us oohed and aahed over the baby for a bit. Mario joined us and, even though it wasn't yet noon, he broke open the Billecart-Salmon Champagne— real Champagne, as Frenchie pointed out with delight. We toasted mother and baby girl.

While Mario departed, entrusted with changing Bella's diaper, Tracy got down to business.

"The reason I stopped by the Sheriff's Office yesterday, Tom—"

"You mean besides to have your next child?"

"Final," Tracy interrupted. "That's final child, Tom."

"Isn't that what you said last time?" Lizzie asked.

"The last two times," Nat pointed out, earning him a glare from the new mother.

"I wasn't talking to you." Tracy said with a smile that ran from her lips to her eyes. "Besides, do you really want to play midwife again, Lizzie?"

Lizzie frowned. "You're right, final."

"What about you, Nat?" Tracy asked.

"What about me?"

Nat appeared tired, distracted.

"Ready for another?"

Nat stuttered.

"Nat's youngest, isn't it, is having some health issues," I cut in.

Nat goggled at me.

"I'm sure everything will work out," I added quickly.

"I'm sorry," gasped Tracy. "I didn't know."

"No need to apologize," Nat said. "It's not something I like to talk about."

"Talking helps," said Tracy. "And I'm talking about talking, not yelling. A kind word goes a long way. And it's Tracy, dammit." She winked at him.

"Yes, ma'am." Nat blushed.

"You were saying why you dropped in besides to drop a baby."

"To tell you that I talked to a friend of mine in the forensics department at ECU. Ryan Deering definitely drowned in freshwater sometime between midnight Friday and six a.m. Saturday."

"Like Currituck Sound," Nat said.

"And it would appear that Isaac Miller suffered a significant blow to the head and suffered a heart attack."

"He didn't have the heart attack, fall and hit his head?" I asked. I felt the Champagne going to my head. I blamed that on Frenchie not providing us with road-trip pastries.

Tracy shook her head. "Nope."

I sat my champagne glass carefully on the table between Lizzie and Nat. I gazed out the floor-to-ceiling windows at the Sound. "Say that again, Nat."

"Say what again, Sheriff?"

"You said Currituck Sound."

"So?" Nat rose and looked out the windows trying to see what I saw.

But I knew he wouldn't.

"Why did you say Currituck Sound?"

"Because it's freshwater?"

"Right. Most of the sounds along the Banks are brackish, Pimlico, Albemarle. Currituck's different," I replied.

"Sure. Everybody knows that," said Nat, although I was certain not everybody did.

River fed, Currituck Sound runs about three miles across at its widest point and approximately forty-two miles long. With little contact with the ocean, it has a very low salt content.

"Could Ryan Deering have drowned in the Currituck?" I turned my question to Tracy, lying in bed with the covers up to her neck.

"No. Too shallow. I mean, what is it, three feet?"

"That's about average," Nat agreed.

"What if he was held under or struck a blow first?"

"In that case, sure, why not?"

"So?" demanded Lizzie, lifting the magnum of

Champagne and emptying the bottle into her glass. "What are you thinking, Tom?"

"I'm thinking every problem has a solution."

"What about zee Navier-Stokes equations, Chief?"

"The what?"

"The Navier-Stokes equations."

"What the hell are you talking about, Frenchie?" demanded Lizzie, stuffing a cracker holding an inch of cheddar into her mouth and biting down hard.

"Fluid dynamics," Frenchie explained. "How will a liquid or gas evolve under varying conditions. I think about theez every day when I stir my coffee."

"You do?" I asked.

Even Tracy was sitting up, intrigued. Mario jostled the baby on his shoulder. I heard her burp. At least, I think it was her.

Frenchie prattled off some physics while we gawked and/or nodded off. Phrases like fluid dynamics, speed of fluid flow, exertion of outside forces— improbable phrases which sounded like they should mean something and probably did. And why Frenchie was familiar with these phrases and concepts and I wasn't, left me dumbstruck. Past my ears flew words like pressure, velocity and gravity. Words I knew but had never heard used in quite this way. More words like turbulence and chaos. Things I was experiencing right then.

"Solve this and you can win one million dollars prize, US dollars," the sergeant concluded.

"For figuring out what the hell happens when you stir your darn coffee?" exclaimed Lizzie, watching her language out of respect for the baby no doubt. "Now I've heard everything."

I sighed. "Tell me something, Frenchie."

"Chief?"

"You can remember all that but you can't remember I'm sheriff?"

"How could anybody forget that, Chief?"

Fortunately for Frenchie and me, I'd left my weapon locked up back at the office.

Still, I had to admit, Frenchie's discourse wasn't without merit. There had been a lot of stirring going on since this investigation had begun. And it wasn't just coffee.

I rested my hand on the Sergeant's shoulder. "You've given me a lot to think about, Sergeant."

"I have?"

"You have. All of you have. Good luck to you both and the new baby," I said to Mario and Tracy. To my team, I said, "I'll meet you all back in the office at two o'clock. We've got a murder to solve. Two murders to be exact."

I started for the door, girding myself in preparation for having to pass through the Junior Wild Bunch once again. Would it be rude to ask if there was another way out of this house?

"Wait for me, Chief. I'm your ride, remember?"

"Fine." Damn, it had slipped my mind. "But we're stopping for pastry."

60

For two hours, huddled in chairs in my small office with Nat and Lizzie, we talked and argued over the details of the Ryan Deering and Isaac Miller murders.

And came to no conclusions. Except the conclusion that we had a lot of threads and no real answers, nothing connecting all those threads into one cohesive means plus motive plus opportunity that would all equal up to one killer. Or even two.

"If it wasn't Harker, or Jeter for that matter, who looks good for this?" Nat wanted to know. He looked and sounded weary.

"Don't forget Lipori," added Lizzie, banging the toe of her boot into my desk. Not caring that I'd asked her a dozen times to stop doing it. "They've all got alibis."

"That leaves Donny Clark and Ariadne Deering," I said, my feet rested atop my desk, reminding me of Tracy in the same position only a day earlier but my feet really needed a break.

"Could be both of them," Lizzie replied.

"I agree," said Nat. "The pair of them could easily have been in this together. And their alibis aren't the tightest."

"We're forgetting Basnight," I remembered.

"His wife vouches for him," said Nat.

"You interviewed her?"

"Yes, sir. She wasn't happy about it. Mrs. Basnight's got a worse mouth on her than Lizzie here." He poked his thumb at the captain.

"Hey, watch what you fucking say about me, asshole." She eased the warning with a wink.

Nat frowned. "I take it back. You, Captain, are the Queen of Foul."

Lizzie grinned like it was the nicest thing anybody had ever said to her. "That's better."

"We know Ryan Deering supplied Lipori with equipment for his illegal gambling setup," I said.

"But we also know he's got an alibi for the time of the murder," Nat replied. "It's got to be the wife and her boyfriend."

"I like them, too." Lizzie sounded surprised to hear herself agreeing with the chief deputy.

"But can we place either or both of them at Lipori's beach house, the beach itself, or even the Bells Island Life Campground?"

"No," Nat answered flatly.

"Not yet," amended Lizzie.

"And how and why did Ryan Deering end up on the beach?"

"The killer tossed off a boat into the Atlantic and he drifted ashore there?" suggested Lizzie.

"According to the experts I talked to, it's within the realm of possibility," Nat said. "But it's just that, a possibility."

"If he was dead, tell me this," demanded Lizzie, "why plant a knife in his back?"

"That's easy," I said.

"Oh, do tell, oh Great Wise One."

"Fluid dynamics."

"Huh?" Nat perked up.

"Please," said Lizzie. "Do not go all Frenchie on us, Tom."

"No, fluid dynamics. Sure, Deering was already dead when he got knifed. The killer did it to muddy the waters."

"Fluid dynamics," Nat echoed. "It did confuse things."

"Yep, that it did." I rooted around in my desk drawers looking for something to nibble on and came up empty. Not a candy bar or even a loose jelly bean. Hell, I'd have settled for an overripe banana.

I stood, heard my knees crack, and stretched my arms overhead. "Can either of you tell me why Isaac Miller repeatedly called Banks Marine the day before he was murdered in his own home?"

Nat shrugged. Lizzie cursed.

"He was going on a boat trip. That is what he told you," Nat finally said.

"Maybe he keeps his boat at the marina?" This from Lizzie.

"Nobody there heard of him, remember?" I shot back. I rolled my neck, something cracked there too. Getting old really was a bitch. "I wonder…"

"What?" Nat climbed to his feet, yawning.

"I want you both to continue pursuing Donny Clark and Ariadne Deering."

"While you're busy doing what?" Lizzie had to know.

"I'm going to get a bite to eat." I also had another train of thought I wanted to pursue but because there were no trains within walking distance, I'd settle for a pirate ship.

This pirate ship of thought wasn't sailing towards Donny Clark and/or Ariadne Jones. In fact, it wasn't aiming for option A, B, C, or D, but something else altogether.

I wasn't quite sure what that other option was yet or how it was possible but I was beginning to think this case wasn't about who and what we'd found. No. Rather, this case might be about what wasn't there and what we had not found.

Put another way, I felt something intangible tugging inside my brain, pulling it this way and that. Whatever it was, I wished it would stop tugging and start spitting out some answers.

I had a hunch maybe the answer to this puzzle wasn't in the pieces of the puzzle we saw and were trying together. No, the answer, the trick, to putting this puzzle together might just be in putting together the pieces that did not exist.

It sounded crazy. That was why I didn't share my idea with Lizzie and Nat. More insubordination, scoffing and razzing I didn't need.

61

Leaving the pair of them to stare at my unflattering backside as I left my office, I waved to get Frenchie's attention. Busy on the phone, he cupped his hand over the receiver. "Chief?"

"If anybody comes looking for me, I'll be at the diner."

"Sure, Chief."

I took my time, counting the paces, enjoying the cool fall air and the sun that lit up the atmosphere, creating one of those perfect Carolina blue skies.

Geraldine "Jerry" Jewell, Vice Chairman of the Board of Commissioners, spotted me the second I stepped inside Davie Jones Diner. Seated at a booth facing the door, a young girl sat beside her.

"Hello, Tom. Join us," invited Jerry.

Even though I'd had my fill of county commissioners, Jerry was one of the good ones. I could hardly say no, even though some me—and my tugging brain—time would have been most welcome.

I removed my hat and set it on the empty bench. We exchanged a friendly kiss that stirred up memories of the handful of dates we'd gone on. "Who's your friend?" I smiled to the blonde girl with striking blue eyes.

I noticed a family resemblance. Jerry's a blue-eyed

blonde too and looks ten years younger than her driver's license claims. A healthy diet, lots of resistance training —I seemed to recall her resisting me plenty at the time — half-marathon running, and good genes, were the combined reasons for that.

"This is Jenny, my sister's daughter."

"I see the resemblance." I slid in across from them. "Beauty runs in the family."

Both girls laughed.

"I should have known I'd find you here at Conan the Vegetarian's sooner or later."

This earned me more laughs.

"Conan the Vegetarian's? That's what you call this place. Does Conan know that?"

"Oh, he knows all right. He has some choice words for me, too."

"I'll bet." Jerry tossed her hair. "I love this place. I come here all the time. I'm surprised I haven't seen you here before."

"Ships passing in the night," I replied.

"Cute. This is Jenny's first time in Davie Jones."

"I've read a lot of books about pirates." Jenny sipped her orangeade. "Did you know there were some famous women pirates too, like Anne Bonny?"

"I did. She grew up down in Charleston, I believe, and operated mostly in the Caribbean. I'd be happy to learn more."

"Jenny's a history fan, like you," explained Jerry.

"I'm surprised you haven't been inside this floating ptomaine tub before."

Slam!

"I must've said that last part too loud." Conan glared at me from the hot grill, bent spatula in hand.

"To answer your question, Jenny is visiting me for the week."

"From where?" I asked the girl who looked all of twelve.

"DC."

"Ouch. Better you than me," I said. "Your mom or dad in politics?"

"No. Pasta," answered Jenny, dressed in a brown suede jacket with a light blue shirt beneath and blue jeans. "They own a restaurant on Dupont Circle."

Jerry was dressed similarly, only her dark jeans were tighter. Ditto her shirt, the collar of which dipped to show just a hint of cleavage as she leaned forward.

Sometimes a hint was all it took.

"Excellent," I grabbed a menu from the end of the table. "Much higher up on the food chain than politicians. What looks good?"

Jenny peered at the menu. "I'm having the cheeseburger and fries."

"You know that's not a real cheeseburger," I explained. "I believe they make them out of recycled sweatpants and used tires. The fries are probably real. Even Conan can't screw up the potato."

"Don't mind him, Jenny," said Jerry. "The burgers are delicious. And they are made with peas and oats, quinoa and lots of other healthy and delicious ingredients, *Tom*."

Jerry bopped me on the nose with her menu. "And the cheese is made from soya. Don't pay any attention to what this guy says. If I had, we'd still be dating."

"You two dated?" Jenny squirmed with delight.

"For a minute," I said quickly. I did not want this conversation going down that road.

The waitress slid by, took our orders and collected our menus. To show what a good sport I was, I ordered the cheeseburger too. Heaven help me.

"You are going to be at the party Saturday, yes?"

"The Halloween thing? Is that Saturday?"

"You know it is, Tom. And you promised." Jerry squeezed her niece's arm. "Jenny will be there. She's making special treats for us."

"Chocolate and peanut body parts," said Jenny.

"Sounds disgusting, but in a good way. You should give Conan the recipe."

"Look, isn't that Sonia?" Jenny stared out the window. Sure enough, Sonia stepped off the sidewalk, crossed the street, and was coming our way.

I slouched down.

"Something wrong, Tom?"

"Huh? No. I dropped my napkin," I lied. I straightened. Be a man, I told myself.

"It's right under your nose, Sheriff." Jenny pointed at the napkin in front of me.

"Right." I moved the napkin in a circle across the tabletop.

"And you're a sheriff?"

Jerry chuckled. "I know, right?"

I heard the sound of the door opening, felt the rush of cold wind crossing over my shoulder.

Sonia had arrived.

Too late for me to hit the Gents. The mermaid nailed to the wall sneered and I knew that sneer was meant for me but didn't know what I'd done to deserve it.

"Hello, Tom. Hello, Jerry. It is so lovely to see you." Sonia, dressed in a black leather jacket, black turtleneck sweater and gray slacks was smiling. But I wasn't going to let that smile fool me.

"Hi, Sonia. Sit. This is my niece, Jenny."

I scooched over and Sonia sidled up beside me. "Nice to meet you, Jenny. Frenchie told me I'd find you here, Tom. But if I'd known you were with someone—"

"No, I'm glad he told you." I couldn't fault Frenchie this time for doing what I'd asked. "We bumped into each other."

"Isn't that nice. You two ladies look lovely. Don't they, Tom?"

"Huh? Yeah. Sure."

Jenny winked at me while Sonia's attention was drawn to the approach of our waitress.

I peeked under the table, in search of a portal to another dimension. Sadly, there was none.

I restored to praying for a miracle and got a Frenchie instead in the form of a phone call. I slipped my phone from the pocket of my jacket. "Hi, what's up, Frenchie?"

"Chief! You gotta come quick!"

"I'll be right there!"

"Don't you want to know why?"

"Right." I glanced at the three sets of inquisitive eyes staring at me, hanging on my every word, and watching my every move. "Why?"

"Chief Deputy Midgett went to interview Donny Clark at his buddy and paint shop. They have zee big fisty-cuffs."

"There was a fight?"

"Who fought?" Sonia asked.

"Yes, Chief. Donny he hits Nat. Nat he hits back."

"Is Nat okay?"

"Nat's hurt?" Sonia asked, twisting her napkin round her fingers.

"Yes, Chief. He has the blackened eye on zee ice."

"And what about Clark?"

"He is in a cell. Medic checked him over. Nat hit him pretty good."

"Good for Nat. I'll be right there." I put the phone away and zipped up my jacket. I motioned for Sonia to let me out of the booth. I stood, pulled out my wallet and threw a couple twenty-dollar bills and an extra five on the table. It was probably too much but getting out of there was worth every penny and then some.

"Sorry, ladies. Got to go."

"Is Nat okay?" demanded Sonia.

"Yeah, he's fine. You know Nat. He gives better than he gets."

"That's a relief."

"Are you going to go Taze somebody?" Jenny's eyes alit on my Taser.

"Not today, Jenny."

Sonia kissed me. "Will I see you tonight, Tom?"

"Sure, If I'm not overwhelmed with work. I'll call you, let you know later how things go."

62

Visiting Donny Clark alone in his cell was like visiting a sad and lonely gorilla at the zoo. No offense to gorillas everywhere. I hate to think of any of the magnificent beasts locked up in a zoo.

Why not stick the Donnys of the world in those cages and pens in their place? Wouldn't folks pay the cost of admission to ogle that? I would.

In fact, the only good thing that sprang to mind that came from gorillas in zoos was Warren Zevon's *Desperado* song. A real classic. Practically the story of my life. All I was missing was the BMW.

And why was it I always felt like I needed a long hot shower and a scrub after visiting creatures like Donny?

Nonetheless and not surprisingly, the visit was a waste of my time. Not Donny's time. He was going to have plenty of time.

Time to recover from the blows I was happy to see Nat had inflicted on him. And time to serve for striking my chief deputy and resisting arrest.

I guess the world isn't all bad. Once you scrape past the surface.

Having missed lunch, okay, having skipped out on lunch before its arrival because I was scared to sit at a booth in a diner with a girlfriend and a one-time girlfriend. And her niece. Who could really blame me?

Davie Jones was a freaking pirate ship-themed diner. Nets hung on those walls. Sabers and other sharp pointy things hung on those walls. An authentic cannon guarded the door.

Being without sustenance all day and on the brink of crashing, I dialed ahead for a large pizza to go from Running On Pizza situated in a small strip mall shared with a kite and bike rental shop, a real estate office and a boutique, in Corolla. Close to home. The pizza had a shot at staying hot until I could safely get it back to my place.

Besides, Ross, the owner, makes the best pizza in the region. He's an old hippie. He earned his living, socking away enough money to retire and open the pizzeria, working as a roadie and then guitar tech for Jackson Browne. Hence the name of his biz.

Running on empty myself, I shot inside the pizzeria, paid, and carried my warm, heavy treasure back to the Bronco, sucking in the aroma, my mouth watering. I'd ordered the pie with everything and then some. Extra cheese, loads of sausage—Bladder Boy loves the stuff—onions, mushrooms, artichokes and broccoli.

I'd have ordered extra calories and extra fat if they'd have let me.

I sped up the beach, racing the dying sun. Bladder Boy greeted me with enthusiasm.

And pee.

There's always going to be pee.

Smelling the pizza in my hands, he quickly did his business and raced up the steps, through the front door and inside to the sitting room, tail wagging, moist tongue dangling.

Bladder Boy and I aren't much for formality. No kitchen table, no forks, no napkins. I laid the pizza box open on the table beside the sofa, grabbed a huge slice weighed down with lots of hot sausage and a wee bit of veggies—especially light on the onions because those did weird things to Bladder Boy's plumbing—and dropped it into one side of his new bowl, the one Sonia had gifted him, and which I had carried over from my kitchen.

I turned to grab myself a slice. As I turned to plop down on the sofa, I found Bladder Boy staring back at me. Bowl empty. Begging for more.

"Fine. Take mine."

I held it out. He leapt, snapped, swallowed.

Before he could ask for another, I pulled one off the quickly diminishing pie and plopped it down in his dish. This time, before going for it, he lapped up some water.

I ripped the top off the box for a plate, grabbed a couple good-sized slices for myself and fell on the sofa.

Of course, my phone rang.

And my phone was in my pocket.

My pocket was attached to my coat.

My coat hung next to the front door.

And, of course, I was the sheriff. I was obliged to answer the phone. Anytime, anywhere, day or night.

Hadn't I recently jumped down Nat's throat about just such a thing?

Hell of a job.

"Shit." I crawled off the sofa, set my pizza on the side table. Bladder Boy's ever-alert eyes went from me to the pizza and back again.

And back again.

The phone kept ringing.

"Don't even think about it," I warned, moving to the phone with more speed and energy than I cared to or felt equipped for.

"Hey, Sonia." I swallowed a couple shallow breaths, which wasn't anywhere near as satisfying as swallowing a slice of Running On Pizza pie with all the works, but it did keep me running.

"Hi, yourself. I thought you'd never answer."

"Sorry, I was in the middle of something." I glanced at Bladder Boy as he danced around the side table. "What's up?"

"First, how's Nat?"

Of course, Nat. "He's fine. Haven't you talked to him?"

"No. Frenchie told me he was home with his family. I didn't want to disturb him. He's probably quite upset. He's such a gentle man. He doesn't like violence, you know."

Was that what this conversation was going to be all about, Nat? And what a great and gentle man he was?

If so, I was finding an excuse and hanging up.

"Will Nat be at work tomorrow?"

"I don't know. I'm not his mommy."

"What's that supposed to mean?"

"Sorry. Nothing. Stop that!"

"What?"

"Huh? Nothing. I was talking to Bladder Boy." The dog had leapt on the sofa and stuck his face smack in the middle of the pizza. "No!"

"Tom? What on earth?"

"It's nothing." I sighed.

Hell, it was only pizza and it wasn't like the

spaniel and I hadn't shared all the germs we probably could at this point. I figured we were practically genetically related by now.

"Was there anything else?" I asked. There sure wasn't any pizza.

"I was going to ask if I could come over but considering the mood you are in…"

"Me? The mood I'm in? The first thing you did when you called was to ask about Nat. Did you ask me about me?"

"I'm sorry, Tom. Did some criminal punch you in the face?"

"You know what I mean."

"No, I don't know what you mean."

Phone in hand, I wandered back to the sofa and inspected the ravaged pizza. Some of it still appeared reasonably edible. Bladder Boy, sated, sat in front of the hearth, expecting me to light a fire to warm his lazy ass.

"Do you want me to come over or not? I could bring some dinner if you haven't eaten yet."

"Dinner? No, I haven't." I glared at Bladder Boy. He averted his greedy eyes. "But you don't have to do that."

"I know I don't have to. I want to. You sound… wound up."

I had to give credit to Sonia. The woman had good ears.

"I don't think I'd be the best company right now." There was no doubt about that.

"That's never stopped me before." Pause. "That's a joke."

"I know. Let's have dinner tomorrow. My place."

"Are you sure, Tom?"

"Yeah, I appreciate the offer but I think I'll go for

a walk on the beach. Take Boy. Believe me, he could use the exercise." Especially after this most recent act of gluttony.

And treachery.

"In this weather?"

By the time I'd arrived at the cabin, the weather had grown cold and a so-fine-it-was-invisible mist filled the air. The weather changes quickly in the Outer Banks.

"This is no time for a walk," said Sonia.

"My god, you're right! I've got to go!"

"Where are you going?"

"I told you. For a walk on the beach."

"Tom, why? You just agreed—"

"Why? Because you are brilliant. And beautiful. Beautiful and brilliant. Talk to you tomorrow. Bye." I ended the call as she was saying goodbye. "Come on, Bladder Boy!"

With Bladder Boy watching me with a pair of sleep-filled eyes, I cobbled together some chunks of chewed and licked over, room-temperature pizza and folded them up in the top of the pizza box as an improvised to-go container.

"Get your greedy butt up, dog!" I called from the door. "We're going for a walk."

63

We trudged up and down the ever-shifting hills. The wind blew in off the ocean, kicking sand in my eyes. I squinted and marched on.

Sonia was absolutely right. This was no weather for a walk on the beach. That invisible mist followed me like a hungry swarm of no-see-ums.

I shrugged the hood to my parka over my head and pulled the strings tight under my chin.

Boy and I stumbled down the dune to the dark beach. No moon. No clouds. No people.

I could make out the dim lights of a few ships miles offshore but that and nothing more.

We were alone but I wasn't lonely. "Come on, Boy." I led him south in the direction of the crime scene. It had long washed away and that was probably a good thing. Not good for tourism, I'm sure.

After about twenty minutes of walking, against the wind all the way, sand and mist recarving the features on my face, we arrived at the spot where I figured Ryan Deering's body had been discovered.

At least near enough. It wasn't like there was some big X painted in the sand to mark the spot.

Bladder Boy padded up to sniff a man-sized chunk of driftwood.

The answer was here, I only had to find it.

"What do you think, Boy? How about using that snout of yours and sniffing out some clues?"

His answer was to begin digging a hole in the wet sand. In a flash, he'd dug a hole half his size. That dog could dig like nobody's business.

I peered in the hole. "If you find anything down there, like buried treasure, it's half mine. You know, like the pizza was supposed to be?" Bladder Boy ignored me, kept on pawing, digging, kicked wet sand up under his belly and over my boots.

Angry ghost crabs skittered around him. Every so often, he turned and halfheartedly snapped at them. It was a game to the crabs as much as it was the dog.

Remembering the pizza I'd been carrying, I unfolded the scrap of cardboard, squatted to lower myself from the wind, which did no good, and ate.

Amazingly, Bladder Boy was so busy digging and crabbing, he didn't even beg for another slice. Not that there were any slices left, only chewed over bits.

Tasted good though. I wiped my sleeve against my lips and folded the cardboard up under my parka.

A million vague thoughts raced across my mind like the million unseen stars I knew existed out there somewhere, obfuscated by the clouds.

The rhythmic breaking of the waves slowed my thoughts.

I could feel threads pulling together. I just had no idea what they were going to build yet.

I listened to my knees crack as I wobbled to my feet.

"Come on, Boy. I don't know about you but I for one am cold and wet and could use a hot drink."

We tread silently back up the beach but for the

susurrus of the waves and the whistle of the wind in my ears.

By the time we slogged up the beach and down the road to the cabin, I was shaking from cold. Bladder Boy appeared to be feeling the effects of the cold and wet too.

I unlocked the door and stepped inside with the dog at my heels. "Freezing? Me, too. We'll light a fire. Warm up."

I tossed a couple handfuls of kindling on the fireplace grill and set on a few logs from the stack beside the hearth. With a trembling hand, I lit the kindling with a long-stemmed lighter and felt a sudden surge of heat press against me like a warm wool glove.

Bladder Boy sank onto his cushion and laid down, resting his head on his paws. He looked miserable.

Taking pity on him, I went to the bathroom for a towel, figuring I'd dry him off some.

Someone banged on the front door as I was reaching under the bathroom sink for a clean towel.

"If you're here to report a crime, it had better be a double homicide!"

"What?" replied a muffled voice.

I pulled open the door. One of these days I'd install a keyhole. I hate surprises. "Jerry?" Okay, this surprise wasn't so bad. I stepped aside. "What are you doing here?"

Jerry Jewel grinned. "Since lunch got interrupted, I thought I'd surprise you." She dangled a bag from Davie Jones between us. "I brought you your cheeseburger."

"You surprise me, all right. But you didn't have to do this."

"Why not? You paid for it after all. The least you can do is eat it. And the least I can do is enjoy watching you try to eat it." She bounced the bag off my stomach. "What's it made of again? Sweatpants and used tires?"

"Very funny." I snatched the bag from her hand. The pizza I'd managed to eat hadn't exactly filled my tank. "Come on in."

"Are you all right, Tom?" Jerry followed me to the sitting room. Bladder Boy was snoring, nose inches from the fire.

"Huh?" I set the bag on the table next to the slaughtered remains of the pizza.

"You're shaking. Your clothes are all wet."

"It's nothing. We went for a walk on the beach."

"In this weather? Are you out of your mind?" Jerry's hand went to my forehead. "And you're ice cold. Damn. Come on."

She spun me around and peeled off my parka.

"What are you doing?"

"What *you* are doing is taking a hot shower and putting on some dry clothes."

"But—"

"But nothing." She picked up the paper sack from Davie Jones. "I'll go warm this up for you and make you a nice cup of hot tea."

"You don't have to. I can do—"

Jerry raised her eyebrow. "Do you want to do this the easy way or the hard way?"

"What's the hard way?"

"Go!"

I went.

64

I stumbled from the shower. The heavenly aroma of a log-burning fire hit me in the face, or at least the nostrils. This scent could only come from real wood, not that fake sterile alcohol stuff Sonia's sorry excuse for a fire feature emits. I also smelled food. And it might have been composed of soiled sweatpants and used rubber tires, but it smelled delicious.

I dried my hair with the towel intended for Bladder Boy, threw on my black flannel pajama bottoms and wrapped myself up in a green flannel robe, tying it tight around the waist. I dug my fleece-lined slippers out from under the bed and slipped my feet inside.

The night was so good I'd call it nearly perfect.

Until things went perfectly wrong.

Reflecting on my reflection in the bathroom mirror, I heard voices. Female voices.

"Hi, Sonia. Come on in."

"Oh, I didn't expect to see you here. Where's Tom?"

Heart pounding, I raced up the short hall, desperate to diffuse the situation and clarify any misconceptions. "Sonia! Hi!"

"Hello, Tom." Sonia's eyes were two hard dark stones.

Wet hair. Bathrobe. Ex-girlfriend in the cabin. I

added it all up.

I was in trouble.

"No, Jerry and I were just about to—"

"I can imagine what you were just about to." Sonia held a bag in her arms. "Here. I thought you might be hungry. I brought Chinese." She shoved it at me.

"Thanks." I fumbled it in my hands. The food was still hot.

Not as hot as Sonia.

"Won't you stay, Sonia?" pleaded Jerry. I couldn't help noticing she'd let her hair down in my absence and removed her coat. Her pink flannel shirt hung loose over some very tight jeans.

Sonia, by contrast, wore a black knee-length wool coat and tall black leather boots, which I could practically feel her desire to stomp on me with.

"How nice of you to invite me, Jerry." Sonia recriminated me with those stony eyes of hers. "No, thank you. I really can't stay."

"Sure you can." I reached for Sonia's hand. "There's plenty. Jerry brought food too."

"How sweet."

Oops.

"Come on," I tried again. "We'll all go sit by the fire."

Sonia pulled free. "No, I have early hours tomorrow."

Sonia pulled the ends of her scarf tighter around her throat and I could imagine she was pretending to strangle me. Maybe Jerry too.

Maybe there'd be that double homicide, after all.

"I'll walk you out." I started to the door.

Sonia yanked it open. "That's sweet. But look

at you." She did, eyes upped and downed me. "You're hardly dressed for it."

Sonia stepped out and shut the door behind her.

"Sorry about that." Jerry stuffed her hands in her back pockets.

"Not your fault."

"Anything I can do?"

"How are your electrical skills?"

Jerry blinked. "What?"

"How good are you at repairing switches?"

65

Two women in the house and I ended up sleeping alone. Got drunk alone. Slept alone. Dog slept by the fire all night.

Alone in my bed. Alone with my thoughts.

I woke up with a stuffy nose, a scratchy throat and a crow tapping out of tune between my ears. The bathrobe twisted around me.

As for Jerry, our ships had passed in the night once more. We'd done some talking to the wine, some staring at the fire. She giggled watching the exaggerated faces I entertained her with as I ate my so-called cheeseburger.

The damn thing was actually pretty good. I was never, ever going to tell Conan the Vegetarian that. He'd never change his menu and I'd be forced to eat the crap the rest of my life.

Then she grabbed her coat, took me around the waist and kissed me goodnight.

Things got fuzzy after that.

Now the dull morning light was beginning to bring life into focus once more.

What that future held, we'd see.

I let Bladder Boy out to prowl while I shaved and brushed my teeth. I was tugging on my boots when I heard him scratching at the door so I stopped and let him inside.

Good thing, too. Because I hadn't put on my pants yet. I yanked off my boots, pulled on my pants, grabbed a fresh uniform shirt and finished dressing.

That crow between my ears kept tapping out the same tune. I wished he'd learn a new song. Like something soothing, a little BJ Thomas crooning *Rock and Roll Lullaby*, maybe.

The last thing I did before checking out was check my phone. No messages. Not that I'd been expecting any but I had wondered if Sonia might, just might call.

I was going to have to make things right somehow. But what that somehow might be eluded me rather like William Butler Yeat's 'glimmering girl with apple blossom in her hair' eluded the poet.

"Don't bother holding dinner for me," I told Bladder Boy. "I might be late."

As per usual, he paid me no heed and went about his doggy day.

I grabbed my parka which Jerry had hung by the fireplace to dry out last night. The Bronco was as cold inside as my refrigerator. I sneezed, cleared my throat and cranked up the heater.

I bumped along the beach, admiring the Spanish horses as they trotted near the blue-gray water's edge. It was early and, except for me and a pair of diehard beachcombers walking a black dachshund with a brown chin, the world was theirs.

I went to Duckees on the Caratoke. I rolled up to the drive-in window and bought two egg and biscuit sandwiches and two large cups of coffee. All for me.

I didn't want to park at the side of the road. I was trying to break the habit. I also wasn't ready to face the office. I texted Frenchie and told him I was reachable by phone and radio if needed and that I didn't want to be needed.

Driving to the Bells Island Life Campground, I parked midway between the pier and the burned-out shell of Isaac Miller's mobile home. A strip of police tape danced in the breeze, one end attached to the side of the door, the other attached to the wind.

The muddy tracks of our vehicles scarred the foreground. One set of which would've belonged to the ambulance that had driven Isaac Miller off on his last cruise. I wondered if he'd requested a burial at sea. I wondered if he had any kin.

I'd have to ask Nat about that. By now, he would have built up an entire six-inch-thick case file on our campground manager. Good bedtime reading if I ran out of history books.

I drank a little coffee, ate a little egg and biscuit sandwich. I must've dozed off because the next thing I heard was the sound of loud rapping on my window. And the next thing I saw was Mitch Green, hands stretched up over the roof. His grin was big as a pumpkin's and his big belly pressed against my door. He wore an unzipped red parka, red flannel shirt and overalls.

Even though my window was rolled up tight, I could swear I smelled sour beer.

"Mitch." I rubbed my fists into my eyes. "Morning."

"You asleep there, Sheriff? I wanted to make sure you was all right. Not dead, are you?"

I rolled down my window. "No. I only wish I was."

"Don't we all, sometime. Whatchyou doin'?"

"I was having breakfast. Come on." I motioned for him to walk around to the other side of my 4x4. "Join me."

"Don't mind if I do."

Mitch squeezed his big form inside and slammed the door shut. I handed him the extra breakfast sandwich and coffee. "Thanks, Sheriff. You find who killed Isaac and that other guy yet?"

"Nope."

"Shit.

"Don't worry." I pulled at my coffee, felt the warmth trickle down. "The day is still young."

"Yeah. But we ain't."

"Amen to that."

"Duckees." Mitch unwrapped and shoved the sandwich in his mouth. Half went down his gullet in one bite. The other half balanced in his fingers, which he promptly licked. "I love these sandwiches."

"Yeah. Do you happen to know if Isaac had any close relatives nearby?"

"Kin?" Mitch rubbed his red, rubbery stubbled face. "Not that I know of. Nobody that came around regular anyway."

I picked my own half-eaten egg and biscuit sandwich off the dashboard and ate. For several minutes, we chewed in comradely silence. I washed the remains down with a sip of quickly cooling coffee. That musical crow between my ears had finally stopped pecking at my cranium. The bird must've found a hole and flown out.

"Can you think of any reason why Isaac might have made a number of phone calls to Banks Marine?"

"Banks?" Mitch burped, releasing a cloud of

fumes. "Sorry." He opened the passenger side door, flapped it like a broken wings a few times then slammed it shut. "I've only been there once, Banks, that is. Pricey. Too pricey for me. Whatchyou thinkin', Sheriff? Think Isaac was looking to buy somethin' or sell somethin'?"

"Yep."

"A boat?"

"Nope."

"You mind sharing?"

"I gave you half my breakfast, didn't I?"

"That you did." Mitch rubbed his jowls some more. Those cheeks of his had more give than two slabs of whale blubber.

Mitch crumpled up his sandwich wrapper and stuffed it into his empty coffee cup. He looked around. "You got a trash bag in here, Sheriff?"

"What? My floor isn't good enough for you?"

66

A sale was going on at Banks Marine, judging by the tree-sized orange, red and yellow balloon clusters swaying like jelly bean clouds twenty feet overhead, and the three fifteen-foot-tall, air-powered boiled red lobsters performing an asynchronous hula up near the road in an attempt to lure buyers in.

In case anybody had any doubt, a giant banner dangling across the floor-to-ceiling plate glass windows of the showroom announced SAVINGS TO END ALL SAVINGS!!

How could I resist?

I squeezed into a Bronco-sized gap between a pair of NauticStar Hybrid 211s running Yahama F150 engines. One wore a Pacific blue stripe, the other a black one. Each held a matching color bimini top.

Plastic pedestal signs beside each promised swim platforms, casting platforms, plenty of rod holders, livewells and baitwells. These babies were even self-bailing. Perfects boats for fishing, swimming or simply tooling around the waters of the sound.

A saleswoman in a red wool coat scurried over, opening the door to my truck before I could so much as reach the doorhandle.

"Good morning, Sheriff," she said, taking me in. Salespersons have keen eyes for detail. I suppose it's important in their line of work.

"Morning, Miss." I tipped my hat.

"Here for the sale?" She couldn't resist rubbing her hands together. She was young, thirtyish with a blonde ponytail sticking out the back of a black OBX ballcap.

"Sorry to burst your bubble." I nodded to the jelly bean clouds. "Or your balloons. I'm here to see Mr. Cassel."

"Oh." Her smile and her enthusiasm faded, but only momentarily. She perked right back up again. A salesperson cannot afford to show any weakness. I could see she was a good one. "Inside. Do you know where his office is?"

"Yes, thanks. And good luck with your sale. Not exactly ideal weather for boating." I began working my way past the black NauticStar.

"Thanks, Sheriff. That's why we hold the sale this time of year. And it really is a once in a lifetime sale!" she hollered.

I turned slowly.

"Good." She grinned. "I see I've gotten your attention."

"Just one question." I grabbed my hat to keep the wind from making off with it and making me look like a fool. "Two actually."

"Shoot. And I don't mean that literally." Her eyes went to my gun, visible because I hadn't zipped my parka. It was a joke I never got tired of—of hating, that is. But she was young and pretty. And kind. Such type always merit a pass in my book.

"What's your name?"

"Hannah."

"Correct." I winked. "Now here's the second question."

"I'm all ears."

"Trust me, you're a lot more than that, Hannah."

"You're pretty smooth for a sheriff. Are you sure you don't want to buy a boat? Impress your lady friends?"

"I'm not so sure how many of those I have left."

"Oh?"

"Long story." And I wasn't telling it. "Okay, Hannah. Question number two." I held up an appropriate number of fingers. "Does the name Ryan Deering mean anything to you?"

She blinked twice. "I know. That dead guy."

"That it?"

"Isn't that enough?" Her question came out on a cloud of cold air.

"Did you ever see him here?"

"Nope."

"You're sure?"

"I'm good with faces."

"Okay, how about Isaac Miller?"

"That's three questions."

"Let's call it two and a follow-up. Isaac Miller's name mean anything to you, Hannah?"

"No." She shook her head slowly side to side. "Should it? Does he want to buy a boat?"

"He might if he wasn't dead."

"Another one?" Her face showed surprise.

"I'm afraid so."

"You sure do attract a certain type, don't you, Sheriff? Tell me, are you part Grim Reaper?" She pulled off her hat, smoothed her ponytail a couple of times in her hands, then reversed the process.

"I confess. It sometimes seems that way."

"No wonder you don't have a lot of lady friends."

"Such is my life." I said goodbye to Hannah for the second time in the space of minutes.

"Hey, Sheriff. You come by and see me before you leave." She thumped the hull of the black NauticStar. "This baby's got your name on it! You won't be disappointed!"

I waved without looking back. Little did she know I preferred the blue one.

"I promise!" Hannah shouted. "We're throwing in over a thousand dollars' worth of extras! I'll even toss in a rod and reel. Your choice up to a two-hundred and fifty-dollar value!"

Hank Cassel sure knew how to pick them.

And I could use a new rod and reel.

I was going to do my best to avoid that woman when I left Banks Marine.

Otherwise, wouldn't Bladder Boy be surprised when I brought home a brand-spanking new boat and trailer.

67

With the temperature inside the showroom of Banks Marine reaching digits usually only seen in the Caribbean this time of year, I felt like I was walking around inside a toaster oven. And I welcomed it.

The scent of coffee and fresh-popped popcorn filling the air emanated from a setup in the corner that included a coffee urn, a three-tap soda dispenser, and one of those old-fashioned carnival red-and-gold popping carts, complete with spoked bicycle tires.

Three huddling salesmen interrupted their conversation long enough to glance at me then went back to whatever was on their collective mind. They'd probably already seen me outside talking to Hannah and knew better than to poach.

Or maybe she'd signaled them through the plate glass window, giving them the heads up that my wallet was empty and my buying power depleted.

Hank Cassel occupied a big, glass-fronted office smack dab in the center along the rear wall of the showroom. His desk faced the ocean blue-tiled showroom floor. Seeing me, he stood and came towards me. "Morning, Sheriff. Good seeing you again."

"You too, Hank. I hope I'm not interrupting, what with the big sale and all."

Hank Cassel grinned. "We're just getting started.

This is only the first day and the day is young." He laid a hand on my shoulder. "This would be the time to buy. I mean, we do have the most inventory today."

"No, thanks."

"Are you sure? If you wait too long, there won't be a lot of merchandise left to choose from."

"Save your breath, Hank. Hannah's already given me the pitch."

Hank Cassel chuckled. "Isn't she terrific?"

"That she is."

"She may be young but she's probably the best salesperson, man or woman, that I've got. Come on in. Have a seat."

I took a chair opposite his desk, my back to the showroom.

"You know your team went all over that Carolina Skiff. Spent hours. I can't tell you how curious we all were, the customers too. Did they come up with anything?"

"Does one big fat goose egg count?"

The marine store owner chuckled. "You mean nothing?"

"I'm afraid so." I crossed my leg over my knee and sat my hat on the other knee. "I know one of my men asked you about Isaac Miller."

"Nat Midgett." Hank Cassel leaned back in his boxy brown leather chair. "We've sold a lot of boats to a lot of Midgetts through the years."

"But none to Isaac Miller?"

"I don't believe anything came up in our records. And before you ask, again, we didn't sell any boat to Ryan Deering. Not a canoe, not a paddleboard. Not even a paddle."

I stiffened.

"Something I said, Sheriff?"

"Yeah. Not sure what though." I tapped the heel of my boot. "What if Deering paid cash?"

"For a boat?" Hank Cassel settled his hands on his stomach, rocked back and forth. His white hair was combed straight back, giving him a forehead like a full sail. His weathered face and neck stood out in sharp contrast to the white cable knit sweater keeping him warm.

"We never say no to cash. But that doesn't mean we don't keep a record of the transaction. I ask you, what kind of businessman would I be if I didn't?"

"A bad one."

"That's right." Hank Cassel pushed forward, rested his elbows on his immaculate desk. "Might give a salesman, or woman, a bit too much temptation. Know what I mean?"

"You ever have a problem?"

"A time or two. I nipped that in the bud."

"Nothing official? No police?"

Hank frowned. "That could be bad for business too. I've got a reputation to uphold. Handled it internally."

I nodded. I had a hunch Hank Cassel could handle anything he made up his mind to.

The ornately-colored and intricately-carved model of a wooden warship stood in the corner nearest the wall. I recognized her immediately. There'd never been another ship like her—or with a story quite like hers.

This was the Vasa, a ship as famous for its size, power and complexity and is it was for its premature and ignominious end.

Commissioned by Gustavus Adolphus, King of Sweden around 1624 and begun a couple of years later, the warship, armed with sixty-four cannons of various types and sizes, left on her maiden voyage on August 10, 1628.

The crew and guests of the Minnow of Gilligan's Island fame had enjoyed a longer voyage. The Vasa quickly sank to the bottom of the Baltic Sea after having traveled a mere 1400 yards or so from its port of departure in Stockholm.

The warship had been built at the incredible expenditure of over 200,000 Swedish dollars, which equaled better than five percent of Sweden's gross national product at that time. I wasn't real good at multiplying and dividing by a lot of zeroes, but I knew that was a hell of an expensive voyage on a cost per mile basis. I'd have liked to have seen the expense report the Vasa's captain turned in at the end of that little journey.

A mere four hundred feet from shore in waters approximately one hundred feet deep, the Vasa sank under the eyes of members of the king's court—the king himself was visiting Poland at the time—and hundreds, if not thousands, of curious onlookers.

A lot of theories were floating around as to why what was then the world's most powerful warship fell victim to a gust of wind. My money was on the one blaming the vessel's high center of gravity.

As the Vasa sailed past the gap in the bluffs at the bay of Tegelviken, she'd been met by a sudden stronger gust that pushed her far over to portside. Seawater poured in through the open gunports on the lower gundeck.

That was the beginning of the end. Thirty people died.

Lost for centuries, the Vasa was later rediscovered, recovered and restored. She now lived on in a purpose-built Stockholm museum.

Noting my gaze, Hank Cassel said with pride, "I built that lady myself."

"I'm impressed. You're good with your hands." I turned my hands over. "Me, I can barely build a peanut butter and jelly sandwich."

"I visited the Vasa Museum in Stockholm in 2005. I purchased the model there. It must've taken me a good six months to complete."

"You've more patience than me."

"Not nearly as long as the two years or so it took those craftsmen to build the original, of course. Talk about patience. Still, the original lasted maybe twenty minutes." He turned the ship broadside. "Take a closer look."

"She's beautiful."

"I've had this lady going on fifteen years or so."

Hank Cassel ran his finger carefully along the side of the ship. "All these intricate carvings tell the story of the Swedish royal family. Underwater archaeologists were amazed when they discovered her remains. Even more so, when they discovered that the wood was ninety to ninety-five percent intact."

"Supposedly," I said, "because the waters there are so cold and oxygen-depleted. This meant less harmful, wood-eating bacteria and worms. Hence, very little rot."

"I'm impressed. Have you been to the museum?"

"No. I spent my previous life in the Coast Guard. Maybe, someday."

"Yeah, the world's filled with somedays." Hank Cassel pulled a Spanish cedar humidor off the top of a fancy teak credenza with shiny brass handles standing behind him. He lifted the lid off the humidor. "Cigar?"

"No, thanks."

I gave the gentleman a minute to perform his ritual. First, he removed a handheld titanium cigar guillotine from a pocket in the lid of his humidor. Carefully clipping the head of the cigar, he brought it to his lips and sucked for a moment or two.

Satisfied, he pulled a wooden matchstick from a box in his center desk drawer and struck it against the side of the desk.

The match burst to life. Holding the cigar at a forty-five-degree angle, he held the flame near the foot of the cigar. Never letting the flame touch the tobacco leaves, he rolled the cigar round and round until an orange glow erupted at its tip.

Locking the cigar between his lips once more, Hank Cassel puffed and smiled. "I know you didn't come here to talk about Swedish history or peanut butter and jelly sandwiches, Sheriff."

Hank Cassel tossed the dead matchstick in his wastebasket. "And we've already come to the conclusion that you do not want to buy a new fishing vessel. Are you really sure about that because I—"

"I'm sure."

"Fine." Hank Cassel puffed, his cheeks moving in and out like an old-fashioned bellows. "You can't fault me for trying."

"No, sir. I can't."

"So tell me." Hank Cassel puffed some more. "What's on your mind?"

68

"I wanted to talk to you about Ryan Deering and Isaac Miller."

"Again?"

"One more time. Hopefully, the last time." I breathed in the distinct aroma of the Dominican-made Montecristo in Hank Cassel's right hand. "I think there's a link between Banks Marine and Ryan Deering and Isaac Miller. It's right in front of me. I can taste it. Feel it. I just can't see it." I crossed my legs. "Yet."

Hank let my words sink in before speaking. "I don't like it. I run an honest business. What sort of link could there be between Banks Marine and those two murdered fellas?"

"Answer that and I'll make you chief of detectives of Currituck County."

Hank grinned. "That's got a nice ring to it. Would you pay me enough so I'd to be able to give up my day job?"

"Something tells me you could retire tomorrow if you wanted."

"And turn this little empire I built over to the next generation?" Hank Cassel shook his head. "Not on your life. Or mine. My daddy started selling used boats out of his front yard, mostly to and for his friends. I said, 'Daddy, I think you got something. You ought to do this for a living.' He told me I should go do it if I thought it was such a hot idea. And so I did."

"Retire? Give all this up?" Hank Cassel poked his cigar at the showroom. "Nope. I'm not ready for that. Neither is my son-in-law."

"Did you know that the first victim, Ryan Deering, had a knife in his back when we found him?"

"Sure, I heard that."

"A Benchmade Griptilian, similar to the ones I hear you were giving away to customers recently."

"Yep, your man, Midgett, asked me about that too. Hell, Sheriff." He tapped some ash into a crystal bowl. "Those knives aren't rare. In fact, we're giving them away again during this sale. I got a good deal from the company. The first fifty customers who spend a minimum of a thousand dollars on merchandise or services, or buy a boat," he emphasized, "get one."

Hank had kicked into salesman mode again. It must have been in his blood. "That and a 94-quart cooler, two life jackets, a year's supply of bait, full tank of fuel, of course, and—"

I waved my hands in truce. "Save it. Like I said, Hannah already gave me the spiel. In fact, she did everything but twist my arm behind my back."

"I might have to raise her commission." Hank Cassel chuckled, blowing short puffs of smoke across the desk. They appeared like tiny clouds moving quickly across the Vasa, making it seem like the ship was sailing. "Just don't tell any of my other sales staff." He winked at me.

"It'll be our little secret." I shifted gears. "Would you mind if I showed your staff pictures of Deering and Miller? Maybe they came in but gave different names?"

Hank Cassel turned his eyes to the ceiling. "I don't know, I think you're clutching at straws, Sheriff." He puffed and pondered. "You ever stop to think this case might just be your one that got away?"

"Not yet it hasn't." I pulled two folded photocopied photos from inside my coat and laid them on the desk. "Look familiar?"

Hank Cassel turned the photos this way and that. "Only from the newspaper."

"And you don't mind if I show them around?"

"So long as you don't interrupt a potential sale." Hank scooped up the photos. "But I'll do you one better. I'll ask my son-in-law to show 'em to everybody that works here, full-time, part-time, none of the time. Believe me, I've got one or two of those."

Hank Cassel cleared his throat. "And if they aren't in today, he'll catch 'em on their next shift. Good enough for you?"

"More than. Are you sure he'll agree?"

"I'm the boss. He'll agree. Let me get him in here." Hank Cassel pulled his mobile phone from his upper righthand desk drawer and hit a number on speed dial. "If he's not in his office, he won't be far."

After a beat, his eyebrow twitched and he held up a finger to me. "You busy with a customer? No? I'm in my office. Come here a minute, would you?" He hung up and slid his phone out of sight. "He'll be here in a minute."

Hank pulled open a cabinet in the credenza behind him. "Buy you a drink? I've got scotch, bourbon, brandy, mezcal, you name it."

He turned and looked at me over his shoulder. "Rum? Even got Coke in the dispenser out there," he jabbed a thumb at the showroom, "if you're one of those who insist on ruining a drink with sugary soda. Not that I'm judging…much." Bottles tinkled as he fished through a collection extensive enough to open his own pop-up ABC Store. "Or are you going to tell me you're on duty? Isn't that the rule?"

"I'm sheriff. I'm always on duty." I leaned across the desk for a better look at the offerings. "If I went by all the rules, I'd never get a drink. Make it a scotch. Short and neat."

"You got it." He reached for the bottle. "Good choice. You fond of The Macallan's, Sheriff?"

"Yep. We haven't come to blows yet." This, however, was the twenty-five-year-old single malt from one of the first legalized distilleries in Scotland. Not the best or most expensive scotch, but it was better than me and cost more than any single bottle I'd ever bought. "Not that I've had the pleasure of this vintage."

"Well, you're about to." Hank Cassel set the bottle on his desk and grabbed two short crystal turret tumblers from the other side of the credenza's interior. "The Macallan distillery was founded in 1824, you know."

"I didn't." I watched as he poured.

A shadow crept over us.

"You wanted to see me, Hank?"

That shadow represented my missing link.

"Leftkowitz?" My fingers locked around the crystal tumbler Hank Cassel had thrust into my cold hand.

"Hi, Sheriff."

"Hello, Jeff." There was no missing the flush rising up Jeff Leftkowitz's neck and coloring his cheeks.

I carefully sat my tumbler down on a four-color Catalina Yachts brochure lying on Hank Cassel's desk, not wanting to ruin its polished pristine finish. "Didn't you tell me you were a broker?"

Jeff Leftkowitz thrust his hands in the pockets of his tan trousers. With the trousers, he wore a blue blazer with a white turtleneck pullover, and tasseled brown loafers. He smiled at Hank Cassel. "I am a broker, Sheriff." He forced a dry laugh. "I broker boats."

"That's the theory anyway," I heard Hank Cassel say behind me.

I kept my eyes on Leftkowitz. "A boat broker. Never crossed my mind." And I'd shut Leftkowitz down when we'd met because I'd been afraid he'd try to sell me a house or get me to sell my grandpa's house.

"What's up, Hank? Why'd you want to see me?"

Hank Cassel's eyes went from me to Jeff to me to Jeff. "You two know each other?"

"We've met a time or two."

"I'm surprised to hear that," replied Hank Cassel. He slumped back in his chair, tumbler pressed to his stomach.

"I'm surprised you're surprised, Hank. After all, it was your son-in-law here who found Ryan Deering's body. Well, Jeff and his family." Which included Hank Cassel's daughter and grandkids. "Didn't he tell you?"

"You did?" Hank ogled his son-in-law. "I had no idea. You mean you and Jinny were the young couple the paper said discovered the body?"

Out of respect for the Leftkowitzes' privacy and to protect them from becoming the target of a murderer, we'd kept their names from the public. Little did I know.

"Why didn't you or Jinny tell me?"

Jeff Leftkowitz glanced into the showroom.

Was he thinking of running?

"We didn't want to upset or worry you," Jeff Leftkowitz finally managed. "What's this all about, Hank?"

"Damned if I know." Hank's cigar rested in the crystal bowl, slowly dying. He hoisted his glass and downed two inches of scotch in a single gulp. "Sheriff?"

My head felt like one of those fast-moving plinko games was going on inside it. The little ping-pong ball was bouncing off the myriad steel rails, this way, that way, that way, this way.

After an eternity of bouncing, that ball representing my brain came to a stop in a slot at the bottom.

Plinko.

Suddenly, I could see.

69

"Last time I saw you, Mr. Leftkowitz, you were washing all that dried mud off that 4Runner of yours out in your driveway. Remember?"

"I guess so." Jeff Leftkowitz frowned. "Why?" He turned to his boss and father-in-law. "That what you called me in for, Hank? To ask me about me washing my truck? Because I was about to call that Honda rep we talked about and—"

"I noticed a truck very much like that outside when I pulled in here."

"It's mine. So?" Jeff Leftkowitz scratched behind his left ear.

"What do you want to bet that even though you washed it, you missed some of that mud? Under the bumper. Up under the wheel wells. Mud can be pretty distinctive too. Like the mud outside Isaac Miller's mobile home." Almost as distinctive as the pig wallowing in it, I couldn't help thinking as I looked at Jeff.

Of course, I wasn't exactly sure how much veracity there was in my words. It wasn't like it was DNA testing. It was mud. Still, I figured there had to be some truth in what I said. And that was good enough for me. Good enough to set his legs quaking and his heart racing too.

"What the hell are you talking about, Sheriff?" Hank Cassel poured himself a second, larger glass of scotch. "What's he talking about, Jeff? What have you done?"

"I haven't done anything, Hank." Jeff Leftkowitz paced the small office. "I don't know what the sheriff here is going on about. So what I washed my 4Runner? That's no crime. Me and Jinny found a dead body on the beach. That's no crime either, last I heard."

He practically shouted that line at me. I could have heard him from the cheap seats.

"No, no they aren't." I rubbed the brim of my hat between my thumb and forefinger. "But murder is."

"Murder!" Hank Cassel spit across his desk.

A waste of 25-year-old scotch but that wasn't his fault. Nor was the fact that he'd sprayed my uniform trousers with the stuff.

"I don't have to listen to this." Jeff Leftkowitz's face turned purple. Wet angry eyes shot pure hate at me.

He wasn't the first and wouldn't be the last to do so. His hate bounced off me like moonbeams. Something I knew were there but were harmless. Couldn't hurt me if they tried.

Jeff Leftkowitz made for the door. I stuck out my arm, blocking his exit.

"This is ridiculous. Are you really going to sit there, Hank, and let this man talk to your son-in-law like this? I'm calling my lawyer."

"Shut up, Jeff." Hank Cassel breathed hard. Fighting to control the tremor in his voice, he asked, "What are you saying, Sheriff?"

"I'm saying, sorry to say, that your son-in-law here is a murderer, Hank." I said it as soft as I could. Still the pronouncement fell on Hank Cassel's shoulders like a two-ton granite boulder.

I watched the old man sag. I felt something inside me give way too.

"Are-are you sure?"

"I'm sure. You see, this case was as much about what I didn't see as what I did see."

"What the hell are you talking about?" Jeff Leftkowitz's butt pressed up against the window looking out on the showroom. "Come on, Hank. You're not really going to sit there and let him accuse me of murder?"

"I told you to shut up, Jeff. I'm not telling you again." Hank Cassel's right hand squeezed his tumbler so hard I was pretty sure I heard something crack. Bone or crystal, I didn't know.

"You see, it was Jeff and Jinny who found the body on the beach. Nobody else even saw it drift ashore. One minute the body wasn't there and the next minute it was."

"Because he washed up, Sheriff. If you lived here long enough, you'd know things have a habit of doing that. All kinds of things, flotsam, seaweed, dead fish, birds."

"Dead men?"

"Sure."

"No."

"Why not?"

"Because Ryan Deering didn't wash up on the beach."

"He didn't?" That came from Hank Cassel.

"No, Hank. I'm afraid Jeff put him there."

"Bullshit," replied Jeff.

"You planted him there, staged the scene. And a good scene it was. A pretty good plan too. You picked one lousy day for the beach. That meant few people around to see what you'd done. Yep, one lousy perfect day for the beach."

"I don't follow," I heard Hank Cassel say.

"And what you'd done is drive Ryan Deering's corpse to the beach in the back of your 4Runner, zipped up inside a standup paddleboard bag."

"You're crazy!"

"That was one of the things that I couldn't quite get a handle on. How do you make a body disappear and then reappear? Every murderer worth his or her salt normally wants to make the body disappear. Period. End of story. So they hope. But in this case, the idea was to make the corpse appear on cue when and where you needed him. That's what you did. But how?"

Both men had held their eyes on me. "And then it hit me."

"The paddleboard bag?" Hank Cassel's voice came out strained.

"Yep, Jeff had a SUP bag spread out on the sand beside the truck like a beach blanket. What you didn't have was a SUP. That's because you hadn't brought one to the beach. You weren't planning on paddleboarding. You were planning something altogether different."

"That's—"

I didn't give Leftkowitz a chance to tell me whatever tale he was about to spin. "You'd brought Ryan Deering's body in that bag. Clever."

"What the hell have you done, boy?" Hank pressed his hands against his desk. He looked rather like a volcano about to go Vesuvius.

"Nothing." Jeff Leftkowitz slammed his fist into the wall, putting a dent in the sheetrock. "This is bullshit!"

"You went to the beach precisely because it was a lousy day for it. My guess is you murdered Ryan Deering out at the campground or maybe back at your house the Friday before."

"The house I paid the damn down payment on?" seethed Hank Cassel. "A wedding present." His fists clenched and unclenched like a pair of pumping live animals.

"You left Deering's car at the campground, drove him home in your truck and what?"

"You took the dead body home?" Hank Cassel shouted. His son-in-law's bizarre behavior was finally sinking in. "To your house?"

"No, not *in* the house, anyway. Too chancy." I answered. And too smelly. "You needed someplace to keep him safely out of sight, away from prying eyes. Probably wrapped the body up and tied him underwater at the end of your dock.

"That would explain both how the Deering's corpse showed signs of being exposed to water, fresh water, like the waters of the Sound behind your house, for days before he was found. Plus, that would explain why they body showed signs of having been lashed."

Hank was spluttering like a boat motor running on bad gas.

"You kept the body underwater—the perfect place to hide him—until you could safely get him to the beach."

"Hold on now, Sheriff, if what you're saying is true, why didn't he just leave him where he killed him?"

Hank asked. "Or drop him out in the middle of the Atlantic for the sharks to eat him?"

"Because he wanted the body found. And he wanted an alibi for his time too—in case anybody had eyeballed him and Deering together, made a connection between the two of them after his demise. What better alibi than spending a day at the beach with the wife and kids and stumbling on a dead man?"

"Are you listening to this fairy tale, Hank?" Jeff Leftkowitz scoffed.

"I think I'm going to be sick." Hank Cassel clutched his stomach. His face was green.

"Ryan Deering was murdered Friday night. My guess is the Catalina that you told me went missing from your marina, Hank, was used by Ryan and Jeff here, to deliver some merchandise to Larry Lipori's beach house."

"You used one of my boats to commit a crime? A murder?"

I suddenly realized that explained the mysterious late night Carova UFO sightings too. The men had been landing and unloading the boat under the relative cover of darkness. The folks who'd seen the lights assumed UFOs rather than crooks.

People, go figure.

Sonia would probably have something to say about that sort of thinking.

I had something to say about it too and I had a hunch it was far less flattering or forgiving than anything she'd suggest.

"Who the hell is Larry Lipori?" demanded Hank Cassel.

"A small-time crook, mostly runs gambling

operations out of pop-up locations, houses, warehouses. In this case a beach rental near my place, Hank. Right, Jeff?"

"Never heard of him."

"Right. Ryan needed a boat and you needed money. So you provided him with one from the inventory here figuring nobody would miss it."

Hank Cassel growled. I had to hand it to him. It was a better growl than I'd ever heard Bladder Boy muster up.

I spun my tale, a tale I figured as close to the truth as I could get without having walked in their shoes. "Lipori met Ryan at the Slowater. The two men got to talking. Somehow, maybe Ryan let it slip or maybe Lipori had done a little digging and found out about Ryan's prior conviction. Either way, Lipori offered Ryan a lot of money, a boatload of money, to supply him with slots and video gambling machines for the house he planned to rent up in Carova, far off the beaten path.

"The ideal location for an illegal vacation gambling den. So Ryan returned to his old ways, hoping to make a big score. But he was worried about hauling everything over the beach. Too many prying eyes. And if he went in at night, what would happen if he got stuck out there on the beach with all those illegal machines? Back to prison he'd go with little or no chance of keeping it short a second time around.

Maybe Lipori told him about the boat dock, maybe he already knew. Either way, Ryan was desperate for a boat. He was asking everybody he knew all across the county for the loan of one but nobody was willing to come through. And that's where you came in." I turned my gaze on Jeff who had pressed himself into the corner, literally and figuratively.

Hank Cassel aimed his ire at his son-in-law. "You took my boat? Jesus fucking Christ." Hank ran the back of his hand over his damp forehead. "Jesus fucking Christ."

"What happened, Jeff? You and Ryan quarrel?" I asked. "What was it about? Money? It's always money, isn't it?"

"Money?" Hank Cassel spat. "Don't I pay you enough? Hell, I've always paid you too much considering what you do around here."

"What I do around here? What I do around here?" Jeff Leftkowitz's bellow shook the walls. "I do every fucking thing around here. I married your daughter. Gave you grandkids. Work for you night and day. Bow to your every word, every command. And what have you ever given me, Hank, huh? You won't even make me GM. No matter how much I do for you!"

"Know what else I did? I kissed your ass!" Jeff Leftkowitz loomed over Hank Cassel's desk. "What have you given me? I'll tell you. No respect. Shitty wages. What was I supposed to do? Huh? Answer me that?"

"You sonofabitch," replied Hank Cassel. "You murdered a man."

"Two men," I corrected.

"Two men?"

"I figure Isaac Miller saw something that night at the campground. Someones, I should say. You and Ryan. What happened, Jeff? Did he see the two of you arguing? Did he see you kill him? Try to blackmail you?"

"What the hell have you gotten Jinny mixed up in?" Hank Cassel shook his head.

"The kids, too, I'm sorry to say, Hank," I added.

"What?"

"They had to be in on it, Hank. Not the murder, but the coverup. After all, they must have seen Jeff and Jinny haul the body in and out of the 4Runner."

"That's sick!" Hank Cassel cried.

I turned to Jeff. "Then what? You waited until the time was just right and told them to start screaming? Am I right? What did you promise them? I spotted a load of new clothes and toys spread around your house. Looked like a post-Christmas explosion."

"You involved my grandkids in this?!" Hank Cassel leapt, sending his chair careening into the credenza. "You sick sonofa—"

70

Hank Cassel lunged across his desk. He wrapped his thick hands around his son-in-law's neck. Jeff shouted and grabbed his father-in-law's arms. He gasped for breath and tried desperately to loosen the old man's grip.

The Vasa went flying through the air as if picked up in the hands of a violent storm. The model struck the wall prow first and exploded into a thousand or more pieces. A jagged section of the busted mainmast bounced off my left cheek.

Both men fell heavily to the floor, Hank on top of Jeff. Jeff rolled over on top of Hank. Then they reversed positions once again. I had to hand it to Hank Cassel, the old guy could sure hold his own.

Fortunately for me, my scotch had survived unscathed. I picked up my tumbler and sipped as the two men wrestled noisily on the floor.

Through the big glass window, employees and customers alike ogled, watching the two men fighting on the floor of their boss's office.

Not something they saw every day.

But no one interfered. Probably because they saw me, the sheriff, sitting there calmly sipping a scotch like he was watching an absurd off-Broadway play.

And I was, sort of.

Jeff punched Hank in the mouth. Hank bellowed and pulled himself up onto his knees. He locked his right arm around Jeff's neck so Jeff was forced to rise with him. Jeff drooled. His face purple as an eggplant. Another minute and I might have another murder on my hands and this was one I didn't want.

If I didn't break this fight up now, the district attorney would be charging Hank Cassel with manslaughter at the very least and there wouldn't be anything I could do to stop him. Why should Hank suffer for something this representative of Homo sapiens had done? He was going to have enough to live with already. This wasn't the sort of thing a person forgets. The experience might fade from memory given time and lots of it but some scars don't ever go away completely. And this was one of them.

Bury Jeff Leftkowitz at sea?

Nope, too many potential witnesses standing, eyes glued to the scene, on the opposite side of the glass.

Shit.

I sighed and carefully set my half-empty crystal tumbler down once more on the boat brochure. With a glance at our audience on the other side of the glass, I stood and tapped Hank's arm. "Hank. Hank."

Jeff blubbered. His eyes bulged like Hank was squeezing a balloon.

"Hank. Time to let go."

"Let me be, Sheriff!"

Jeff lurched to one side. Hank Cassel cursed and squeezed with all his might.

I pressed my hand into the crook of Hank Cassel's arm. "Come on, Hank. He isn't worth it. Besides, if I lock you up, who's going to take care of your grandkids when this one's in prison?" I could have added his daughter in there too, but they say don't kick a man when he's down, and this man was down.

"Fuck." Hank wiped at the blood spilling from his split lip. He released the arm he'd been using to squeeze the life out of his son-in-law.

Jeff fell forward, striking his forehead against the front of Hank's desk with a loud thump.

I stuck out my hand and helped Hank Cassel to his feet. "You okay?"

"Yeah." He combed his fingers through his hair, breathing hard. I steered him to his seat and poured him a refill. "Drink this."

Huffing and wheezing, Jeff crawled on all fours to the side wall. His shirt was undone and both his jacket sleeves had been torn loose. He rested his head in his hands and cried.

Hank Cassel drank noisily and banged the glass down on his desk. His disheveled clothes were sweat-soaked. With a sweep of the arm, he cleared the Vasa's debris from his sight. "Why, Jeff? Tell me why."

Jeff Leftkowitz sat hunched over on the office floor like a Rodin marble statue representing the failure of man, knees pulled up to his chest, tears spilling down his face.

He was missing a shoe.

"I told you. I needed the money."

"For what?" demanded Hank.

He sobbed in his chair on the floor. Jeff cried like there was no tomorrow. Of course, for him, there wouldn't be.

I didn't have the heart to tell Hank that his daughter was in trouble too. She was an accomplice.

There was no getting around that.

As for the kids, I felt sorry for them. They'd only done what their sick parents had told them to do. They probably thought it had been a game. Maybe when all this was over, they'd be living with Grandpa.

"For Jinny and the kids. They wanted stuff, expensive stuff and it's not like you pay me a whole hell of a lot."

"I pay you plenty. More than enough!"

Jeff snorted. "Yeah, right. If Deering hadn't gotten stingy and Miller so damn greedy, I could've made plenty. Enough to get away from you, asshole!"

Jeff charged Hank, knocking him out of his chair. The two men hit the desk and slid across to the floor.

Hank was quick. He grabbed Jeff by the arm and threw him across the room. Hank Cassel leaned forward, hands clamped to his knees, huffing and puffing and sweating like he'd just run a 5k.

Not knowing when to stay down, Jeff bellowed and charged again. Both men fell to their knees. Hank Cassel managed to snake his arms around Jeff's neck once again. I couldn't help lowering my opinion of Jeff even further. The idiot had fallen for the same trick that almost got him killed the first time.

And it looked like this time, it might really just do that—get him killed.

Hank Cassel was once more choking the life out of his son-in-law. With a frown, I finished my scotch. Jeff's face was all purple again. What came after purple on the way to dead?

Better not to find out.

I figured I'd better put an end to the activities before we all found out.

Plus, with that crowd—which I noticed now included Hannah who'd given up chasing a new sale in favor of the show—watching from the showroom floor, it wouldn't look right if I just let their boss kill this clown.

71

I stormed into the Sheriff's Office and ran to my desk.

Frenchie shot up from his desk. "Everything okay, Chief?"

"I need to finish those budget reports. That insufferable Jenkins from Finance is right behind me. Can you believe it? He followed me all the way from the damn courthouse."

I'd gone to file some papers relating to the Ryan Deering and Isaac Miller murder case. Jeff and Jinny Leftkowitz were in my jail, separate cells, awaiting transfer to a larger facility. Jeff was charged with a double homicide, Jinny as his accomplice. They'd both lawyered up. They weren't talking to me. Hell, they weren't even talking to each other.

As for their kids, after a lot of hollering and arguing—much of it being done by me—they were under the care of Grandpa Hank.

They'd also been ordered to undergo counseling. Sonia met with them late yesterday evening, after the arrests of their parents. She said the kids were doing well under the circumstances. And that was pretty much all she said to me, except to say that she wasn't talking to me.

Frenchie followed me into my doorless/hingeless

office. I was becoming a bit unhinged myself. "Why would he do that, Chief?"

"Because he spotted me. Cornered me in a hallway at the courthouse—I mean, what the hell was he doing there?

"He threatened that if I didn't file the report in twenty-four hours, he'd see that our budget gets slashed twenty-percent." I grabbed the PC and punched it to life. I threw myself down in my chair and swiveled the monitor my way.

"But Chief—"

"How the hell does this screen keep ending up every which way but where I'm looking?"

"Dunno, Chief." Frenchie helped himself to a chair.

The coffee he held in his hand didn't smell great but, the state I was in, it smelled good enough to steal.

"I wanted to tell you—"

"Not now." I threw up my hand. "And if you don't offer me a cup of that coffee soon, I'm taking yours, Frenchman."

"Coming right up, Chief!" Frenchie sat his coffee mug on the floor, ran off to the coffee pot and returned with a cup for me. Nobody in the office brews a halfway decent cup of coffee but surly sheriffs who haven't had time for their first shot of caffeine of the day cannot be choosers. Wasn't that the saying?

"Thanks." Using the mouse, I scrolled through the folders. There were more today than yesterday. Did the damn things breed overnight? "Where's the folder with the budget report? The one with the projections?"

"That's what I've been trying to tell you. Got them done, Chief." Frenchie smiled and sipped his coffee. He slipped a rabbit-shaped couque de Dinant cookie from his trouser pocket, extracted it from the plastic bag, took a big whiff, smiled and then gnawed on an ear.

Frenchie tossed a second one to me like it was a bone. Those sweet Belgian cookies his wife bakes up are hard as a bone too but I loved them and he knew it.

As Frenchie had originally explained to me, the couque de Dinant is traditionally made from two very simple ingredients, wheat flour and honey. Bakers press this simple, firm dough into carved wooden molds. They place these filled molds in the oven and bake the cookies at a high temperature, so that the honey caramelizes and the cookies take on a deep, golden color —and the consistency of a brick.

"Thanks." I cracked my tooth biting into the cookie. It was worth the dental bill. The couque de Dinant is meant for dipping so I followed the bite with a gulp of caffeine. "Now, where are those—" I slammed my couque de Dinant down on the desktop. It did more damage to the desk than the cookie. "You got them done?"

"Mais oui, Chief."

"Even the projections?"

"Oui, even zee projections. Two years out and they only wanted eighteen months. But I thought what could this hurt?" Frenchie bit off a chunk of cookie. I couldn't imagine how he did that. The man had a genuine steel-trap jaw.

"Are you kidding?"

"About what, Chief?"

"The budget reports."

"Sent them over first thing this morning."

"But how? I've been working on those reports for

weeks." Months, actually.

"Piece of cake, Chief. Even a third grader could do it."

I let the comment go on the grounds that it could and did incriminate me and my IQ and might and could cause Frenchie grievous bodily harm. Something I was loathe to inflict on him, especially considering he'd just served me coffee and a homemade cookie.

"You've been busy with other more important matters, Chief," Frenchie hastened to add, as if reading my thoughts. He wiped a crumb from the edge of the incipient moustache he was trying to grow.

"Thanks." For the first time this morning, I relaxed, sipped my lousy coffee. "No joke? You really did?"

"I swear at you, Chief." Frenchie raised his right hand and made a peace sign. Or was that a V for victory sign?

Whatever.

"All of them?"

"Yes, Chief."

This time, I really did relax. I stood and dumped my coffee in the wastebasket. "If anybody needs me, I'll be at the beach."

"The bitch, Chief?"

My eyes fell on my broken doorframe. "Damn. I should've put in a request for a new door."

"Solid mahogany with a brass name plate, Chief." Frenchie was working on his second bunny ear now. The poor rabbit looked beat up.

"You kidding?" I fondled my couque de Dinant. In the wrong hands, one of these would make an ideal murder weapon, the unexpected, untraditional blunt object. And you could eat the evidence—or at least run it through your tree shredder.

I blinked to make sure I wasn't dreaming or hadn't entered some alternate reality. Everything looked the same. "Give yourself a raise."

"Already did, Chief."

I kept moving.

I didn't know if he was joking or not.

I didn't care.

"Wait until you feast your eyes on that name plate. Two-eench tall letters," Frenchie said, following behind. "Chief Thomas Edge."

I admit I flinched a little there and my fingers choked the life out of the combination little Belgian bunny rabbit couque de Dinant/blunt murder weapon but I still kept moving.

I still didn't care.

I'd stop by the cabin and pick up Bladder Boy. There was a beach out there waiting for us. And if he couldn't find something to piss on, I would.

ABOUT THE AUTHOR

Glenn Eric

 Glenn Eric is the critically-acclaimed and best-selling author of many novels under his own name and numerous pen names. He is also a musician and singer-songwriter. He can be contacted through his website at: www.glenneric.com.